i

# Wake of Darkness

## Megan Winkler

Wake of Darkness
© Copyright 2012 by Megan Winkler

Cover design by Megan Winkler
Cover Image ©*zdenek kintr*– *Fotolia.com*

Published by The Brainy Babe Micro Pub
Visit www.thebrainybabe.com

To Mike, with love.
Somehow I wrote you before I knew you.

# Wake of Darkness

## Megan Winkler

*C'est la guerre.*
That's war.

# Chapter 1

Present Day—A Small College Town in Texas

Sophie didn't speak to anyone, not so much because she didn't want to, but because she really didn't *have* to. She struggled with Herculean effort to listen to the last words of the professor and ignore the thoughts of the guy next to her—they were familiar, faintly disturbing, incredibly irritating—but tuning out the thoughts of others wasn't always the easiest thing to do. Today it was proving to be extremely difficult. If she really concentrated though, she could block the voices out...sometimes.

She debated idly if she could pound some sense into him and smiled darkly at the thought, imagining it. She thought about what it would be like to rip his throat out, but she wasn't that strong. Granted, she'd never actually *tried* to rip someone's throat out...She glared at him through narrowed eyes and a subtle growl from deep within her chest found its way up to her throat.

No, as much as she might like to resort to violence, it wasn't the answer...or so that's what the proverbial "they" always said. She sighed despite the boiling frustration and closed her eyes, rubbed the sides of her head and tried to block him out, hoping it would work. After a fruitless moment, she dropped her hands on the desk in frustration. Today it just wasn't working. She wondered again, as she had on so many previous occasions, if she was alone; if anyone could truly understand what she went through on a daily basis. Wasn't there anyone else in the world who could hear every single, intimate thought of those around them? More importantly, if there were, then where *were* they?

If she thought about it too long, the other terrifying question that haunted her would creep into her mind. It was the one she hated to ask, but the one that was the most persistent: what if there *wasn't* anyone who could empathize? She shook her head

1

quickly to chase that demonic thought away; she wouldn't let herself go down that road again.

Her classmate grinned at her until he finally paid enough attention to her eyes for the black look in them to register. They locked stares and he immediately looked away and shifted nervously in his seat, avoiding her glare. She rolled her eyes and tried to shift her attention back to the professor. When the eternal hour was finally up, her eyes bored into the same guy, precisely at the moment he was checking out her butt, catching him in the act, and completely off guard again. The same growl threatened to claw its way upward, but she held herself together as she hastened to the door, relieved to be outside before the rest of her classmates, and away from the lewd mental comments she was being bombarded with.

She took in a deep, cleansing breath and reveled in her liberation from the classroom before anyone else. Escaping outside, she sighed in the fresh air. Sophie found her transient peace in moments like this, just before the rest of the student body poured out of doorways like hundreds of little ants, scrambling to get away from the dreaded classrooms, their minds swirling freely.

*And...here they come,* she thought.

She froze where she stood, regardless for those filing around her, closed her eyes and concentrated on not hearing the unfiltered chaos of thoughts which swarmed around her. She didn't care that people had to stop short and swerve quickly in their path to avoid hitting her—she could feel the insanely subtle movement of air around her as her frustrated peers dodged her. Today was a bad day, and it took all she had in her not to scream at the insanity of it all. One therapist had suggested meditation as a means for exorcising the voices that he hadn't really believed were real anyway. Sophie didn't have a mantra though.

Their thoughts flooded her mind. Sophie imagined what being trapped in a whirlpool was like. She figured it wouldn't be much different: disorienting, chaotic, choking. Sometimes it felt like she was drowning. She'd been crazy to think she could lead a normal life; that she could go to school and be a typical co-ed.

*College was a bad idea,* she thought to herself for about the millionth time.

Taking a deep breath, Sophie forced the useless thoughts from her brain and focused instead on her breathing, rubbing her temples with her fingertips. Soon, she felt a tentative calm settle over her, but part of herself waited for the calm to suddenly retreat as it invariably did; the peace was always too short.

She reluctantly opened her eyes when she knew she *could* walk away from the building. She looked around. A strange feeling crawled up her arms and burrowed itself into her brain as she scanned her surroundings. Life had taught her to be aware of people lurking in the shadows. She was always the first one in a crowd who knew when something was off, when something didn't feel quite right, but she didn't often feel the strange urge that she was being watched—until recently. As she experienced this still new sensation, she knew that she wasn't in danger...at least she didn't *think* she was, but she definitely felt like someone was watching her.

And as she scanned the façade of the buildings towering over the little courtyard in which she now stood, Sophie was struck with the strangest feeling that maybe she didn't *want* to go. That maybe, she wanted to run back *inside* the building she'd just emerged from. She'd been so relieved to be out of the history building moments ago—as always—but at the same time, she felt the imperative urge to turn back. Without thinking, she instinctively turned back towards the structure. The impulse was so strong that she had to consciously fight the urge that nearly sent her back to find the source of the *itching* desire. She dreaded facing all of the people she'd run into along the way, or rather, *hearing* all of them, and that dread inevitably won over, but just barely. She shook her head quickly in a futile attempt to chase the nagging feeling away and continued stubbornly on her path away from the building determined to keep her eyes from it lest she be tempted to turn back.

Sophie walked along the sidewalk out of the courtyard towards the little downtown square that was her destination nearly every day at this time. She always liked to escape the mental hustle and bustle for a quiet cup of coffee whenever she could. Try as she might, Sophie couldn't keep herself from glancing back up at the building, looming down at her in its majestic modernity. She was certain someone was watching her—she could feel that presence on her back. She thought that maybe, *just maybe*, she'd seen a familiar face staring down at her from the second floor. Through the foggy tinted windows of the retro structure, he seemed to be someone she recognized, but she couldn't tell precisely *why* he was so familiar. The most unsettling part was that she couldn't hear what he was thinking. She couldn't figure out why he was staring at her. The realization made her shudder. She dragged her eyes away as quickly as possible, pulled her sweater around her body and wished, again, that she were invisible.

*No, I take that back,* she thought to herself. *I wish I were somebody else.*

She shivered. As the chills threatened to shake her to her core, she didn't try to figure out if it was the weather or the man who caused the reaction. She tried to put the thought out of her mind as she hastily walked towards the square and concentrated again on relaxing her body and mind, refusing to think about the man who was so familiar and whose mind was completely silent.

Instead, her thoughts drifted back to the frat boy who'd been ogling her in class. If he'd only known what she'd heard in his disgusting little brain. She laughed bitterly at the thought as she walked along, hoping to ease the stress that tensed her body like a violin sting. It didn't do any good for her to be so keyed up. It was moments like this that her temper was quicker and her emotions hotter than usual. She inhaled the brisk, chilly air heavily, feeling it dry and sting her throat as it helped clear her mind.

Today the downtown square was bustling with art students and jocks tossing footballs on the courthouse square. Drug-stained kids of ex-hippies played bongo drums on the corner, their audience snapping at the end of the interpretive song. Sophie chuckled at their beatnik mimicry.

It was a day like any other in her town. The thoughts of the people here sounded much more like what she would think the hubbub of a crowded lecture hall would sound like to a normal person. Occasionally, something was shouted in someone's head loud enough for her to hear, but most of the time she was able to tune the madness out to a dull, minimally distracting roar.

It was an eclectic sort of town where old men gathered at the courthouse on Saturday mornings to play bluegrass on the lush, green front lawn in the shadow of the archaic Confederate soldier monument. Where the local burger joint—built from an old filling station and garage—played host to several different types of people, depending on the day: Friday nights belonged to local college students; Saturday evenings to empty-nesters; and Sundays to guest musicians who took over the make-shift patio strung with multi-colored lights made for Christmas trees. It was the kind of town where everyone talked to everyone else walking around the square. Geeks wandered shamelessly into the comic store, hipsters argued outside the record shop. Everyone greeted each other with small-town hospitality which wasn't a relic of American antiquity here; it was an everyday reality.

Her favorite coffee shop sat on the square, on her favorite street: Pecan. She ducked into Bean There, giggling to herself at the name once again, and ordered a tall, black coffee, careful to concentrate on not listening to anyone's thoughts. It was easier with so few people around, to ignore their thoughts, but it still took a great deal of exhausting concentration not to hear the private secrets of those around her

She made random eye contact with a fellow student and his face broke out in a wide, friendly smile. She hesitantly smiled back, seeing herself in his mind's eye. Her shockingly bright green eyes looked at him from her porcelain face slightly paler than "normal", and her auburn hair was what this man considered sexy: slightly wavy, full, and hanging just past her shoulders. He contemplated walking up to her as his eyes ran up down her dancer-like figure, and asking for her number, but her quickly diverted eyes discouraged him and he soon turned to walk out of the coffee shop. She sighed to herself as she listened to him, relieved that his mind didn't automatically turn to less appropriate thoughts, as was usually the case with men who encountered her. She smiled to herself: There was hope for men yet.

She paid for her coffee and stepped reluctantly back outside to brave the chill in the air, to sit on the little teetering heart-shaped wire chairs right outside the doors. It was really too cold for that type of behavior, but she could be relatively alone there; the thoughts of passing pedestrians were easily confused for vocal utterances outdoors, and that was comforting. Of course, she knew from experience that she could hear spoken words better than the people around her. Too many times, she'd caught the grumbling of a professor as he muttered something under his breath, or the sigh of an exasperated cashier from a few hundred yards away at the grocery store.

Today, the discomfort of sitting out in the chill was worth the peace it afforded, the streets were largely uninhabited. She gripped her coffee and watched the steam billow from the slit in the lid, relishing the act of normalcy, because—as Sophie was keenly aware—she was decidedly *not* normal. She let her mind wander for a while: people watching, taking in the sights of the square, surveying the courthouse and its stately granite façade, noticing a shop she kept meaning to step into, and feeling the wind tickle her hair, before her roving eyes slowly settled on someone she hadn't noticed before, someone sitting opposite her on a bench on the courthouse lawn. She picked him from the crowded streets because he didn't look natural, or more accurately, he looked out of place. He was massive and built like an athlete, and should have been hurling a football to some of his friends, but instead, he just sat there, pretending not to watch her. She'd initially failed to notice him because his mind was silent to her; it hadn't demanded any of her attention. A shiver went up Sophie's spine as that realization hit, but she couldn't pull her eyes from him immediately, as she was certain she *should*. There was nothing that logically screamed danger about his posture, but she was really starting to get creeped out.

Ever since the start of the semester, it seemed like there were continually men staring at her, although not in the same way that guys looked at her in class. She knew—as she watched him— that she'd seen him before. He'd followed her to the library one afternoon after class; had watched her cross the street a few days before that, as he stood silently under the shade of a building on campus. There was no menace, no sexual undercurrent; no real danger to his manner. She'd been an unwilling student of human behavior for too long not to understand simple body language. There was something else completely different about these men specifically—*And why had it only been men?* she asked herself— who simply watched her, and she could never get a reading off of them. That was what haunted her the most. Well, that and the fact that she couldn't turn the corner without running into some gorgeous sandy-haired guy. The irony over the situation was not lost on her. Weren't hordes of admirers every girl's dream? Her own admirers, or watchers, as Sophie affectionately dubbed them—because "stalker" wasn't all that flattering, and really pretty frightening if she thought about it—seemed to be at every turn. She never seemed to be able to go anywhere without one of them being.

*Of course!* She thought, not oblivious to the fact that the jock in cowboy boots started in his seat at just the exact moment of her revelation.

Her mind raced forward, putting the puzzle pieces together. She hadn't realized it before, but the man in the window was precisely the same guy she'd seen almost every day since the start of the semester. He was everywhere. She'd seen him at the library, glaring—but *not quite* glaring—at her over the tops of books; under the shade of an ancient oak tree; in the Union, and of course, today. And now there was this one, subtly staring at her from across the street while he perused the newspaper.

*And who reads newspapers now, anyway? Doesn't he have a tablet, or an iPhone, or something?*

He moved from his spot, standing as if to approach her, and she started feeling the prickly feeling of the fight or flight response kicking in. Her breathing accelerated as she further connected the dots. She could tell she was starting to freak out, on the verge of having a panic attack, if she wasn't careful. It felt like there were little pin-pricks at the back of her neck, her hands became clammy, and she was going to start seeing spots if she didn't make a concerted effort to chill out.

*Calm down, Sophie,* she thought to herself. She closed her eyes and concentrated on steadying her breath again. It didn't stop her from getting up from her seat, though. She opened her eyes quickly and abandoned her coffee without a second thought, yielding to the instinctual response that coursed through her veins.

She headed out of the square, but not before shooting him a brave, albeit dirty look for ruining her afternoon beak. She resolutely turned her back on him and walked from the square, feeling the warmth under her skin boil to the surface. She breathed a sigh and the heat slowly faded.

"Temper, temper!" one of her foster mothers—when she was still a small child—had chastised gently when something small would set her off like that.

After she'd walked about half a block, and had glanced behind herself enough, Sophie was satisfied that she wasn't being followed. Her overreaction *may* have been a little unjustified, but she wasn't about to stick around to find out, just in case.

She hated the fearful part of herself that had recently surfaced in reaction to these mysterious men. The vulnerability they elicited was unsettling to say the least, and she'd been through enough in her life to be the type not to run away. Normally, she fought back—running away was unacceptable—but not today. Not *ever*, with these people.

The wind whipped through the trees around her as she walked along, whistling almost silently through the branches and leaves. There was a rare cold front, even for a Texas mid-November afternoon, in the air. As she walked up the slanted sidewalk, she pulled her sweater together over her chest and crossed her arms to keep the chill out. She chastised herself for attempting to wear one of her favorite chiffon tops on a day like today, as she walked back towards campus along her favorite downtown street. She took a deep breath and slowed even more, taking in the welcoming sights of the historic district. Since she'd reasoned that she wasn't being followed, she was not going to waste the opportunity to walk up the street on the way back to her dorm, no matter how far out of the way it was.

Everything about that street was a familiar comfort to her and the only sound today, aside from the occasional car passing by, was the crush of acorn tops under her feet on the pavement as they rolled almost therapeutically under her toes. She loved all the old houses; each one was different. She felt a strange connection to them, but she'd always chalked it up to her interest in history and her silly tendency towards nostalgia, rather than giving the feeling any other significance. Such old houses conjured up her unrealistic ideas about the perfect family with a mom who loved to cook— and incidentally stayed at home, a dad who proudly brought home the paycheck every week, brothers and sisters playing in the yard, and a dog lounging on the porch. Never mind that Sophie's version of the perfect family was something right out of 1950s television, complete with home-baked cookies, crisp aprons, tire swings, and white picket fences. To her—the serial foster child—it was the closest thing to heaven she could imagine. She longed for a family of her own, one way or another; a place to would belong.

She passed the brown gingerbread house, whose twin stood further up the street on the opposite side; the huge white mansion built at the turn of the century with its deep, curvy, wrap-around porch, arched doorways and windows; and the red brick colonial claimed to be haunted, because despite being well maintained, there didn't appear to be anyone living there most of the time. Of course she knew a cute little old man who religiously wore blue Dickey's coveralls lived there. He took great pride in his beautiful lawn as he rode around it on his glowingly pristine riding mower. There were the smaller cottages and the mid-century homes with their Asian influenced designs scattered along her path. And then, *then* there was the house on the corner.

Why this one wasn't supposed to be haunted, Sophie could never tell. It stood on the corner, on a little bit of a hill, the windows always dark, looming over passers-by. It was the only house with a storm shelter in the yard, visible to the street, and it was one of those imposing Victorians—perfect for a horror flick, complete with high-peaked eaves, lightning rods, and stone lions— that one always sees in historical neighborhoods. She had always admired it for some reason, despite its creepiness, and she'd always wanted to see the inside. It had always drawn her in a very specific way, to the point of longing for it.

She turned the corner to walk alongside the white house on her way back to campus, and a fierce wind hit Sophie full on, taking her breath away for a moment and burning her throat. In the same instant that the wind struck her, Sophie thought she heard her name. In fact, she could have *sworn* the sound was mixed into the whirl of the zephyr.

Turning towards the direction of the voice, she scanned the imposing façade of the white mansion. She shook her head, laughed at herself, and turned away, when she distinctly heard the whisper again, a bit louder this time. Looking back over her shoulder, slowly turning towards the house, she caught the glimpse of a woman at one of the always-vacant windows, staring down at her. A chill ran through Sophie's body, making the hair on her arms stand on end as—yet again—she quickly determined that she couldn't read the woman's thoughts.

This was the first sign of life from the house and it was focused on getting *her* attention. She looked straight ahead, towards campus, ignored the woman, and briskly continued on. Once she reached the next intersection, she realized with dread that she had to wait for the light to turn before she could cross the street without effectively becoming road kill mere yards from campus. Sophie nervously bounced on the balls of her feet without understanding the anxiety her instincts demanded, without questioning the thousands of tiny hairs that stood on end along her neck and her arms. It didn't matter; she never second-guessed her gut reactions. She just knew she needed to get out of there. Fast.

When she glanced back over her shoulder, feeling like she was being watched, she suddenly wished she hadn't and froze in a blank stare. She could feel the adrenaline rush through her chest and into her limbs, threatening to buckle her knees as she stood transfixed. A man who looked like he stepped out of Roman mythology stood about thirty or so feet behind her, still as stone. Beside him stood a tall, willowy redheaded woman who was a still as he, except for her wild hair that danced in the wind like a flame around her head. They might as well have been statues; Sophie couldn't hear a single thought from either figure. She took an unconscious step backwards and the man held his hand up gently, as if to tell her she didn't have anything to be afraid of. He was massive, his broad shoulders draped with a buckskin coat, his shoulder-length blond hair rustling in the wind.

Sophie heard the change in the traffic light as soon as it mercifully changed. She strode too quickly across the intersection, hoping for a brief and foolish moment that she wasn't too obvious—really, what did it matter if they caught her being quick trying to get away? Was she worried about *offending* them?—and once on the other side of the road, she turned around to see that they had vanished into thin air. With trembling hands, Sophie pulled her sweater even tighter across her chest and rushed to her next class, trying to shake off the feeling that she'd seen them before.

\*

Something was different; something was wrong. Her sharp eyes canvassed the room, her quick mind listening to the minds of everyone in the large lobby.

*...I wonder what I should wear tonight...*

*...Damn, there goes that average...*

*...I gotta score a touchdown Saturday...*

*...My mom's going to kill me if I don't call her today...*

*...I really want a Big Mac, but I should stick to my diet...*

*...Dr. Andrew is so freakin' hot...*

*...sum, es, est, sumus, estis, sunt...*

*...Who cares what x equals anyway? It's always different...*

As usual, the thoughts of each person moved around her. She was on-edge already, but something was definitely not right.

She pushed the second set of glass doors open and felt the pressure change as the air from the outside world forced its way around her body and into the space. Through a process of elimination, she examined everyone, deciding if they were a threat or not. It wasn't immediately apparent what the danger was.

A couple of girls looked at her and then looked away in jealousy. She pulled her mind away from theirs, as images of herself mingled with unkind thoughts in their brains.

Sophie didn't recognize any of the few students that were scattered about the first floor of the building, and that actually surprised her a little, given the events of the day so far.

There was a male student in the lobby who leered at her from the corner, his mind filled with disgusting images. His thoughts were familiar, faintly disturbing, and they suddenly made her angry. She debated idly if she could pound some sense into him.

She smiled darkly to herself, imagining it. Of course he misinterpreted the smile and acted as if he were going to walk up to her and she scowled at him. She'd *like* to rip his throat out, but she wasn't that strong.

*Of course*, she thought, *I've never actually tried to rip someone's throat out.*

She glared at the guy through narrowed eyes and a nearly inaudible growl from deep within her chest found its way up to her throat. Startled by the noise, she stopped her rage in its tracks.

She sighed wearily against the boiling ire and closed her eyes. She rubbed at the side of her head and tried to block him out, hoping it would work. Of course it didn't. After a fruitless moment, she dropped her hand in frustration and rolled her eyes.

The hair on the back of her neck stood on end as she looked around, and she knew that her instinctive hyper-awareness wasn't without reason. In her sweeping eye, she caught sight of the student in the corner again. He grinned at her until he finally paid enough attention to her eyes to recognize the black look in them. They locked stares; he immediately dropped his eyes and shifted nervously where he stood, avoiding her glare. She rolled her eyes again.

*Stupid boy,* she thought, but he wasn't why she was edgy.

That's when she felt other eyes on her. She glanced back over her shoulder, and saw no one there. A chill ran up her arms and she was suddenly overcome with a serious case of déjà vu...or maybe it was something different. Whatever it was, it didn't feel right; even the air around her felt...*off.* She looked around anxiously and suddenly felt uneasy, like she was walking into a trap, which was ridiculous.

*Or, was it?* She asked herself; her stomach churned in knots of faint, unexplainable nausea.

She looked around the room and her eyes rested on a random guy standing in shadows of a doorway, directly opposite the first corner she'd looked in. She spun on her heel to face him. She licked at the little beads of sweat that gathered on her top lip. She focused her sharp eyes on him, as if he was the only thing in the scene that mattered for a fleeting moment. She gripped the strap of her bag where it crossed her chest, folding the stiff canvas as she crumpled it in her hand. He was leaning against the wall and staring at her, sending a chill up her spine as she scanned his face. He was no random student. He was there for a purpose.

His was smooth and pale, not totally unlike hers, but also not quite right. He was unbelievably thin, almost anorexic looking. Despite the distance, she could tell his eyes were unnaturally black as coal.

He had a menacing, dangerous look in his eyes and she instinctively shied from him, even from across the large expanse of lobby that spread mercifully between them. She looked about, and found that she was suddenly, *utterly* alone, except for this man. The lower level of the building had emptied of bodies almost all at once.

Had she been late to class? She wondered fleetingly, but she didn't take the chance to look away from him to her watch. *This* was the most crucial thing now. *He* was the most critical.

He meant to harm her; there wasn't a question of it, and she didn't take time to analyze the logic at play. She felt the blood rush from her face as her heart pounded, sending the adrenaline rushing painfully through her limbs. Her eyes flashed quickly to one side and then the other, seeming to focus more sharply on her surroundings, unwilling to turn her body completely from her predator. Where were her kind stalkers now?

His lips spread into a slow, snarling smile, a faint hiss almost impossibly touching her ears. Little bumps ran up and down her limbs, and the adrenaline that coursed through her veins quickened her breathing, as the fight or flight response kicked in with more ferocity than usual. She didn't second-guess herself.

This was serious.

There was *no way* she was over-reacting, and her instinct was to run.

She took one step backwards from him, but he was suddenly at her side, gripping her arm and dragging her back into the darkened hallway with lightning speed, so fast no one else would have been able to track his movements. He hissed like a devil in her ear.

*NO!!!!* She wanted to yell, but couldn't find the words in her surprised throat. Every fiber of her being shouted non-existent words in protest, but her voice failed to utter more than grunts and gasps as she clawed frantically and uselessly against his iron-tight grip.

He tossed her like a rag doll against the wall, knocking the wind out of her chest. She gasped painfully for air and clutched at her ribcage where a jarring pain stabbed her before it slowly began to ebb. She fought to remain standing through the pain, grateful for a moment that her back was against a literal wall.

"Well! What do we have here?" he snarled, circling in front of her. He didn't break eye-contact, and focused intently on her as he moved.

Gathering what little strength she could muster, Sophie pushed away from the wall in spite of her protesting back and broken rib. She stepped to the side to run around him. When she tried, he caught her in his hard grasp, bruising her ribs further, and knocking the breath out of her again in the same painful instant. She screamed.

"I don't think so," he hissed in her ear, feeling her squirm in his crushing grasp. She gasped in pain.

"Please..."

He shoved her against the brick wall with such force that the rough edges of the bricks dug into her skin through her clothes, drawing warm, sticky blood. Its scent filled the air, mixing with his smell of decay.

The newly-identified smell—because it just occurred to her that he smelled like rot—coming from him swirled around her like heavy, disgusting perfume. He carried a putridly sweet odor, smelling something of sugar and of death. When he breathed in her face, it washed over her and she fought the urge to vomit at the repugnance.

She saw his eyes nearly glow in anticipation of something that only her soul understood. She whimpered in pain and closed her eyes against the inevitable for a brief, but seemingly eternal, moment.

*Oh no! Please! No!* She silently begged to no one and retreated into herself for a breath's length.

She'd heard about victims doing that, but had never understood how it was possible. She never thought she would be the type to just disconnect like she did for a moment, there in his arms.

Yet just as quickly, she mustered what remaining mental strength she possessed, regained control, and opened her eyes. She was determined to face her killer, and at very least look him in the eyes as he killed her, if she couldn't fight back.

He leered at her, and literally *licked* at the air. His eyes rolled back into his head like a Great White's before an attack. Her hands pushed against his chest as he craned his head blindly toward her neck. His lips trembled in excitement as his hands coursed lustily up and down her arms.

Panicked breaths rose in her lungs and she tried to push against him with all the force she could muster, using the inexplicable anger that suddenly boiled in her hot, healthy veins. A feral growl ripped through her throat as she felt his body being torn away from hers, by a force that was not her own. She looked down at her hands in confusion.

A familiar man hurled the attacker into the opposite wall, denting the metal door that caught the weight of his thrown body. She tried to run, but her rescuer wordlessly grasped her arm and pulled her into the fire escape stairway around the corner before she could argue. She was completely stunned when he pulled her close to his own body before speaking to her in a quiet, calm voice.

"Close your eyes," the deep voice commanded as he pulled her closer and cradled her head against his chest. He was much taller than she'd originally taken him for when she'd first seen him weeks before.

But Sophie couldn't gain control of any part of her body— let alone her eyes—so she stood limply in front of him, her arms hanging lamely at her sides. The very muscles in her face seemed to have been paralyzed, and so she just stared up at him in shock. He released an irritated sigh and covered her eyes with his hand before she felt a gust of wind swirl around them. And almost as suddenly, his hand was gone, revealing where they stood.

She would have collapsed into a puddle on the floor if he hadn't been holding her up. He held her tight against his chest as he growled quickly into his cell phone. She couldn't focus on the words, but he didn't sound happy. She straightened up a little, but he still held her too closely for her to move away from him. She wasn't a petite little thing, but his shoulders were easily twice as wide as hers, and she couldn't move. Her eyes, at least, were free so she looked around the unfamiliar room.

"What happened?" an oddly frail-looking woman asked, suddenly appearing from around the corner.

She had dark, straight hair and fragile features, and spoke in a brisk, strangely metallic voice. Sophie recognized her immediately.

A younger girl was fast on the other woman's heels. The man she'd seen earlier on the corner with the redhead was suddenly there; it was like they popped up out of thin air. Sophie still struggled to pull away from her rescuer, as she looked from one familiar face to another.

*What's going on?* She thought, in a half-shocked state. *Where am I?*

She glanced out the front window, her sharp eyes taking in the houses that stood opposite the house. Her breath caught as she suddenly realized where she was. A tremor of shock, something close to fear shot through her as she tried to figure out how she had gotten there, who these people were—everything. She felt like she was having an out-of-body experience and the room began to sway a bit before the world suddenly flipped sideways.

"What's happening?" she asked weakly.

It didn't make sense for the world to suddenly turn on its side, and her mind was usually quicker than that. It took her a few seconds longer than usual to realize that the man who had rescued her was suddenly scooping her easily into his arms. He moved swifter through the space than he should have been able to and soundlessly placed her on a couch in the next room before she could protest.

He ignored the comments of the others and quickly inspected her for injuries as she gaped at him like an idiot. He brushed her hair back from her face, and turned her arms over in his firm hands, looking quickly at every inch.

When he let go, Sophie folded her arms across her chest; she didn't like the way he scrutinized her, and she squirmed a little under his gaze. He smiled subtly as if she'd spoken her thoughts out loud. She narrowed her eyes at him incredulously. His green eyes looked over her body, looking for blood and broken bones. His slightly curled blond hair fell haphazardly across his serious brow. He was dressed for work, in slacks and an Oxford with the sleeves rolled up. As she watched him, Sophie was struck by his seriousness until his voice cut through her reverie.

"Laney," he suddenly said to the young girl, "bring me a washcloth, please." His voice was deep and strong and rang with authority, yet it was also non-threatening.

It was safe.

"Are you alright?" he asked, carefully reaching up to smooth Sophie's hair back from her sweaty forehead as she stared at him.

A stunned, pathetic nod was all she could manage as she flinched back instinctually from his touch. She wasn't used to men touching her, even in a non-romantic, medical kind of way. Not that it ever actually happened. She'd always had perfect health—so perfect in fact that she never remembered having ever gone to the doctor.

Out of the corner of her eye, she caught a glimpse of a big athletic, frat boy looking guy that she'd seen earlier on the courtyard. He'd literally come out of nowhere—not unlike the way she'd gotten there, once she thought about it. He was followed into the room by the exceptionally graceful redhead who moved like a dancer. Her shocking blue eyes watched Sophie carefully from her towering height—she was easily as tall as the men, but her heart-shaped face and delicate features seemed better suited for someone much smaller.

"Is she okay?" The jock asked, as he stood behind the couch with his hands on his hips, watching her with mild concern.

"She seems to be alright," the older looking woman said in a calm voice with a frantic, uncontrolled wave of her hands.

Sophie watched her in fascination. Even through her shock, the other woman's contradicting actions didn't make any sense to her.

The one called Laney—a bright-eyed teenager with an impossibly high ponytail—came bounding back in the room and handed Sophie's rescuer a wet washcloth. He took the washcloth from Laney and then handed it to Sophie who suddenly wished she knew his name.

"Here, use this to cool off," he commanded before looking back at Laney. "Will you check her back and make sure the bleeding has stopped?"

Sophie watched numbly as the younger girl danced to her back. Laney paused, the hem of Sophie's shirt in her hand. Sophie looked questioningly at the man who sat in front of her. How did he know she'd been bleeding? Her shirt was black and wouldn't have shown any of the blood.

He stared back into her eyes for too long of a moment. "I could smell it."

"I'm gonna lift up your shirt a little back here. Is that okay?" Laney asked, oblivious to the fact that the guy had just read Sophie's mind.

"Um, yeah," was all Sophie could weakly respond, as the edges of her vision threatened to blacken.

The man gently took the washcloth from her limp hand and dabbed at her cheeks and forehead. All she really wanted to do was lay down for a minute. The redhead watched Sophie carefully through concerned eyes, leaning over the back of the couch.

The details of what had happened started to flood back into Sophie's brain. She'd been attacked—she was absolutely sure of that—but, by what? *That* was a mystery. Whatever had attacked her, it certainly wasn't something natural...or human.

Laney quickly checked any wounds that Sophie may have had, before letting the shirt fall gently back into place.

"She's all but healed. She'll be okay," she confirmed. "There's some bruising on her ribs, but she'll be good soon."

Sophie breathed a quiet sigh of relief and fatigue.

The older woman came and soundlessly sat on a couch opposite the one Sophie occupied and tried to rest her twitching hands in her lap. The man who had saved her noiselessly rose and left the room as Laney slipped down to sit beside her with a gentle smile on her face. The younger girl watched her carefully, as if she was ready to catch Sophie if she suddenly fainted.

Sophie looked at the woman who sat across from her. The woman seemed disproportionately frail. She had a presence to be sure, and despite the tinted lenses she wore, she wasn't blind by any stretch of the imagination. In fact, Sophie felt utterly exposed sitting before her as if in one instant, she'd been stripped naked. Absentmindedly, she touched her pant leg, just to make sure.

She knew where she was of course. She'd often paused in front of the large white Victorian on her way to class. She'd been inexplicably drawn to the structure and had often wondered what it looked like on the inside. As she scanned her surroundings, she found the interior of the great white house to be as intimidating as the gloomy façade outside. A wide, shining mahogany staircase tempted visitors upstairs. Large windows ran from floor to ceiling and a fireplace yawned on the back wall. The rooms were filled with antiques and gauzy curtains caught the breeze of the air conditioner when it clicked on.

The strange woman scrutinized Sophie who shifted uncomfortably in the seat across from her, trying not to over analyze the situation. Once Sophie had gotten her bearings, and the pounding of her heartbeat receded into background noise, it only took her a moment to realize how quiet it was here; that here she heard absolutely *nothing*, without even trying to block the thoughts out.

It was oddly disorienting. Even in the company of one person, she had never been able to escape a mental thought from someone else. But here she sat, facing this strange woman, and she heard absolutely *nothing* from her or from any of the others in the house.

"Yes, I know," the other woman said suddenly.

Sophie jerked her head back to the woman and gaped at her with wide, confused eyes. The other woman gave her a condescending smile before she elaborated.

"I assure you: you will not come to any harm under this roof. I realize that it must be *quite startling* for you to be unable to read my thoughts. Everything will be revealed to you in good time and in proper manner of course," the woman explained in her strangely accented way of speaking.

It was now Sophie's turn to scrutinize this woman, but she didn't know what to think, or even how to respond to what she'd just heard.

"Do not be alarmed," said the European looking man in a voice as thick as honey.

Sophie jumped.

He was suddenly perched on the arm of the couch opposite Sophie. She hadn't even seen him come into the room.

"No, do not be frightened…" the woman added.

"How…? What…*happened?*" Sophie interrupted, looking from one to the other. She swallowed, trying to keep the panic from rising from the pit of her stomach. "Who *are* you people?"

"You are entirely safe here," the woman continued. "You have survived a rather vicious attack I think, but you will find security here in this home."

Sophie stared at her.

"I don't understand."

Her heart pounded in her chest. She was so completely lost, and the quiet around her was distracting and unnatural. It made her uneasy. She kept waiting for one of them to sneak up behind her. She couldn't figure out why she couldn't hear their thoughts, but it was obvious that they could hear hers.

The woman cackled. "You *truly* believe you are the only one who is able to hear others' thoughts?"

She was laughing at Sophie, but as soon as she made eye contact, the woman caught herself quickly and began again. Sophie glared at her through narrowed eyes and waited for an explanation, swallowing the anger that rose in the back of her throat. Even if she were the type to attack, she was lucid enough to realize the futility. She was outnumbered here.

The woman smiled insincerely. "But I have been *terribly* inconsiderate. Please excuse me; I have not introduced myself," the woman said, gesturing to herself and to the man who was perched next to Sophie. "My name is Catherina, and this is Dante." She pronounced the names with a slight accent, rolling the "r" in her own name.

The introduction had pulled Sophie's attention away from her previous thoughts, and her frustration quickly disappeared.

"Welcome to our home," Dante said with a slight bow to her. He pointed to the others in the room. "These are Zoey, Laney, Jim, and Alexander," he said and Sophie gazed at the last one mentioned—her rescuer. "May I bring you anything?"

"Um…some water?" She had just become aware of her parched throat, dry from her stress.

He nodded in response and was gone so quickly that even Sophie's quick eyes couldn't follow his movements. As he left the room, Catherina looked back to Sophie before beginning her explanation.

"Please do not let it frighten you. As I have said, you will not come to any harm here, although some of what I have to tell you will shock you. I must begin with the confession that I," she looked pointedly at Sophie, "or rather, *we* are not, nor ever have been human."

# Chapter 2

"*Excuse me?*" Sophie asked, her mind racing, trying to put two and two together. She tried to wrap her head around what Catherina was saying.

She had always felt human…*hadn't she*? She *had* always known that she was different, but something other than human? But, what was "human" anyway? Wasn't that just like asking "what is normal?"

Catherina raised an eyebrow at Sophie, reading her thoughts.

Sophie's eyes shifted quickly about the room. Her heart refused to stop racing, but it didn't seem like she would have the chance to try and calm down.

Catherina settled further back into her seat to begin her story. She smiled ever so slightly before saying, "Today, you survived an attack by a vampire."

Sophie stared at her. A firm hand was laid gently on her shoulder and she looked up to see Zoey, the willowy redhead, looking at her calmly. She smiled down at her empathetically.

Catherina continued. "I understand that to *you*, having lived in a very human world, this sounds like the stuff of nightmares or science fiction. If you have any residual doubts after today - which I suspect you do not – you must know that you may trust me when I tell you that they are in fact a reality."

"Okay…" Sophie replied incredulously.

"We are related to them, but we are most certainly not vampires. Indeed, we are something quite different from their kind, and the human beings who surround us."

"And I'm included in that '*we*'," Sophie deduced.

"Yes."

"Great," Sophie murmured.

"For now, I am tired. I am sure Zoey would not mind showing you to your room," Catherina continued.

"Wait," Sophie said holding her hand up. "What exactly do you mean about my room?"

"You'll be staying here," Alexander said from where he had been leaning against the door frame.

Sophie stood. "Like hell."

He straightened his posture and met her gaze. "You seem to misunderstand."

"No, I think it's you who misunderstands," she replied, feeling the blood boil just beneath the surface of her skin. "First you kidnap me…"

"That's a fine way to describe me saving your ass," he replied.

"You still dragged me here against my will—in some bizarre, supernatural way. Now you expect me to kowtow to the group of you just because you tell me I'm related to some mythical creature?"

"They're not mythical," he replied. "They're real."

"I'm not staying."

"I'm not letting you walk out the door just to get killed. I've spent too much time watching your back to let that happen now."

"Yeah, and what the hell is that all about?" she asked.

"We had to keep tabs on you to make sure you stayed safe," the big guy, Jim, said.

Sophie turned on a heel to glare at him.

"Hey," Jim said with a shrug, "you're still breathing because we've been keeping track of you."

Sophie considered it and suddenly felt the anger wash away from her. "You're right. But I can't just move in here."

"Well, you can't just leave here either," Jim replied.

"Are they looking for me?"

"You're on their radar now, kiddo. If they can take you out, they will."

"Why?"

"It's a long story," Jim said.

"Yes, and one which we will explain to you if you will just sit down," Catherina replied harshly.

Sophie looked suspiciously at Catherina but sank down to the couch. "I'm listening."

Catherina sighed and looked to Dante, who turned his eyes to Sophie.

"There is a war coming," he said.

"A war?"

"Yes. Between our kind and the vampire covens."

"Why is that?" she asked incredulously.

Alexander stepped into view and her eyes were immediately drawn to him. "Because a very long time ago, Catherina angered one of the coven leaders—the same coven leader who has ties much higher up on the food chain that we would like."

"What do you mean?" Sophie asked.

"It is a long story," Catherina replied.

"Yeah," Sophie said, becoming angry again. "I get that—could someone actually get to the story, instead of just talking about it?"

# Chapter 3

Present Day—Outside New Orleans

He strummed his fingers on the hardwood desk. The light was low, but still glimmered off of the worn surface, polished by decades—maybe even centuries—of use.

"We have a problem," said a voice from the gloom. Another man stepped forward.

He looked up. "Of course we have a problem you *connard.* They're running rampant in the streets, killing our brothers and sisters. And now, *your* daughter"—he jabbed a finger at a woman standing nearby—"has just joined their little band of villains."

"*My* daughter?" she asked. Her voice was light and clear, but her eyes were the antithesis. "I don't have a daughter."

He tossed his head back and a low ripple of laughter started to roll out of his throat. It was bitter and harsh. "Of course you do; you just didn't realize it, Leslie. When you turned, you released that thing into our world, and your maker hadn't a clue what to do with it. So, it lived."

Leslie looked at him incredulously. "Jacques, I don't know what you're talking about."

His smile faded as he leveled his empty eyes at her. Leslie took a step backwards away from him, holding her hands up in wary apology.

"What's wrong?" he taunted. "Are you afraid of me?"

"I...uh..."

He suddenly shot over the desk. He pinned her against the wall as the rest of them backed away from the scene. "You. Should. Be." His breath spread across her face. Though she was as undead as he, she felt the chill of the air that seeped from between his lips.

"If you want to remain with us here, you'll kill your daughter as she should have been killed at her birth," he said.

"But, I..."

"No excuses!" he spat. "You know you are nothing without this coven. You know you would die within days at the hands of our enemies. Get rid of her or never show your face here again."

She stared into his black eyes and felt the edges of the room soften and fade into a haze. "Of course."

# Chapter 4

The ashen gray stones, corroded with age, reflected none of the light from the sconces flaming on their façade. The cold echo of footsteps danced off of the cold stones of the floor, the walls. Emerging from an intersecting labyrinthine hall, she crept into the crypt and looked at no one. She slowly floated towards the window wall, overlooking the little hamlet below; the safest little niche in remote Romania with its lofty guardians of darkness overlooking them like lords.

"My queen," a hollow voice greeted.

Remaining with her black-cloaked back to the speaker, her raspy voice called out: "Leave us."

Most of the collective—gathered in casual groupings around their ancient thrones, languishing in antiquity—began to disburse. Those who slinked swiftly into the shadows glanced with their dead, black eyes over their shoulders at the remaining figures in the room as they made their hasty retreat.

Without warning, she spun viciously on a heel to face those who remained, even before the door to the circular chamber had swung shut on its archaic hinges. Her black robes spun around her frail body, a glimpse of her royal blue gown showing as the cloak shifted on her frame. The costume was cliché, but it scared anyone around her and that's why she liked it. Her sharp, violent eyes glared at the one who had spoken, as he stood in the exact middle of the cavernous crypt.

"Adonis," she said aside, in a more gentle tone, to one of the remaining observers. She continued to stare down the one in the middle of the room.

A favorite, Adonis stepped swiftly to her side, his black hair cascading to his black draped shoulders, the fire on the wall reflecting off of his devilishly preternatural skin.

"My queen," he replied with a swift bow of his head.

She reached her talon-like hand out to grasp his arm.

"I shall require your *specific* expertise," her tinny, haunting voice advised before turning to the one in the center of the room.

"Cusick," she quickly said.

He lifted his eyes to meet hers before quickly bowing his head submissively once more.

"What is your report?" she asked, without acknowledgement of his obligatory deference.

"They are moving, my queen," he quickly answered, his voice heavy with peculiar accent of someone speaking English for the first time.

"No doubt they have already done so," she concluded, unimpressed.

She looked to Adonis as he stood at her side.

"I would send for the others, my queen," her favorite advised.

She turned quickly to the other observer who had remained.

"Brynja," she addressed the female hovering in the shadowed corner, "fetch Sloane and Bennett immediately."

Brynja bowed, her icy blonde hair falling forward in sheets, before she spun and spirited from the dank room before the queen's eyes left her subordinate.

She turned to Adonis and as a unit, the two floated towards the window which overlooked the scurrying humans in the village below. Bowing their heads close together, their lips moved so swiftly as to resemble perfect stillness, as they conferred with one another regarding their North American concerns.

"Hero," Adonis could be heard informally saying, "You must do what is necessary to save our kind in America. Do not hesitate to do what you know you must."

He spoke to her in tones as none other would have dared, having been an advisor to her from the very beginning of time and something more for many centuries since.

The air pressure in the room altered and the queen and her advisor raised their dark eyes to the group entering the chamber.

Brynja entered, and bowing, resumed her place in the corner once more, as two others stepped forward: Sloane, a tall, well-built man with a distinguished air, classic features and silver hair, and Bennett, a lithe and willowy woman with freckles and slightly amber curling hair, to join Cusick where he stood in the innermost point of the cave. The two additions bowed: Sloane in a sweeping movement, Bennett in a more reserved submission.

The queen stood before them, glaring down her nose at them while they waited.

"There seems to be a problem in the United States with our old enemies," she began.

Bennett and Sloane nodded in agreement as Cusick watched his sovereign carefully through dark, skeptical eyes.

"What has been your assessment of the situation?" she asked, suddenly turning to Bennett.

She quickly nodded her head in confident acquiescence.

"My queen, they are gaining in strength and news of their exploits has spread as far westward as the Pacific coast. Members of their kind and ours are becoming extremely aware of the situation and of their...*mission*, as they call it," she answered in her tinny and sharp, but ultra-feminine voice.

Hero turned to Sloane. "Are you of the same mind? Have you come to the same conclusion?" the queen demanded icily.

Sloane offered another swift, sweeping bow.

"Yes, my queen, I have. Word has traveled quickly and those within my territory have also heard rumor of their...*work*," he answered in a thick, New England accent.

The queen straightened and turned to Adonis once more. She glared into his eyes for a fraction of a second, before turning without warning back to Cusick. She flashed in front of him in a movement that would have gone unnoticed by human eyes; a human would have simply seen her in one place one instant and mere inches from Cusick in the next.

"If your man cannot clean his mess up, you shall have some explaining to do, Cusick," she warned acridly.

He nodded, understanding the warning was no empty threat.

# Chapter 5

1704—Old Swedes' Church, Wilmington, Delaware

"Are you here?" she whispered into the darkness. She looked around the corner of the church building, her blonde hair falling like a shroud before her eyes.

"Of course," he replied in her ear.

"Oh!" she exclaimed; he was suddenly standing right beside her. "You startled me."

"I am truly sorry," he said.

"No matter, my love. It is time."

He eyed her belly, knowing a child grew within it. "Astrid," he replied, "you must wait until you are delivered. I do not know what the transformation will create."

"What do you care of it?" Astrid demanded, ripping her hair back away from her face. "Are you not *vampyr*? What do you care for a puny little babe—especially one that has ceased to move within me?"

"What?" he gasped.

"Yes," she replied, reaching for his face. "My husband's son is dead. You needn't wait for me to deliver for fear of what will come forth. I am ready, my love. Take me."

His coal-colored eyes searched her face for any sign of dishonesty, for any sign of hesitation. She ran her fingers up his neck and into his pitch black hair and bent his neck towards her.

Vampires weren't supposed to fall in love with their prey, but she had turned her violet eyes on him the night he was to make a meal of her, and in that moment, he suddenly remembered something from his human life, something he couldn't put his finger on. She was familiar and he longed to have her by his side forever. The one predicating event was for her to deliver her child—he didn't know what kind of monster might come from a baby born to a woman who became a vampire, one of the undead. Even worse, he didn't know what another body within hers would do to her. If it were a living creature, it stood to reason that perhaps the baby would take the transformation instead, and in the exchange of blood, the baby could be made the vampire and Astrid could be lost.

But if the baby were dead already...

She drew his head to her neck, sweeping her long locks away from her shoulder. Her breasts rose and fell in her inappropriately revealing dress—as if she'd tried to be as alluring as possible—as her breathing increased. With the excitement of the situation, her blood coursed faster, her heart pounded harder, and the veins—always easy for Lisandro to see—were even more apparent under her delicate skin. The smell of her life was overpowering and his mouth watered at the thought of tasting her. There was one last second where he could have stopped what was happening, but it was swiftly gone and his eyes rolled back in anticipation. His teeth tore precisely through the sweet flesh and Astrid gasped. She pulled his head harder against her neck and arched her back into his embrace.

She moaned and let out a delirious giggle as her knees collapsed. He held her, his tongue lapping at the sticky sweet fluid that poured from her flesh. Its warmth coursed through his body like delicious electricity, and he trembled against the sensation.

Astrid's breathing slowed and became shallow. He pulled away from her neck, wanting more, but knowing that if he were to take it, she wouldn't survive. He gently laid her on the ground at his feet, her rotund belly looking like a tiny mountain in comparison to the rest of her drained body.

With lips still covered in her blood, he tore at his own wrist and cupped her head towards the wound.

"Drink, my darling," he cooed.

Her tongue swept across it tentatively before her lips closed on it. In her relative weakness, her draw against the wound as she sucked the blood from his body felt like the most delicate of kisses. She pulled harder against the cut; blood trickled from the corner of her mouth and down her jaw, resting near the wounds he had inflicted.

He watched her eyes carefully, waiting for any sign of the change, worried that it wouldn't happen. It shouldn't have been taking this long.

But suddenly, her eyes widened in shock. Her back arched and she bellowed a guttural, hellish scream. Her body convulsed and he tried to comfort her, but she lashed out at him, bit at him, threw her arms towards his face. He could do nothing but stand aside and watch in horror as his golden angel fought against the convulsions of death.

Suddenly, she folded in on herself and tore at her belly with still human-weak fingers. And with another convulsion, her back arched and what seemed like a river of blood and fluid spread out from beneath her heavy skirts. Lisandro watched in horror. His creator had never told him the terrible nature of the transformation. He was terrified that something was wrong. He watched the light go out of her eyes.

And then, he heard something crying. He stared blankly into the night as his normally swift brain struggled to process the sound. It wasn't Astrid, who by now was pulling herself up and taking in the visions of the night with her new eyes.

Lisandro looked at the soaked ground that lapped up the blood from Astrid's womb as surely as she had lapped the blood from his wrist moments ago. A tiny creature kicked at the night. Her hair was as black as his own, but her eyes were violet like Astrid's had been in life.

"Dear God in Heaven," he gasped, staring at the baby in horror. "What have I done?"

He reached down tentatively and scooped the baby up into his arms. She wiggled in his embrace and smile slowly crept across her baby pink lips. Lisandro looked up at where Astrid had been standing. She was gone.

"Astrid?" he asked the too-still night. "Astrid?!"

He spun around, forgetting the fragile creature in his hand. Astrid was nowhere to be found. And in that moment, had Lisandro had a heart to break, it surely would have destroyed him. She had abandoned him.

The baby squirmed in his arms and cooed at him. He looked down when he felt a tiny tug at his long hair. Their eyes met and she smiled again. Lisandro was entranced by her eyes, so much like his love's, and he smiled back.

"And what shall I call you, little kitten?"

Something in the night caught her eye and she seemed to be cataloging the stars with her little newborn mind. A name came back to him, from a place far away and a time he had all but forgotten. His mother's name: Catherina.

# Chapter 6

Present Day—Texas

Catherina pled fatigue at Sophie's insistence to hear what she had to say, prompting her to exercise self-control—she didn't think it would do anyone any good to attack the matriarch in her own home. So, Alexander took Catherina's vacated place with a quick glance at Zoey, who still sat silently on the floor, playing with the golden cross that hung from a thin gold chain around her neck.

"I shall be brief," he began, looking Sophie directly in the eye. "Catherina tends to be a little…"

Zoey raised her eyebrow at him. He shook his head, mumbled something under his breath and started again.

"You must know what you are—what we are: We are the product of a human mother and a vampire creator."

Sophie shook her head in disbelief. "That's impossible," she protested.

"Nothing is impossible," he countered. "We are not the biological child of our vampire parent. My mother was changed into a vampire while I was still in the womb. At the time of her death and transformation, I was aborted from her body, but not before I inherited traits from my vampire father. It's the same with you."

"And with me," Zoey added.

"How does that work?"

"Basic biology," Alexander said. "We are not entirely sure of all the mechanics, but a mother's blood mingles with her baby's. When a pregnant woman is changed into a vampire, three blood types are exchanged within the mother's body."

Sophie nodded. "Okay. So, let me get this straight. A vampire bites a pregnant woman, but what do you mean three blood types are exchanged?"

Alexander exchanged a glance with Jim over her shoulder before answering.

"The transformation requires an exchange of blood," Alexander replied.

"An exchange of blood?" Sophie asked incredulously. Her eyes brightened with recognition as her mouth twisted into a grimace. "You mean she drinks the vampire's."

"Yes," Zoey answered.

"Oh, alright then," Sophie replied. She suspected she could be going crazy.

"The physical traits we inherit from our vampire parents vary," Alexander continued, "but we do know that the powers we possess are as varied as our vampire parents."

"Catherina met her father—her vampire father—not long after the start of her thirty-third year. After a few years together, he took her hunting with him; he taught her to kill. She found that the new life she embraced gave her incredible strength. The local coven of vampires warned her father against such things, but neither heeded the warnings. Her father tried to kill Jacques, their leader, but when he was unsuccessful, he fled New Orleans, leaving Catherina to fend for herself. And then Gabriel—one who is like us and made a play for her in the past—came back for her. He hired members of Jacques's coven to help kidnap her—they had it out for her already, so they were easy to pay off. Gabriel held her captive and raped her repeatedly, trying to create an offspring of our kind through a more natural course."

Sophie stared at him in horror—the horror of Catherina's actions and the horror of her capture combined into one. Zoey nodded sympathetically at her as Alexander continued.

"Catherina soon learned what happens to one of our kind who begins to live like a vampire. Without blood to sustain her, her natural strength and ability over the vampires disappeared. She became weaker even than a human being against their kind. Luckily for her, there were several such humans on board the ship on which she was being kept prisoner. She lured him to his death and through his blood gained her strength. Fueled by the blood that newly coursed in her veins, Catherina was able to escape the bonds that held her.

"She leapt from the ship and swam to shore. She found that she had been moored in the Mediterranean, and she very soon thereafter found Dante. Once together, Dante and Catherina traveled the world. They enjoyed many years with one another and she slowly regained some of her strength, *without* the consumption of human blood. However, she has never been the same since.

"Having failed in his efforts to create a super-monster if you will, Gabriel turned his sights on capturing Catherina for himself. Whether his actions were out of spite or out of something less sinister, we have never known. Living for so long, members of our kind occasionally fixate on something or someone for lack of anything better to do. It usually results in *someone's* death," he paused, remembering something else, but his mind was still closed to Sophie, so she didn't notice much of a pause. He continued.

"Gabriel surprised Dante and Catherina one day while they were traveling through Paris. Having tracked them throughout Europe, when he knew that he had them cornered there, he informed Catherina that he held her father, Lisandro, captive. Gabriel knew that nothing, not even Dante, could have kept her from trying to rescue her father.

"His bargain was simple: Lisandro's freedom for Catherina's captivity. He wanted to possess her for himself, and he understood that his scheme was the only way he possibly could attain her."

Alexander watched Sophie shiver at his words and he smirked. "You are not going to faint again; are you?" he asked, bitingly disdainful.

She froze and looked at him like he had physically slapped her in the face before she quickly recovered herself. *What the hell did I do to you?* She reflexively thought, feeling the heat of embarrassment move through her body.

Despite his better judgment, Alexander was instantly sorry for his words. He felt himself becoming emotionally concerned for Sophie, for her well-being and feelings; he was quickly approaching dangerous territory. Zoey sighed heavily at his feet.

Sophie looked at him coolly. "No, I'm not going to faint again."

Laney scrutinized Alexander for a half-second before saying, "You should be nicer to her, you know," with a knowing smile.

Alexander grimaced as he glanced sideways at the younger girl; he was decidedly not in the mood. Shaking his head, he continued: "Catherina was able to trick Gabriel into his death."

"How?" asked Sophie, and her serious tone disturbed him in ways it shouldn't.

"Quite simply, she seduced him. When the *fool* believed her, she killed him," he quickly explained.

"But...how? I mean, she's lived for so long. I assumed..."

"...That we cannot be killed?" He shook his head. "I am afraid that we can be. Our beating hearts drive blood through our veins just like the hearts of human beings. It is *nearly* impossible to kill one of us, but there is one way to successfully do so."

Sophie nodded. The answer was so simple; she knew it instinctively. "She bit him." It was not a question.

"Yes, but that act alone was not enough of a cause to lead to her problems, which are now our problems. No matter what vampires are paid or promised, no amount of money, no gain whatsoever, will lead to absolute loyalty with one of *our* kind," he explained. "Ultimately, Gabriel meant little to Jacques and his company; they were simply trying to make a profit out of the necessary situation they had found themselves in.

"Dante spoke of a coming war, and as melodramatic as it seems to you, we undeniably shall face certain danger soon. It is important that you understand what has transpired to lead us to this point.

"Gabriel's blood gave Catherina new life; so much so that she believed she was transformed. Somehow, she knew immediately where Lisandro was, as if she had absorbed some of Gabriel's knowledge along with his blood. When she arrived at the designated location, though, she found that Gabriel's vampire cohorts had killed her father of their own accord—it did not matter that they were on Gabriel's payroll.

"Her new strength raged in her as deeply as the anger that coursed through her veins. They had looked for Gabriel's arrival; they had planned to collect their payment and go. Perhaps they would have killed him; perhaps not. Regardless, Catherina was the last being they expected to see walking through the door.

"She struck before they knew what hit them—I once saw the memory in her mind. None escaped death except Jacques. She slew his friends and his mate, Delphine. And now we are dealing with *that* unfortunate fact," Alexander explained. He sat back into the couch and waited for Sophie to process what she'd heard. His watched her carefully.

"So what's the big deal with this guy, and why is everybody talking about not much time left? What's happening? Does it have to do something with this Jacques guy?" Sophie asked, the stream of confused questions coming out before she could stop herself.

"The Council is the self-appointed governing body of vampires. From a dark cavern overlooking a little-known village in Romania, they keep careful watch over everything, and I do mean *everything*. They maintain and ensure vampire sovereignty in the world. They are everywhere and nowhere, investing in large corporations, influencing governments across the globe, and staunchly retaining their ruling status in the world. While they move about with the upmost discretion, they are freer now than ever before: the modern world does not believe in monsters any longer, but has chosen to give those they still *would like* to believe in, a beautiful face."

"Yes, but I don't underst…"

Alexander cleared his throat. "Every society eventually evolves to the point that it needs a government to keep order. That is what the Council is for their kind. Humans haven't the least inkling of their existence, and vampires have become something appealing in pop culture," he scowled at the last sentence.

"The Council has facilitated our extermination, in a way. Jacques has convinced them that Catherina, Dante, and the rest of our family must die for Catherina's crimes and unjustified vengeance against his coven. The Council has sanctioned the action and will support Jacques in his endeavors, though they will remain detached from it as long as events proceed Jacques's way."

Sophie looked at him, horrified. "What's their motivation for just going along with him?"

Jim cleared his throat. "Well, y' see Sophie, there are some of us out there who hunt and kill vampires," he explained, "and that makes the Council kinda mad."

"To say the least," Laney chimed in, suddenly appearing from nowhere.

"When did she...?" Sophie asked, pointing towards the doorway.

Alexander swept a dismissive wave at her question.

Jim kept talking: "And then there's Jacques, who's got a burr under his saddle for Catherina, so the situation fits pretty nicely into the Council's grand design. They figure if they let him take us out, then fewer of their friends get killed on a regular basis."

"Jacques has been spotted by friends of ours," Alexander added. "He is looking for Catherina, which means he is looking for all of us. She killed his family, so he will kill hers."

"Great," was all Sophie replied before concluding, "So...the Council's blessing gives him a legitimate excuse," she sighed. "But when did all this first happen?"

"A little over a hundred years ago."

"And he's *just now* causing a problem?"

"Not exactly," Alexander explained. "He has been pursuing her for decades." He glanced at Jim and then back to her. "Sophie, what you must understand is that time means something entirely different to us than to humans. In your world—or rather the one you have been living in—a century is an unimaginable length of time to hold a grudge. In ours, it is a mere pittance of time."

"'Cause, when you live forever..." interrupted Laney.

"Precisely," Alexander said, and Sophie nodded in understanding. He watched her carefully for any sign of panic; any sign of shock or fear.

Jim nudged her with his elbow. "Makes you feel a little like Alice in the rabbit hole, huh?" he joked.

Sophie loosed a hysterical little chuckle and shook her head in disbelief. Zoey smiled sympathetically at her.

"We shall discuss further arrangements at a later time, but we will be moving on soon after we make contact with the other one here," continued Alexander. "And you are welcome to..."

"The other one?" Sophie interrupted, looking quickly from Alexander to Jim, searching for an answer.

Jim turned to her. "Laney thinks there's another one of us somewhere close, but she's not really sure. We'll leave after we deal with him or her."

Sophie nodded numbly, attempting to absorb it all.

Alexander felt an inexplicable urge to comfort Sophie as he watched her. She seemed in better control of herself than before, as she processed everything she'd just learned.

# Chapter 7

The family's patriarch looked down at Sophie. "You must do what you believe best, but we would highly recommend that you remain here with our family. We are sorry to have brought you into this situation, but please understand that we believe you are safest here. Jacques and the others will not pass you by simply because you are not with us. You are *one* of us, you know us, and that is all the justification he needs to strike. He will come here looking for our family; we have been in the area for too long already and if we leave you behind, it would be disastrous for you. We offer you a home and a family with those who understand you and who share the same life you do. I sincerely hope that you will accept it."

To Sophie, who had been known to jokingly call herself the perpetual foster kid, the temptation was great. She could have a place to belong, but as she contemplated it, her attention was pulled to Laney. She sat Indian-style on the floor, chanting to herself.

"Safety, safety, safety. Safe in the nest. The eggs will break. Crack, crack, crack." Her lips barely moved. Her closed eyes suddenly popped open. "Yes, Sophie, you have to stay."

Sophie watched her in baffled silence.

Jim chuckled under his breath. "Laney is…uh…*interesting*," he whispered conspiratorially. "She's pretty weird, actually. You'll get used to her."

With that, Laney jumped up and was suddenly planting a sisterly kiss on Jim's cheek.

Sophie shook her head hoping to regain her concentration. "My safety?" she asked, turning to face Dante.

"Once we become aware of our nature, we begin to naturally rely on our talents; we utilize them to a greater extent than before. That makes us easier to find—we stand out more you might say," Dante explained. "You have just recently shown up on their radar, for lack of a better metaphor, and to make matters worse, they will know that you are associated with us. There are members of their kind who actively seek our family out in an effort to eliminate us, but none of our kind are safe from them—our existence is the only threat to the lifestyle they prefer to lead."

Sophie drew in a ragged breath and glared at him. Dante seemed unaware of her sudden change in temper, but Sophie's mind had connected the dots faster than she'd realized.

He was the leader of the family. He'd dragged her into this mess, and now she had no hope of being free of it. Even with the crap fest that her life usually was, no one was ever trying to kill her. Now she'd been assured of a premature death for just having known this hodge-podge of a family.

Laney flashed to Sophie's side, holding her hand up, palm out, toward Sophie. Alexander took a step closer to her, placing himself more between her and Dante while nonchalantly removing his wrist watch and pretending to wind it. He watched her out of the corner of his eye as she struggled against the unexpected anger that shook her limbs. Zoey stood slowly, keeping an eye on Sophie.

Alexander took another subtle step towards her; he would stop her if she gave in to the instinctual fury towards Dante. All she wanted to do was lunge for his throat in a rage at the circumstance she'd been dragged into. Yet, she suddenly felt heavy, like she was made of lead. An uncomfortable but weak sensation came from the general direction of where Laney stood, as if something were trying to push her backwards.

"Sophie, please calm down," Dante pled soothingly. "It is for your own good that we have introduced you to our life."

She gritted her teeth against the unseen force that held her back, and then huffed a sigh of frustration through her nose and slowly unclenched her fists. She exhaled carefully. After regaining some measure of self-control, she looked at the assembly around her. Once the fog of her anger cleared and she was able to think about things logically again, she had to admit to herself that she *did* feel completely safe there. The thought of spending the night alone in her dorm room was a little more unsettling than spending it here among these people, since her attacker was still on the loose.

"Can I sleep on it?" she asked.

Dante nodded.

Laney's lips suddenly burst into a smile. "Jim can take you home," she cheerfully volunteered.

Jim grinned at Laney and then at Sophie. Nothing kept those two down, apparently.

"Let's do it," he answered before Sophie had a chance to object.

Alexander's eyes shifted quickly to Jim as he replaced his watch on his wrist. "The old-fashioned way," his deep, intimidating voice commanded before he turned and strode out of the room.

Sophie stared after him in wonder.

"Aw, alright," Jim grumbled.

She made a mental note to remember to ask what the difference was between the "old-fashioned way" and whatever Jim had in mind for transportation. She was inclined to assume that it had something to do with the method that had gotten her there in the first place. He grinned down at her. She couldn't have been too far off.

Nevertheless, Sophie sighed with relief that Alexander wasn't taking her anywhere.

Jim chuckled, shook his head and looked from Sophie to where Alexander had been standing.

She grimaced when she'd realized he caught that thought. She wasn't used to being transparent. And, she still couldn't hear any thought that passed through the minds of the family who lived there. As she followed Jim towards the back door, she wondered idly to herself how they blocked her out.

"We'll teach you!" Laney called as she danced herself into a handstand and grinned at her new-found friend.

Sophie glanced over her shoulder incredulously at Laney and at Zoey who clearly didn't seem to think there was anything odd about Laney's behavior, before she followed Jim silently to his huge red Dodge pick-up truck. Climbing in, she folded her hands awkwardly in her lap as he backed the truck into the road.

"Um…so, what's with Laney?" she asked carefully once they were on their way, hoping they'd be out of earshot of the house.

As they traveled further from the Victorian structure, she felt an empty dread creep into her soul, a coldness that she couldn't explain. She almost desperately wanted to go back—pulled like a magnet to the residence.

Jim chuckled again.

*He does that a lot*, she thought. But, no matter how much taunting she received from him, Sophie couldn't deny that this man and his family were the family that made sense to her. It would be nice to have a big brother who poked fun at her. She really didn't have anything to sleep on.

Jim shrugged. "Honestly, we don't really know what's up with Laney," he answered, talking to her as if they were old friends, steering the huge truck easily through the tiny on-campus streets. "She's like this weird little wonder child or somethin', but she's got an old soul, I guess you could say."

"You love her."

He looked at her and smiled an endearingly crooked grin. "Who doesn't love their little sister?"

*So, that's what it was like: a brother-sister thing*, she thought, sorting things out. He didn't respond.

"How about Zoey?" She asked cautiously.

"Ah," he replied. "She's different. She doesn't say much, but when she does, you'd better listen."

Sophie nodded. They continued in silence until they reached her building, but thankfully, it was a comfortable silence. As soon as he cut the engine, Jim looked around them, inspecting everything down to the very shadows for anything unusual.

He came around to the passenger side of the truck and hustled her indoors as quickly as possible, keeping a hand on the small of her back. Once inside, he maintained his vigilance, quickly double-checking all of the dark corners in the hallways.

Sophie would get in so much trouble if one of the resident assistants found out she had a guy up there, but tonight she didn't care. That fate was much safer than not having Jim check her place out, hoping that nothing was waiting for her inside. How quickly her priorities had shifted. Ascending the stairs, she let them both into her room.

He held his hand out to her. "Lemme see your phone."

She silently handed her cell phone over to him. His fingers moved over the keys quickly before he handed it back to her. She raised an eyebrow and looked at him for an explanation.

"I programmed our phone numbers into your cell," he explained. "Call us if y' need anything or if you change your mind before tomorrow morning. You've got mine, Zoey's, Laney's, Dante's and Alexander's in there."

She unconsciously grimaced at the mention of Alexander's name.

"You know, you should really let up on Alex," he said all of a sudden, "or...*Alexander*. Don't let him hear you call him Alex. He doesn't like it."

"What are you talking about?" She was puzzled, but his mind was silent to her.

Jim sighed and then he smiled. "He really likes you, is all," he supplied, his tone softening into brotherly affection.

"Yeah, *right*," she mumbled, toying with her phone absentmindedly. It hardly seemed possible, and she was fairly sure that she didn't want him to think of her like that.

"You might be surprised, kiddo," was his response.

She frowned. "But he's so..." *Irritating, angry, disgruntled, grumpy...* The words shot through her head before she could make them stop. She looked at Jim warily.

He frowned. "You *really* don't know what you're talking about," he warned in a calm voice, coming to Alexander's defense. He spoke with the kind of calmness that shot more of a warning through her body than any shouting could have done.

"Sorry," she muttered.

He shrugged. "I'll be back in the morning to get you," he said, sure that she would make the decision to join their family.

Sophie simply nodded.

"We'll be around, you know, keeping an eye on everything," he said, looking meaningfully towards the window before opening the door to leave.

"Thanks, Jim," she replied, looking down at her hands. "And," she added quickly as he stepped out, "it's really good to meet you."

"You too, kiddo," he replied and stepped through the doorway, closing the door silently.

Sophie sighed when she was finally alone, and probably—hopefully—safe. It felt like her legs were made of lead as she walked slowly to her window and gazed out at the courtyard below. The night was settling around the buildings and there, on a bench below her window, sat Alexander, looking extremely bored. She hadn't expected to see him there. As she watched, Jim walked up to him and Alexander rose in greeting. Sophie could tell they were discussing her; they glanced up in her direction a couple of times as she watched. Jim seemed to be cheerful, but Alexander just appeared to be annoyed. He couldn't possibly like her—Jim had to be wrong.

She reluctantly pulled herself away from the window and walked in slow, aimless circuits around her room, looking at everything without really seeing any of it. As if she could sense his presence, she knew Alexander would stay there all night. That knowledge comforted her to an extent. Surely she was safe—but hadn't she been assured of her safety this morning? That fact kept the nervous energy kindled in her blood, coursing through her veins.

Sophie had a lot to consider…but in reality, not a lot to decide. So, she slowly started to pack her things.

"What other choice do I have?" She murmured.

*Vampires are real.*

As much as she wanted to pinch herself and disbelieve what she'd experienced, she knew it was the truth. She sank down onto her small bed and curled up against the wall, her knees under her chin.

*What should I do?* She thought to herself, over and over.

She was now on the vampires' hit list. That mere fact threatened to make her blood boil. The collective vampire community knew that she was associated with Catherina and the rest of them. Sophie would probably be eliminated the second one of them left her alone, thus the need for the unarmed guard down

below…she glanced toward the window again, but she knew he
was still there; she could feel him.

She shivered.

The reality was hard to digest. In one afternoon, her world
had been turned upside-down. Across the hall, she could hear some
girls gossiping and talking about cute college guys.

*They have no clue,* she thought. They were just as clueless
about the world as she had been that morning.

She was part of the supernatural world now.

Vampires were hunting her now, along with everyone else
she'd just met this afternoon. Even without the threat, the
possibility of everything Catherina and Dante had to offer was
undeniably appealing. They offered her a family, a home. She'd
never really had either of those.

She pushed herself off the bed. Biting on her thumbnail,
she slowly walked back to the window. She looked down at
Alexander, who stood with his back to her building now, his arms
crossed, and leaning against the back of the bench. She
absentmindedly stared at his back, watching his head move slightly
from side to side as he watched the seemingly still night around
him.

She watched as his hair caught the nighttime breeze, and
the stronger gusts disturbed the hem of his coat. He wore a black
trench coat and she would not have been surprised if he were
wearing a fedora as well. His posture and appearance were slightly
antiquated, but not in a bad way; he looked like an old-fashioned
movie star.

He must have heard that she was thinking about him,
because he suddenly turned around and met her eyes without
hesitation. She froze at the window and returned his steady gaze
with one of her own. Even from a distance, he was intimidating but
she wasn't going to let on to that.

She forced her eyes away from his and turned back to her
small room. She contemplated the concept of "home" as the rooms
around her gradually, one by one, fell silent in the night until she
knew from just listening that she was the only person on the floor
still awake.

Time seemed to mean something different to her that night.
She wasn't sure when she'd made the decision, but at some point,

she turned back to her bed, pulled a duffle bag out from under it, and began resolutely and systematically emptying the contents of her dresser into it.

*

"I'm ready to go," Sophie told Jim early the next morning.

She left her dorm room for the last time, and followed Jim silently back to his truck, looking around nervously.

*You've got nothing to worry about, little sis. We'll take care of you,* he told her silently.

She smiled at him, relieved to be trusted with his thoughts. She let him put his arm around her shoulders, and was glad for the protective gesture. She was nearly as tall as he was, but he was easily twice her size, and she felt instantly safe in his presence.

When they walked through the door of the house just a few minutes later, a further sense of security enveloped her. All of the tension seemed to melt away from her. Jim chuckled again under his breath as he walked up the stairs, her bags over his arms, leaving her in the vast entryway below.

*Why does he keep doing that?* She thought, watching him ascend the stairs.

Something caught her attention from out of the corner of her eye and she looked to her right to see Laney, awake earlier than any teenager had a right to, perched precariously on the arm of one of the sofas holding her hands up in front of her face. Sophie edged quietly around the end of the sofa to get a better look at what she was doing. Between Laney's hands was a silver spoon, floating in the air.

*What the hell?!*

"Hi Sophie!" Laney said immediately, making the spoon spin in mid-air and then letting it fall into her hand.

Sophie laughed in amazement, which edged toward hysteria. "That's crazy," Sophie whispered.

"Oh pah-*lease!*" Laney exclaimed. "After *everything* you've heard? And *seen*? *This* freaks you out?" She skipped out of the room, her pretty laugh floating after her as she went.

Sophie exhaled and gaped after her. She shook her head. Laney had a point, but she couldn't help it if she felt like she'd stepped through the rabbit's hole yesterday.

Something caught her attention from the opposite corner. Her eyes darted to where Alexander sat staring at her. He was seated in one of the many chairs spread about the front room, an anciently bound book lying lazily across his lap. Her eyes met his and she suddenly couldn't breathe. She felt a strange, magnetic-like attraction that seemed to be emanating from him.

But unlike what she'd felt the day before when she'd been close to attacking Dante, this force didn't compel her to stop. It didn't push her back, and it didn't serve as a warning. It beckoned. And she wanted to follow it.

*You're kidding me,* she thought.

His eyes narrowed at her a bit, scrutinizing her. He made no move to stand. He simply stared at her with the penetrating gaze that seemed to see everything.

"Welcome home, Sophie," Catherina called from the large stairway.

The greeting wasn't a warm one; it was more a statement of fact. It took all of Sophie's effort to force her eyes from Alexander's, but another part of her brain told her that Catherina probably wanted her to follow her.

Sophie turned slowly, suddenly conscious of her every move as she walked to Catherina. She could still feel Alexander's stoic eyes on her back. Catherina's mouth curved into a small smile. Sophie shot a quick look back over her shoulder to where Alexander had been sitting. He was gone.

"I hope you like the room we have prepared for you," Catherina said, pulling her attention away from the now empty room. Sophie wondered if Catherina really cared if she liked the room at all, or if she was just trying to be cordial.

Catherina frowned at her but didn't say anything.

It took them a while to climb the massive staircase together; Catherina moved slower than Sophie was used to walking. The first floor was comfortable and modern in a generic sort of way, but the second floor's rooms were decorated in a varied array of themes.

They passed a room that must have been Laney's and another that was probably Zoey's. Up a second flight of stairs was Jim's room, and then Alexander's.

"And here is your room," Catherina finally said, indicating the next door. "Jim has already brought your things up for you."

Sophie stepped inside the doorway and let out a little gasp. It was beautiful. It was as if Catherina had stepped into her mind and discovered exactly what she'd love. Everything was soft, white on white textiles—a place she could really let her mind wander. Sophie even had a towering bookshelf already quickly on its way to being filled with books she suspected she would enjoy. Everything else in the room suited her perfectly. They had really done their homework on her.

"Those are from Alexander's personal collection," Catherina said, watching Sophie examine the books. "He believed that you would like them."

Sophie looked at Catherina incredulously. Her mind immediately raced back to the man who she knew was probably on the other side of the wall. "I really don't understand."

"He is quite interested in history as well, and can be a bit of a bookworm himself," Catherina explained with a weak shrug of her fragile shoulders and then looked away. "I am gratified to see that you like it here."

Catherina turned to leave, but then hesitated. She faced Sophie once more, as if she'd forgotten something. "I shall leave you here to rest, since you seem to have neglected sleep last night," she added coldly. Without waiting for an answer from Sophie, she walked off slowly, mumbling strangely to herself like a lunatic in an asylum.

Now that she was alone, she didn't fight the yawns that had been threatening to make an appearance all morning. She walked around her room, taking it all in, allowing her fingers to touch everything lightly despite her lethargy: the cotton on her new bed, the satin of the lampshade, the antique wood of the door and trim until she made her way back to the bed and slumped down on it.

She curled up and reviewed the events of the past twenty-four hours slowly. Despite everything that had happened, she felt strangely relieved. She didn't know what to make of it all, but for the first time in her life, she felt like she was somewhere she belonged. She sighed and relaxed onto the bed and before she knew what had happened, she had drifted off to sleep.

*

The sun traversed the sky into late afternoon. Sophie awoke with a start, sitting straight up. Her fitful sleep had taken up most of the day. It took her a few moments to get her bearings, but once she had, Sophie hugged her knees to her chest and closed her eyes.

For the first time since she had been here, Sophie truly listened. She rocked back and forth absentmindedly as she focused on everything around her. She listened so intently that she could almost feel the others around her.

And that's when she heard it *all*.

When she really listened and no one was guarding their thoughts, she found that she could hear everything.

She found Dante first. He was down in the kitchen, cooking spaghetti for dinner. She was thrilled by the small revelation and grinned at herself.

She concentrated again and the entire picture downstairs opened up to her as the information flooded her brain.

*Catherina sits on a stool in the kitchen, watching her companion; watching him cook for his big family. He calls her Rina; this is the name that only he is allowed to use. She smiles at him. They are discussing when they think the other one might show up.*

Sophie smiled to herself. All along, she just had to figure out how to become attuned to their minds. She excitedly decided to try someone else and almost frantically searched for another target; Jim seemed like an entertaining choice. Closing her eyes, Sophie concentrated again until she found him. It didn't take long. He and Alexander were silently arguing somewhere in the house.

*So when are you gonna tell her?* Jim asked. He sounded happy, even in his thoughts.

*Now James, whatever do you mean?* Alexander's silent voice asked back. Sophie thought that—just maybe—Alexander was taunting him.

*Jim,* was the firm, correcting reply.

*As you say.*

*You know exactly what I mean. Our new little addition. She likes you too, but she's not gonna admit it.*

"What?" Sophie gasped to herself. She suddenly wanted out of the eavesdropping hole she'd fallen into. She frantically tried to stop listening, but she couldn't pull her mind from *his* now that it was there, no matter how imperative the action seemed to be.

*I hardly believe what you are saying. Besides, she seems terrified of me,* Alexander answered casually distracted, though Sophie thought that maybe he sounded a little sad.

"I don't want to hear this," Sophie sang to herself, as if she were able to block it out that way.

*Well, yeah! You sit there in the corner and stare at her like you're gonna eat her or something. I'd be pretty damn terrified too, Al.*

*Alexander.*

Jim laughed. *Whatever. So, when?*

*Do you* not *realize that she could be listening?*

*You think? Why don't you go surprise her?*

Sophie's heart raced so quickly that she thought it'd pound out of her chest. She wasn't ready for that. What would she say to him if he decided to follow Jim's suggestion?

*No, no, no,* she wanted to argue back. She didn't want anything to do with him in that way.

"Hi Sophie!"

She froze. In her panic, Sophie's usually quick brain couldn't keep up with the sound well enough to decipher the speaker's voice.

She didn't dare open her eyes. She sat with her forehead still on her knees. *Please, please don't let that be him,* she prayed silently.

Without raising her head, she peeked with one eye at the person in her doorway. She breathed a sigh of relief. Laney skipped over to her bed and planted a kiss on Sophie's cheek as she stared at her in wonder.

Laney frowned. "You okay?" she asked.

"Yeah," Sophie replied absentmindedly. "Thanks."

"Who'd you think I was?" Laney asked, cocking an eyebrow at her. "Wait. Never mind. Dante said dinner's ready, so I want to show you something really quick."

Sophie smiled at her and thought she had to be the most adorable girl she'd ever met.

"Thank you!" Laney replied with a big grin. "Now listen: you're gonna love this! We all have a special gift. Well, more than one, but whatever! The vampires can run really, really fast...almost fly, fly, fly, right? So...we can move from one place to another *without running!*"

Sophie watched her warily. Laney laughed at the look on her face.

"The only catch..." Laney began to say, but her eyes glazed over. She was lost in a wayward thought, but was back to normal just as quickly.

"Are you okay?" Sophie asked.

"Yeah, sorry!" She grinned sheepishly at Sophie. "What was I saying? Oh, yeah. The only catch is that we have to have seen where we want to go before we can get there, and sometimes we're too far from where we want to go, so it does limit us *a little*, but it's really cool. We call it jumping 'cause we don't know what else to call it, and it happens just like that"—she snapped—"Like a blink of an eye, quick as a jump!" She giggled in the middle of her breathless chattering.

"What are you talking about?"

"Watch this. I'll think about standing in the hallway."

Sophie watched as Laney closed her eyes, took a deep breath and then a split second later was standing in the hallway. Sophie gasped in complete disbelief as Laney smiled at her, several feet away from where she'd started.

"Now you try. Come to me. Just close your eyes and envision the hallway. Then all you have to do is want to be there," Laney instructed.

Sophie didn't completely trust her, but she figured it was worth a shot. She closed her eyes and thought about the hallway. Almost an instant later, she felt a sudden breeze hit her face.

"Whoa!" she exclaimed.

Laney reached out to grab Sophie as she took a step backwards in shock.

"You okay?" Laney asked.

"Uh..." Sophie began, "yeah, I'm okay." She giggled to herself. She was more than okay; she was elated.

*Excellent job,* thought Dante, now that they were all in sync with one another.

*Way to go, Sophie!* Jim thought from somewhere else in the house.

"Is that how Alexander got me here so fast yesterday?" She asked Laney.

"Yeah. Pretty cool, huh? Now, try it again, but try to go downstairs this time," Laney said.

The only room she'd seen downstairs was the front room.

*Okay, here goes nothing,* she thought to herself.

Laney nodded in encouragement.

Sophie drew in a breath, trying not to worry that everyone would be watching or listening for her next move. Closing her eyes, she saw the front room in her mind's eye. She felt the air move out of her way, but she was prepared for it the second time.

What she wasn't prepared for was what happened next. She opened her eyes with a gasp and stumbled backwards from Alexander. He was so close that she could feel his breath on her cheek. She tripped over the rug behind her in her haste. Without thinking, he reached out and caught her hand before she could fall back into the glass table. He pulled her into his arms in an effort to steady her.

Her sharp ears heard the steady beats of his heart in his chest, obviously unaffected by the encounter. Sophie, on the other hand, had to hold her breath to keep it from escaping her lungs too quickly.

Out of the corner of her eye, she caught Catherina shoot a sideways glance at Dante. She'd missed the silent communication, but Alexander hadn't. He frowned and roughly dropped his arms from Sophie and marched into the dining room, leaving her behind, stunned. She let out a shaky breath and hugged her arms around her chest, rubbing them where he'd held her. She turned around, and her eyes widened in shock. He had kept her from crashing into the glass table behind where she stood.

"That was awesome!" Jim yelled from the top of the staircase, snapping her attention back to the moment.

Sophie could feel a smile spread slowly across her face as she looked up at him. "Thanks, Jim."

Zoey was there instantly and laid her arm across Sophie's shoulders. "You're doing very well," she said.

Sophie remembered what Jim had said about the redhead – she wasn't very talkative, but what she did say meant something more. Sophie smiled to herself; she didn't think Zoey would have said anything complimentary just to be nice.

*You're right,* Zoey answered her silently.

Sophie nodded gratefully.

"Come on," Zoey said aloud and walked with Sophie into the dining room.

Catherina smiled vaguely at Sophie as the pair walked into the vastly windowed dining room. Laney and Jim were already there; it would take her a while before she was comfortable traveling in any other way than her slow, human method of transportation.

Catherina took her place at the head of the table with Dante on her right and Laney to her left. Alexander sat at the foot of the table. The chairs to his left and right remained empty. From the opposite ends of the table, the two exchanged a cold look but didn't say anything to each other.

# Chapter 8

The room was hauntingly quiet and Sophie was alone. A library in and of itself was nothing unfamiliar to her, but she sat silently in this one for the first time, playing absentmindedly with the silver cross that hung around her neck. Zoey had brought it to her soon after her arrival, but it had been unclear who the gift may have been from.

She ran her fingers along the edge of the book's pages where it was spread in front of her on the table. The musty odor of ancient books hung in the air with the dust motes that danced in the slanting sunlight. She had, of course, been given free reign of the house and Dante had encouraged her to come here almost immediately after her arrival. She'd made a habit of studying there; learning everything she could about this new, alien life in the few weeks that she'd made the Leone family home her own.

She perused the shelves in search of something promising and was about to give up for the day, when her eyes fell on a very thin, dusty book in the corner on one of the highest shelves. When she'd pulled it down, she found that it was an old journal of Catherina's, all but forgotten. It was really more of a memoir than anything; she wondered if Catherina had written it for herself or for others. Its words were sentimental, but they sounded oddly instructive at the same time, as if the writer had suspected that she might not always be around to tell the tale.

Flipping the pages aimlessly, the book fell open arbitrarily near the middle of the volume. There was no date for the entry, but the words caught Sophie's eye and she began reading Catherina's musings. She learned more about the woman in a few paragraphs than she ever had in talking to her, but it felt voyeuristic to be reading something so personal.

*I shall always remember the first time I saw him. I stood on the pier in Venice; the day was bright. His name came to mind once more and I closed my eyes. The beautiful breeze from the water rose up to run through my hair; the sun was warm on my face, bright on my eyelids. I breathed in the sweet smell of the Mediterranean and was lost in the beauty of such a place. When I opened my eyes, I knew I was being watched and there I beheld him. It was like coming home.*

*After our first meeting, it was difficult to be separated from Dante, and the feeling was mutual. It is as if the human emotion of love is greater within us. I do not truly understand the reason, but I do know that our companion is not a choice, not a conscious decision. He or she is shown to us in a time which is not our own. I believe that we are paired with another in order to help strengthen us.*

*Dante's strengths compliment my weakness and my strengths compliment his. Thoughts flow more quickly between us than between any other beings, and we are intimately attuned to one other. At any point in the day, I know exactly where Dante is and what he is doing, and the same may be said about him with regards to me. There have been times that Dante and I have faced an adversary together, and in those instances, we have functioned as a single entity, rather than two individuals. The alliance between companions is stronger than any other I have ever experienced – it even rivals the relationship I had with my father. Given the choice between one's companion, and another individual, it is one's companion who invariably is chosen in the matter. That is the choice I would make; I would choose him over any of my other acquaintances or family. This is not to say that I do not love the rest of my family. It simply means that Dante is my other half and without him I would cease to exist.*

Below this entry, in Catherina's antique handwriting, was a translation of Dante's name: *everlasting*. Sophie was surprised that Catherina hadn't filled the rest of the page with girlish scribbles, like the kind girls always scratched on their notebooks in high school. Sophie half expected to see lines and lines of "Mrs. Dante Leone" filling the page.

She sighed, stretched, and rubbed her eyes as she leaned back in her chair. She'd been reading for the better part of the afternoon, catching up on the common knowledge already shared by those of her new family; she felt alarmingly behind the learning curve.

"Ugh," she mumbled, rubbing her head. "My brain is fried."

She needed a break and some time to think. She wasn't about to try "jumping" up to her room though. She needed a little more practice with that, since the last time she'd tried it, she nearly landed in Alexander's lap. She probably would have too, if he'd been seated.

She pushed back from the table, and was about to stand when the door creaked open and the subject of her current thoughts stood in the entry. She jumped.

"You scared me," she said automatically. She still couldn't hear his thoughts; she'd had no warning that he was just feet away from her.

"My apologies," he replied. He looked about as uncomfortable as possible, watching her from the doorway. "Er...," he said, finally finding the apparently elusive words, "Are you finding all that you are looking for?"

"I think so," she responded slowly, sitting back in her chair. She wondered what he wanted, but she didn't ask.

He cleared his throat and deliberately walked around the table to look on the shelf behind her. She refused to look around and struggled to keep her breathing even. Her hyper-sensitive ears heard his breath, his whispering footfalls, and then the nearly silent scrape of a book being pulled from a shelf behind her.

"Ah, these are so dusty," he said to himself regretfully, blowing the dust from the cover.

He placed the book on the table in front of her. Sophie looked down to see that it was one of the volumes that she'd intentionally skipped.

"Yeah, I can't read Latin," she blurted out matter-of-factly.

"I can."

Her jaw dropped open before she shut it with an audible snap. She resisted the urge to get lost in the confident smile he wore as he spoke to her.

63

He turned away from her to look at the dusty tome, and he started turning the pages. He was still standing over her, leaning over her, really. As he slowly leaned on the table, his hand almost touching her arm, Sophie was extremely aware of the closeness of his body next to her own. She glanced briefly over her shoulder at him, but his eyes were steady and serious as he thumbed through the pages from above.

"These are Dante's memoirs," he explained, glancing at her quickly.

She caught her breath as she stared back into his very green eyes. Thankfully, her mind was blank so he couldn't read her thoughts, but her heart audibly pounded in her chest. She could hear it, so she knew he could as well.

He turned back to the book as if he hadn't noticed the flush in her cheeks and the catch in her breath. She tried— unsuccessfully—to ignore the warmth of his body, so close to her own. She rolled her eyes. This was getting ridiculous.

Dragging his finger across the page, jumping from the end to the beginning of sentences and back again to the beginning as one has to do when reading Latin, he translated the strange writing for her quietly.

"It says, 'My first encounter with a vampire was in the year 1432. Holding Mass, I perceived a different sort of parishioner in my presence'," he began, pausing from time to time to jump around the page, piecing the words together.

"Wait," she said, holding her hand up to stop him. "Dante was a priest?"

"Yes," he replied. "He devoted his life to the church until he determined the futility of continuing on in such a conspicuous profession—while not aging. After a time, it simply raised too many questions. Our safety in many ways depends upon our anonymity."

She nodded. It made sense. "Sorry," she apologized. "Go on...please."

He smiled quickly before turning back.

"'When the congregation filed out of the chapel, one single individual remained. He was deathly pale and looked to be suffering from some sort of disease. I feared the plague for the sake of my parishioners, but knowing that I would be free from harm, I approached him.

"'What may I do for you, my son?' I asked him.

"'Father,' he begged, 'I need your help.'

"'I encouraged him to continue. With some hesitation, he told me what he had become and how he thirsted for blood. He had not made the decision to become a vampire, as it had been forced upon him. He explained to me that to his understanding, an unwilling individual was the only type of vampire who possessed remorse for what they had become; at least that was the case for him. He pleaded with me to free him from his existence.

"'I responded that I could not make such a decision lightly and told him to return the next morning.'"

Alexander hastily flipped the next few pages.

"Wait, what are you skipping over?" she asked quietly, but her words stopped his hand as surely as if she'd shouted them.

"His meditations regarding whether or not he felt that he could kill someone who was not human; if it would be considered murder or mercy," he explained.

"And did he?" she whispered.

"Yes, in the end," he answered, holding her gaze. "It says that after he had complied with the vampire's supplication, he had to contend with the fiend's creator. It was the beginning of Dante's quest as he hunted the vampires within his parish. Soon, he found it to be overrun with the devils," he explained. He never looked away from her as he stared relentlessly into her eyes.

Sophie traced every contour of his face with her eyes. Every feature was familiar, even the glint of gold in his piercing green eyes. Her heart pounded against her chest. He leaned toward her, but didn't seem to be aware of his own movements.

She suddenly looked away and stood up, pushing the chair back so quickly that it would have fallen if he hadn't caught it without looking, refusing to take his eyes from her. She exhaled heavily and ran her hands through her hair as she walked to the window, fighting against the feelings that were surfacing.

She massaged the sides of her head as he turned to sit on the edge of the table, rubbing his hands together softly and watching her.

"Are you alright?" he asked quietly, articulating each word carefully and folding his arms across his chest as he watched her.

"Uh…yeah, I've just been at this all day," she tried to convince him. She folded her own arms across her chest, but quickly dropped them when she'd seen that she was mirroring his posture.

He nodded and sighed with a chuckle to himself. "I'll leave you alone," he said before turning to leave the room.

"Wait," she said suddenly, stepping towards him and then hesitating, adding, "…please."

He stopped mid-stride and pivoted on a heel to face her. His abrupt compliance startled her.

She took a deep breath. "You said that the vampire Dante killed was unwilling. What did he mean by that, exactly?" she asked.

"Ah," he responded, nodding, "I am not surprised you asked. I shall explain. Please sit," he said, gesturing to a chair at the table.

She shook her head. "Uh…that's okay, I'll stand," she answered awkwardly. "Thanks."

He shrugged and sat in a chair on the opposite side of the table, nearest the door. *As you wish.*

He cleared his throat and leveled his eyes at her. "The mechanics of transformation are quite gruesome."

She nodded and sucked in a breath. "Tell me."

"Do you recall what Dante told you about the exchange of blood between a human and a vampire?"

"Yes," she said, swallowing hard against the tightening in her throat as she took an unconscious step toward him. She hadn't liked that bit of newly-learned information—it was just too creepy.

"A vampire *typically* stalks a victim for some time before striking, to decide if they are worth the transformation. Vampire relationships are rooted in the blood; they are especially binding and extremely strong. A wise, and usually older, vampire may even take the time to make friends with a human being before changing one. He convinces the human that he can be trusted. Some have even been known to reveal themselves completely to their chosen prey before striking; some believe that it smoothes the transition more easily. Regardless, a human who becomes a vampire almost always has to make the conscious decision to become one of those…those *fiends*. There are some, however, who are simply left too weak at the point between life and death to make the choice."

"What do you mean?" she asked, walking towards the table.

"The vampire strikes, draining his victim of a majority of his blood," he explained. "At that time, the human is given the choice: either surrender and die, or…" he hesitated, "…*partake* of what the vampire offers." A disgusted look spread momentarily across his face.

She slowly sank into a chair across from him, still holding his gaze.

"If a human takes in a vampire's dead, cold blood in exchange for his warm, wholesome, human blood, then his soul is lost," he answered coolly.

She dropped her eyes to the table where they traced the microscopic grooves and scars in the wood.

"In this way, the human takes the unholy into himself, to become one of the fallen. The devil's kind, as I have heard someone once say."

Sophie was quiet for a long time, her head swimming with the implications. He waited, letting her sort through her thoughts.

It all boiled down to one question, and it was a question that she knew she'd never be able to answer unless facing it firsthand: If the devil offered you life for death, evil as that life may be, would you be seduced into accepting his offer, as you stared the Grim Reaper in the face?

"So…" she proceeded slowly trying to make sure she understood everything correctly. "The ones who are remorseful, they didn't make that choice, right?"

He nodded. "Yes, that is correct. A vampire may *force feed*…"--Sophie felt nauseous--"…a victim his own blood, thereby depriving him of his free will in the matter. Some choose to live, while others--like the one who sought Dante out--wish to die, remorseful of what they have become, regardless of their lack of blame in the matter."

"Wow," she whispered, gazing out the window and shaking her head. "That *sucks*."

"Indeed!" He laughed at her unintended pun. The sound startled her; she'd never heard him laugh before. She had somehow thought he never laughed.

She couldn't keep herself from laughing along with him, immediately breaking some of the tension in the room. They looked at one another and their laughter faded when he caught her eye again. He cleared his throat and watched her as they fell silent. A few awkward seconds passed which felt like an eternity.

She looked at him seriously. "How many have you killed, Alexander?"

He became very somber again. Her heart accelerated as he gazed at her. There weren't words to express what he seemed to be able to do to her without even trying. She shifted uncomfortably under his gaze, waiting for his answer.

He sighed. "Too many to count," he finally answered in a soft voice.

He stood and silently walked out of the room, leaving her in silence.

She turned and gazed out of the window to her right, thinking over everything he'd said, her head spinning. It meant something more now that she knew that the vampires they faced, the ones that would happily attack her on the street—in broad daylight, no less—had made the conscious decision to take up the lifestyle; to become a monster. She still didn't know if she could kill one of them, but she also couldn't see them in exactly the same way as before. What she'd learned had changed things drastically.

How Catherina had ever lived with one—and *like* one— for so long, boggled Sophie's mind. The mere thought of something like that disgusted her, affecting her on a core level in ways she hadn't anticipated.

She stared out the window until she'd finally calmed down. She definitely needed a break. Sophie didn't even try to figure out what had her so frazzled. She told herself that it was the stories she'd heard, but she knew, as soon as she'd had the thought--at the very moment the excuse had entered her mind--that she was lying to herself. She turned from the window and left the library, closing the door softly behind her.

As she passed his closed door on the way to her own room, she paused.

*What do you want, Sophie?* Alexander asked gently, although his thoughts affected her as if he'd yelled the words.

She froze. Had he been listening for her?

*I'm sorry*, she thought apologetically. She listened for his response, for some small thought from his mind.

But there was nothing.

It was just as well, she supposed, she wasn't interested in getting hurt and she wasn't interested in complicating relationships. She thought he'd warmed to her in the library, but now he was back to giving her the cold shoulder and the whole situation left her utterly confused.

But she'd stopped at his door. Because no matter what she told herself, what he thought actually mattered to her.

She almost hated that she had come to want to be near him, to be in same house as him. It felt like she was losing her independence, her self-reliance. But, was she really?

She knew one thing: she was confused. These feelings were so new and strange that she didn't know how to describe them. She certainly felt better in the house than not, and she was inexplicably more at peace when he entered the room. She felt an almost Zen-like sensation when she was at home.

"Home," she whispered to herself, liking the way the word sounded. It was a new concept.

She suspected the calming feeling—the sense of completeness—had more to do with Alexander than she cared to admit. In fact, she could *feel* the exact moment he walked in the front door.

She always wanted an answer, a plan to things. Once she'd become an adult, and finally after so many long, difficult years, she actually had a say in what happened in her life, but everything seemed out of control.

Stewing over the situation, she asked herself if it was really so bad to be drawn to someone like she was to Alexander. Her own personal history had taught her that any sort of attachment to another person could be dangerous. You got attached to someone, started caring about them, and before you knew it, you'd ceded control of parts of yourself to that other person irrevocably. She'd lost herself like that before. She walked into her room and shut the door softly.

*Am I being stupid?* She asked herself as she gently brushed her fingers along the wall that separated her from him.

Sure, she hadn't had great luck with guys; they had the tendency to be assholes. They acted one way on the outside, but their minds were usually in the gutter…not that they ever realized Sophie knew it. She'd certainly had friends who resisted the temptation to be with someone…but all it accomplished was a delay in the inevitable.

And what was developing *felt* inevitable, undeniable—irrevocable. It felt…inescapable.

"Ugh!" she moaned, plopping down on her bed, burying her face in her pillow, and hitting the mattress with her fist. "Forget about him," she told herself. *What is he to me?*

She flipped over and rolled the question around in her brain. She didn't know the answer, and more questions just sprang up uselessly in her head in revolt and her thoughts continued to drift back to him.

# Chapter 9

Two Months Before—The Same College Town

The cafe was one of her favorite haunts, and she'd slipped away during her break between classes again. She sidled up to the counter and paid for her coffee before heading back outside to walk back to campus.

She let her mind wander for a while: people watching, feeling the wind tickle her hair. She lost track of time that way and it always had a calming effect on her. Her sharp eyes roved around the little green area next to the English department's building across the street. It was a slightly sloping, tiny little park in the midst of all the concrete and brick of the university. The leaves had begun to dust the still-green grass, but the pretty scenery wasn't what caught her eye. She picked him from the crowded sidewalks because he looked out of place. He was tall and catlike, built like a runner, with the bearing of a soldier. She froze.

She had initially failed to notice him because his mind was silent to her; it hadn't demanded any of her attention, but she had soon found him, as if she'd known he was there. His intense green eyes held her gaze. He was everywhere.

*Why do you keep following me?* She thought.

*To keep you safe.*

She hadn't expected a response.

"What?!" she shouted across the street, not caring who heard her. There had been months of being followed by several strangers, but they had never let her into their heads.

A panicked look swept across his face in a flash, before he returned to his usual stoic behavior. She wasn't supposed to have heard that; she was sure. She walked towards him, crossing the street without looking to see if the way was clear; she had to know who he was.

She was in the middle of the street when the car horn blared. She jerked her head to the side. A punk kid with dyed black-blue hair was flipping her off.

"I'm sorry!" she shouted, and backed out of the way.

The car passed with a flurry of foul language and grinding gears. Once it was gone, Sophie looked up.

The man was still standing there, just a few feet away. A look a horror was frozen on his face. Her eyes met his again, and she was obviously okay. He visibly relaxed, and a faint smile appeared on his lips. Sophie looked to the left and right before starting across the street once more, but when she looked for him again, he was gone.

She ran across the street and stood in the green space. She turned circles as she looked around, but he was gone.

She kept her eyes peeled for him the rest of the day. But he was gone, and she irrationally felt like she was going to cry. She was possessed with such emptiness that she felt hollow inside.

# Chapter 10

"This cannot stand!" one of them shouted from the gloom. His voice echoed around the dark, circular chamber, his Slovak voice ringing rough with rage.

"We shan't allow such an outrage! Something *must* be done!" a shrill female voice called into the crowd, pounding her fist against the chair she sat in, exciting those around her into hisses.

They commenced arguing amongst themselves—a cacophony full of fury and agitation—until a louder, more maniacal hiss broke the commotion. The room fell into a tense quiet. Those who had been standing took their seats; their archaic thrones. The light footfalls, barely audible on the rough stones, stopped in the middle of the nearly dark room. Shadows danced off the figure from the sconces of flame that adorned the walls. She raised her head and eyed the assembly with a dark look.

"My children," the ancient, lyrical female voice began, "I know that the news of our losses pains you; however, we shall not act at this time."

There were mutinous rustlings among those gathered. She continued to speak regardless of their disruption, as a monarch of perceived divine right.

"What has occurred *is* a travesty," she said, carefully pronouncing the words in her heavy Romanesque voice, "but we shall move *slowly* forward in an effort to contend with these…individuals."

The audience rustled around her at the perimeter of the room. One brave individual stepped tentatively forward, his long robes grazing the uneven stones underfoot. He stooped in a slow, sweeping bow even though her back was turned to him.

"But, my Queen," his grave voice protested in supplication.

She spun, her robes flaring out from her shoulders as she moved. The movement of fabric was the only sound in the room. She glared at him with a sharp, piercing eye and dared him to speak with a look. Her severe features added to her menace as she looked down her razor sharp nose at him.

Stepping back, he bowed his head and spoke no more.

She stepped forward and closed the space between them. "They *shall* be dealt with," she vowed, leveling her eyes at him and spat her words out. "However, we *must not* send more of our lambs to the slaughter. Let us refrain from action for the present and let our lost ones' souls rest for a time as we deliberate on our next course of action." She sank into an instinctual crouch at the perceived challenge.

"Your Highness," a Celtic, male voice submitted, clearing his throat. "Perhaps we send a warning?"

She straightened from her crooked posture, and looked to him with a thoughtful, black eye, debating the wisdom of his words. She nodded her head slowly.

"Yes. Hmm…perhaps that *is* the best way. We shall send a warning. Perhaps it will tempt them to forgo their lifestyle, surrender their so-called mission, and save more of our brothers and sisters from destruction."

She looked to all the faces in the round room, and nodding, she gave the command, ignoring the tangible skepticism of those surrounding her.

"Make it so," was the command.

# Chapter 11

Dante waited at the dining room table. He and Catherina had called a meeting. Laney was the first to appear. She came bouncing in from the backyard, fresh from some time outdoors. She laughed for no apparent reason in her light, childlike way. Dante smiled to himself and looked proudly at his sweet daughter.

His eyes moved to Catherina who hovered in the corner. His smile faded. The years had been difficult for her in ways that they shouldn't have been. Her body suffered greatly for the choices she had made early in her life. She had been so strong. Now, she sat silently and wrung her hands together—as she rocked back and forth slightly—waiting for the others to arrive. She glanced up at him and smiled, a wave of calm clearly washing over her. He relaxed into a smile in return.

Zoey appeared in her seat at the table with a smirk on her face. *They're so stubborn,* she thought.

Dante winked at her as Jim lumbered into the room with Sophie gliding in on his heels. Alexander made an effort to appear nonchalant by slowing his stride and putting some distance between himself and Sophie as he walked in. The latter ignored him gracefully.

Dante chuckled under his breath at his brother, whose behavior was so out of character. Alexander had never allowed himself to be ruled by his emotions before, and the change in him was profound.

*Alea iacta est,* Dante thought. *The die is cast.*

Alexander glared at him and shook his head once in stiff defiance. Dante suppressed the desire to smile in response.

"Everyone, please be seated," Dante instructed. Their customary places were taken and six sets of eyes were suddenly on him. "Catherina believes that the new one is here already."

There were inquiring looks across the table and Dante began to answer the questions as they silently came to his mind.

"Sophie, a university is a large attraction for individuals the world over—both human and supernatural," he answered. "That is why we have been so fortunate to find you and we are now waiting for another in the same place. The cosmopolitan atmosphere attracts individuals of *all* sorts."

Alexander exhaled deliberately.

"I do not know when, Zoey," Dante replied. He looked to the youngest girl at the table.

"I do not know why you did not see it, Laney, but that is why Catherina wanted us to come together. We hope that Sophie is able to help you both."

Sophie shot a confused look at Dante. He looked to Catherina, who rose slowly and walked to Sophie's side. The older woman took her hand.

Zoey looked from one woman to the other. "Is that wise this early?"

Catherina glared at her before turning back to Sophie. "Come with me for a moment. Do not be alarmed," she said.

Sophie hesitantly rose from her chair. Laney bounced out of her seat to take Catherina's other hand and the three stood in a small triangle.

Zoey held her breath. Jim sat on the edge of his chair, eagerly watching what was happening. Alexander sat back in his seat, arms folded across his broad chest, silently watching from under his eyelashes, tense with anxiety. In all of their centuries together, Dante had never seen him in such a state.

Catherina explained: "Our power increases when we make physical contact and work together as a unit, one with the other. Laney and I have enjoyed great success in the past and we are hoping that with you, the three of us will be better able to focus our energy. We females are gifted with extra talents which enable us to do this."

"What about Zoey?" Sophie asked.

The tall redhead shook her head. "My gift is different," she replied calmly.

Sophie shrugged and looked back at Catherina and Laney. "What do I do?" she asked.

"Here," Laney chimed in, "take my hand. Then, close your eyes and concentrate. Catherina will direct our thoughts since she's seen this guy or girl before in her own visions. Just relax. It'll be really cool. Cool, cool, cool...as... a cucumber!" She glanced sheepishly at Sophie who was staring at her in disbelief. "Sorry."

"It's okay," Sophie whispered back, wide-eyed.

The trio of women stood in a circle, joined hands, and closed their eyes.

"Now, concentrate," Catherina murmured to the other two.

The others, still seated at the table, watched as the other three began to sway subtly. The motion increased until they all appeared to be on the verge of losing their balance when suddenly, all three became completely still.

Catherina began speaking slowly, "There...are..."

"Three," Sophie suddenly interjected. All eyes shot to her, though her own remained closed. Even Catherina and Laney came out of their trance and watched her. They kept a tight grip on her hands.

Zoey and Jim exchanged a look.

"*Three?*" Alexander demanded suddenly and loudly, his voice booming through the stunned silence.

Dante shot him a look of warning, but Sophie was already responding automatically to Alexander's question.

"...walking down the street. Two...women, one man...looking, searching...for...something... Us?" She answered very slowly, sounding unsure of herself.

"What are their names?" Dante asked cautiously. He glanced hopefully at Alexander. "Perhaps we know them."

She shook her head.

"Can you sense what their names are, Sophie?" Catherina asked quietly.

"Not...uh...no, I'm not sure."

"Come on Sophie, you can do it. Who are they?" Laney prompted in a gentle whisper.

Again Sophie shook her head, the frustration building as her cheeks became flushed with the effort. She was faltering; her breath increased and she was about to lose the image.

Jim started lightly pounding the table with the side of a closed fist, unconscious of the action. He looked at Alexander, his face full of anxiety. *Three?* Jim thought. *This could be bad.*

Alexander simply remained as he had been, watching and waiting.

"Try, Sophie," Catherina begged softly.

"I…I…can't," Sophie began, starting to panic, a small tear sliding between her eyelids in frustration. She was trying desperately to focus, but couldn't regain control of the vision.

Alexander suddenly pushed off of his chair to stand. He walked to Sophie and stopped directly behind her. Dante and Jim exchanged a look.

"Sophie. What are their names?" His voice was commanding.

She seemed to visibly relax. "Masumi," she responded immediately. "…Celia." Alexander stiffened, but almost immediately sighed in relief. "…Charlie, no *Chaz*."

He placed his hands carefully on her shoulders, glancing quickly around the room before speaking again. "Good work. Now, what else do you see?" he whispered in her ear, calmer this time.

Laney looked at Dante. *What's he doing? It's going to wear her out. She looks like she's going to pass out. The first time is always the hardest.*

The patriarch shook his head, *Wait. He knows what he was doing; how far he can push her.*

Sophie's breathing slowed and her head sunk to her chest. Dante watched as she swayed ever-so-slightly from side to side like a monk in meditation. Laney and Catherina kept tight hold of her hands and watched her warily while Alexander continued to grasp her shoulders.

"Celia's tall…curly hair…really thin and she likes to wear black."

Alexander nodded in recognition as she continued. "Masumi is…closer to…Laney's size…Japanese…she walks like a dancer…Chaz is Celia's companion…She's the leader…They're on their way here."

"That's very good, Sophie," Alexander encouraged. "Look around. Can you see anything else?" he asked gently. "Perhaps something of their surroundings?"

Her brow furrowed in concentration, but suddenly, her eyes shot open and she was falling, her legs folding underneath her. Alexander and Laney caught her. Sophie looked around, confused. Zoey and Jim were immediately at her side.

*What happened?* Sophie thought. She'd lost the image altogether.

"You have done remarkably well, Sophie," Catherina answered before Dante or anyone else could, looking down on the younger woman who had sunk down to the floor at her feet. Sophie still leaned against Alexander.

"Are you alright?" Dante asked, stepping closer to her.

"I think so," she said rubbing her head before suddenly realizing who she leaned against. She shot out of his embrace so quickly that Dante caught her so she wouldn't fall.

"Geez, Soph. He won't bite!" Jim exclaimed with a chuckle.

"Unless you *want* him to!" Laney joked, her laugh ringing through the air.

Alexander stood and straightened his shirt as he stared emotionless at Laney. Sophie was mortified. She could feel her face burning with embarrassment.

*Why won't they all just leave me alone about him?* She asked herself.

Jim and Laney had teased her about him since she'd arrived and she didn't fully understand why.

Zoey smiled sympathetically and looked from her to Alexander and back again before returning to her seat.

Dante helped Sophie back to her chair.

"*Amor tussisque non celantur,*" Dante murmured under his breath with a meaningful glance at Alexander. *Love and a cough are not concealed. Perhaps it is not love, but it will be easier for you both to admit the connection.*

Alexander glared at his brother and shook his head once. "Do you know when they are coming?" he asked Sophie calmly, watching her carefully from his adjacent seat.

Catherina interjected, "I believe they will arrive in a week," though she couldn't be sure because Sophie wasn't exactly sure of the timing herself.

Sophie closed her eyes and tried to slow her breathing down, pinching the top of her nose between her eyes as she fought off the dizzy feeling that had overcome her. She sighed. "Okay, would somebody please tell me what the hell is going on? What just happened?" She sounded weak.

Jim pointed to Catherina. "You want to know why Catherina's the leader here? That's why," he said.

*What? What does that even* mean? She thought back and dropped her hands on the table in frustration.

"Sophie," Dante began gently, "the females of our kind are gifted with many special talents. One such talent is that in groups, you may more finely attune your telepathy. I must say though, that I have never seen it have such a powerful affect on anyone as it has upon you. It is quite interesting."

Sophie snorted. *Interesting, huh?* She tried to understand what had just happened as everyone talked. Her mind was so hazy and later, she didn't remember much of what they talked about. She just remembered that if felt like a swirl of sounds flooding her senses.

"How are you, Sophie?" Laney asked—her voice saturated with concern so mature it took Sophie a moment to recognize it when her voice that cut through the confusion.

"It's weird. When I first came out—or came to, or *whatever* that was—I wouldn't have been able to tell you what I saw. It's starting to come to me, though...I *think*. It's starting to make more sense," Sophie said, but really she was just talking to herself.

"Do we have anything to fear of these three?" Catherina coolly asked, pushing Sophie for the fleeting information.

"No," Alexander answered for her. "I am...*familiar* with Celia. She is, no doubt, simply passing through," he explained, disgust in his voice.

"Yes, I noticed you seemed relieved," Zoey said, exchanging a knowing look with him.

"They're looking for us," Laney pointed out.

Alexander sat back in his chair suddenly. He pursed his lips in thought.

"What do you mean you're *familiar* with Celia?" Jim asked, narrowing his eyes at him.

"From many years ago," was all Alexander answered.

Dante nodded in agreement. Jim looked at him for an explanation, but Dante just shook his head.

Sophie sighed heavily and put her face in her hands, her elbows resting on the table, and she closed her eyes. It suddenly felt like she would fall over; she was so weak.

"Are you alright?" Catherina demanded briskly.

Alexander glared at Catherina.

"Uh...yeah, I think," Sophie replied weakly, looking between Catherina and Alexander, wondering about the dynamic there, before realizing she didn't care and adding, "I need some air."

She stood up and started walking towards the front door. Jim and Dante exchanged a look while Alexander scowled at Catherina.

"Do not look at me like that," Catherina said. "*You* were the one who pushed her."

"Damn it Catherina..." Alexander yelled back at her, slamming his fist on the table.

"*STOP HER!*" Zoey yelled before she disappeared.


Sophie walked down the front steps. She saw a man standing on the street corner; the movement barely caught her eye. He sneered at her.

"Gotcha!" he yelled triumphantly and started barreling towards her.

Sophie backed away from him, toward the house, but the stairs behind her tripped her feet out from underneath her body. She landed on the wood steps with a crack and gaped at her would-be attacker. He was now pinned against a tree with a piece of stray wood lodged in his chest.

Sophie looked up to see Zoey standing over her. The redhead's hand was still in mid-air, holding the vampire's stake in place by using some unseen force.

"Oh my God!" Sophie yelled in surprise. Alexander suddenly appeared, placing himself between her and the vampire.

Jim was there too. He stalked towards the vampire who was spouting profanities in their direction. Zoey followed close behind him. Her hand was still raised and she walked slowly, gracefully, and with a purpose towards the vampire.

"Are you alright?" Alexander asked, offering Sophie a hand.

She took it and hauled herself off the ground. "Yeah," she replied in a whisper, watching Zoey and Jim.

The vampire was staring at Sophie with his coal black eyes. A cold rush of adrenaline shot through her body.

"Don't you want to know where your mother is?" he yelled.

"What?"

The vampire started cackling. "You're all going to die."

Jim pulled a long knife out of his belt and ran it swiftly under the vampire's chin. "You first."

The vampire's head bounced to the ground. Zoey's shoulders relaxed as the dead body slumped over the makeshift stake.

"I'll take care of it," Jim said to her.

Zoey turned back for the house without saying a word.

Sophie stared at her. "How did you know?"

"I heard him," Zoey replied simply, before walking back inside.

"Come on," Alexander said, tugging at her arms.

She couldn't look away from the bleeding body. "He said something about my mother."

"It does not matter," he insisted gently.

She glanced up and saw him looking down at her with a pained tenderness she didn't understand, but she was too distracted by what Jim was doing to let her eyes linger on Alexander for too long.

Jim gathered the dismembered body parts and started to walk around the house. Sophie stumbled forward and peered around the corner, leaning against Alexander.

"What's he doing?" she asked.

"Burning the body," he replied quietly.

Her knees threatened to buckle under her. The adrenaline had dissipated so quickly that it left her feeling weak.

"I think I need to lie down."

"You've had a busy day," he agreed, before steering her back towards the house.

She leaned instinctively against him. It was nice to be able to lean on someone.

*Why is the world spinning?* She thought to herself.

"You'll be alright," he whispered.

He practically carried her up the first flight of stairs, and she barely noticed when he swung her up into his arms effortlessly to carry her up the second flight. They were in her room a moment later. She was somewhere between consciousness and sleep, but she could tell that she was lying down when he pulled a quilt out from the trunk at the foot of her bed and tucked it around her body to keep her from shivering; she was nearly in a state of shock after the experience.

She opened her eyes and tried to smile; he was being so nice to her. He paused when he realized she was staring at him.

"I'm sorry," she quickly whispered.

He shook his head and opened his mouth to say something. She held up a hand to stop him.

"No, really. I mean for earlier; for jumping away like that. It just…startled me, is all. You know—when I woke up or whatever in the dining room." She shook her head. Her mind just *would not* be clear, but moving it in the hopes of finding clarity had been a mistake; her head was pounding. "I can't make my brain work."

"It's okay," he whispered and kissed her forehead quickly, his lips barely brushing her skin.

She stared up at him, wide-eyed in disbelief.

"Rest for now," he said in an equally quiet tone and was gone before she'd recovered, disappearing before her eyes.

Sophie pulled the blanket closer and stared at the door, but her mind was blank, like it was trying to catch up to what had happened: the trance she'd been in, how the vampire who knew her mother had almost attacked her, Zoey's unreal speed, and then Alexander's behavior. She wasn't sure which one had shocked her more.

The bed felt like it was spinning. She closed her eyes and tried to breathe. She didn't know how long it took for her to slip into unconsciousness, but at some point, she fell into a deep, dark sleep.

# Chapter 12

Sophie had only been passed out for about half an hour, but she felt as rested as if she'd gotten a full night's sleep. She threw the blanket off of her body and swung her legs down on the side of the bed. It took a few seconds for the blood in her body to keep up with the quick movement, and she felt light-headed.

"Whoa," she said, and tried to steady herself.

"Hey kiddo," Jim said.

She looked up quickly to find him in the hallway outside her door, where he'd stopped in mid-stride as he'd walked past. She smiled warily at him.

"You okay?" he asked, leaning forward through the doorway, his hands bracing his weight on the doorframe.

"Yeah," she replied, nodding. "I feel pretty great actually." She exhaled and looked around the room in thought.

"Good," he interrupted. "You ready for round two?"

"Round two?" she asked cautiously, standing up and walking towards her new brother of sorts. "Do I want to ask?"

He grinned wickedly at her. Suddenly Alexander was there, appearing behind Jim's shoulder.

Sophie glanced down at her feet and then raised her eyes and smiled sheepishly at him, not knowing what else to do. A smile played at the corner of his mouth as he nodded to her.

Jim looked from her to Alexander and chuckled under his breath, shaking his head.

"Let's go see what you can do," Jim said and held his hand out for her to take.

"Um," she hesitated. "...okay."

She placed her hand firmly in Jim's and suddenly found herself outside of what looked like an old storm cellar in the backyard. With a rush of wind that hit her in the back, Alexander, Zoey, and Laney had joined them.

"You wanna warn me next time you do that?" Sophie asked, gripping his arm to steady herself.

"Where's the fun in that?" he asked, and she playfully punched him in the arm.

Jim typed a code into a small keypad to the right of the door and it suddenly opened to a dark, damp, gaping entrance.

"Come on," Jim said and led the way; flicking lights on ahead of them.

Laney, the last one in, turned and pushed a button and the large metal door slid silently shut behind them. They followed Jim down a steadily sloping hallway that dead-ended in a large, brightly lit room lined with what at first glance looked like gym equipment. On closer examination, Sophie saw shelves of weapons mingled with medicine balls, punching bags, and weight benches.

"Seriously cool," Sophie whispered.

"This is where we train," Jim said.

"Train?" Sophie asked skeptically.

He shrugged. "You can't decide to go fight vampires without learning how to do it first. It's pretty obvious that they're not gonna leave *you* alone."

"True. I guess it would be nice to learn how to use a stake or something." *Then I wouldn't feel so helpless.*

Alexander stepped forward. He took a deep breath. "We are going to see what your *abilities* are. Before we start, please do not take offense to anything. We have to provoke you to elicit a usable response from you."

"A *useable* response?" she asked incredulously.

"Think of it as…" he looked to the others before turning back to Sophie, "a diagnostic exam."

"Okay," she replied and took a deep breath. "But, I don't really understand."

"Our abilities are very connected to our emotions. Our emotions tend to be…*volatile,* but through channeling them, we learn to harness our abilities, to use them to our advantage," Alexander explained.

"Huh?"

Jim grinned. "We have to piss you off to see what you're capable of."

"Oh, well *naturally,*" Sophie replied with a sardonic shrug.

Alexander looked at Jim. "Do not forget how raw the emotions are at this stage," he warned him.

Jim nodded and grinned at Sophie.

Laney jumped over to the opposite corner and perched on a weight bench to watch. Zoey silently glided over and took a seat beside her. Alexander turned to Jim, communicating silently with him in a way that Sophie couldn't hear.

*That's a nice trick,* she thought. She looked at the other girls questioningly.

"Don't think," Laney replied. "Just run on instinct."

Zoey nodded.

Sophie was still looking at the girls when she heard something whizzing towards her. The faint sound of the air whistling out of its way became more noticeable as it got closer. She couldn't tell exactly *what* it was, but she knew it was coming right towards her head.

She turned just in time to see an arrow cutting through the air. Alexander stood behind it, a bow in his hand. She stepped to the side and snatched the arrow from its flight as it flew past her head. It twirled on her palm and she hurled it back—arrowhead first—directly at Alexander's head. He swiftly "jumped" out of the way just before it hit him, disappearing and reappearing a few feet away.

"Dodge these if you can!" Jim taunted.

His words alone infuriated her, but she turned just in time to see him fling two handfuls of throwing stars at her, one after the other.

Somewhere deep within her chest, a snarl crawled its way up her throat uncontrollably. She crouched like a lioness about to attack, her hands held out at her sides. She saw him through the tunnel vision of her fury and something instinctual inside her took over.

Counting a total of eight stars without thinking, she sidestepped the majority of them with a spin on her heel. Her hand fell upon one of the shelves of weapons to her left and she reflexively grasped something long and metallic that lay there.

"What the hell are you doing?" she roared at them, her eyes flaming.

"Get ready," Alexander warned Jim. He dropped the bow and crouched closer to the ground.

"Are you trying to *kill* me?!" Sophie screamed at them.

She rocked back on her heels and then barreled towards closer of the two of them. Jim jumped quickly at the last second, disappearing only to reappear behind her. She whirled and tried to grab him from behind. He jumped out of the way right in time. Reappearing several feet away, he turned and charged Sophie. She held her hand up in warning half a second before barreling towards him herself. Her instincts told her that she was in danger; she reacted to them without thought.

The two struggled. Sophie clawed at his face, and Jim just tried to keep her off of him long enough for someone else to help. As she began to gain an advantage over his brother, Alexander suddenly sprang to action. She suddenly had a silver stake in her hand and was about to plunge it into Jim's neck.

Alexander tackled Sophie. The situation escalated faster than he'd anticipated.

The two fell against the opposite wall in a snarling ball of aggression and flesh. He tried to pin her down for her own protection and the safety of the rest of his family. Jim stood up and dusted his shirt off. He ran over to stand between Laney and Zoey. Laney jumped to her feet in horror as they watched Alexander try to wrestle Sophie under control.

"Should we do something?" she asked Jim.

"Just wait," he said, holding her back and refusing to turn away from the wrestling match.

Laney remembered her own such test; she never had the amount of fury that poured out of Sophie now. It was astounding.

Sophie's flaming eyes looked at Alexander, but didn't see him. He struggled to control her.

"NO!" she roared, another animal snarl ripping through her chest. She disappeared and was suddenly out of Alexander's arms and standing over him, about to strike.

He jumped and was immediately behind her, his arms around her waist. She lost her grip on the stake and it fell from her hand to the ground with a metallic ring. Laney saw it, and with a gesture of her own hand, she sent it rolling across the room and out of Sophie's grasp.

"Watch her!" Jim warned just as Sophie jumped again and was behind Alexander this time.

He turned on a heel and grasped her arms at the wrists securing them in his iron grasp behind her back.

"Get off of me!" she screeched and hissed, trying to kick him off of her.

He took three steps forward and finally had her pinned between his body and the wall.

"Stop it!" he warned. "Stop it, now!"

She huffed her breaths out furiously and glared up at him. Her lips curled back from her clenched teeth as she stared at him, trying to wrench herself free.

"Calm down, Sophie," he ordered sternly, his face mere inches from her own.

Her chest heaved with her frenzied panting. He held her there, against the wall, against his chest, keeping the rest of his family safe. She pressed her heels into the concrete wall behind her, trying to launch herself off of it, but he was stronger than she was. She struggled to pull her arms out of his grasp, but he had the advantage of leverage against her.

"Calm down!" He ordered again at an ear-splitting volume.

"I'll *kill* you!" She vowed, spitting mad. She tried to shove off the wall again.

"Oh, I know," he assured her in a commanding tone. "But I would appreciate it if you wouldn't."

Jim snickered. He exchanged a look with Laney who watched the pair nervously.

*She's a fighter,* Zoey thought.

"Calm down, Sophie," Alexander commanded again. "We are not going to hurt you."

He felt some of the tension leave her body as he spoke to her.

"Get control of yourself," he warned. "You *are* safe, but I won't let you go until you are safe for the rest of us."

Sophie took a few deep breaths. The muscles of her face relaxed slowly as she stared back into his eyes, violently at first. She struggled against him periodically, but sanity seemed to be returning to her.

Alexander sighed and began to relax himself.

"Everything good?" Jim asked from across the room.

"Yes," Alexander replied, still not moving from his position. He didn't look away from Sophie.

Laney, Zoey, and Jim glanced awkwardly at each other. "Uh…" Laney asked. "Do you want us to stay?"

"You may leave," Alexander replied.

He and Sophie were instantly left alone.

"I'm going to let go of your arms now that they are gone," he warned and slowly released her wrists, watching her warily for signs of her previous fury. His hands slid down to hers, unwilling to release her just yet. "Do not try anything sudden."

Her eyes had never left his and in a few moments, they blinked back to recognition. His strong hands no longer felt like a threat; his presence no longer felt deadly.

As she calmed down and her heart rate slowed, it became obvious how close they were to each other. Her body pressed against his with every breath.

"What were you trying to do?" she asked suddenly, still breathing heavily.

"Exactly what I did."

She watched him for a moment through suspicious eyes. "Which was what?"

"I—*we*—needed to see how you react to attacks," he explained, "now that you know you are not an average, defenseless person and you understand your instincts better. That vampire would not be so lucky if he tried to attack you now that you know exactly what your potential is."

She leaned back against the wall a bit, losing more of the tension that had coursed through her veins like a drug just minutes before. Her breath still came out in frustrated huffs as she watched him.

"And did you learn anything?" she asked sharply, raising her eyebrows at him.

He chuckled under his breath. "It was educational. I have never seen someone react *quite* like you have."

Sophie's eyebrows furrowed. "What do you mean?"

"Most of us are more human than vampire, but some of us can access that other side more *easily*."

"Great. And I'm one of those," she replied flatly, grimacing.

"Yes," he answered softly.

"You're not gonna hurt me," she said more for herself.

"No," he vowed. "Never."

She nodded and felt a little more normal as her temper cooled. She couldn't ignore the intensity in his voice.

"I'm okay," she assured him breathlessly, nodding her head.

"I know," he said and released her hands.

He placed his hands on the wall, on either side of her shoulders, still leaning over her in case her temper flared again. "How do you feel?"

She stared into his eyes, the fury replaced with something else. "A little dizzy…" she admitted and laughed at herself as she pushed away some of the hair that had fallen into her face.

He reached up and caught a strand she missed and pushed it back from out of her eyes, letting his fingers graze her cheek, a tingling flash of heat traveling along his touch. He ran his fingertips along her jaw line. She froze as her heart pounded against her ribcage in anticipation.

He suddenly dropped his hand and pushed away from the wall with a heavy sigh and began to straighten the room after their grapple.

She slumped against the wall a bit and ran both hands through the top of her hair.

"What is it?" she asked firmly.

He turned and looked at her with a strained look on his face. He was so difficult for her to read sometimes. It irritated her when he was so cryptic.

He shook his head slowly and turned away from her.

She sighed. "Can we do this again sometime?" she asked.

He turned and looked at her skeptically.

"I mean, can we work on some techniques? So I can actually use that anger for something other than trying to kill you when you piss me off?"

"It was not anger," he began.

Sophie looked around the room, glancing at the destruction. "Um…" she snickered. "I'm pretty sure what I was feeling was anger there."

"No," he replied simply. "What you were feeling was pure instinct. We inherit it from our vampire parents."

"Then…" she began, sorting through everything. "Do they all react like that?"

He nodded, placing up-ended metal shelves back in their spots with ease. "Most of them do."

"Okay…so *instincts*, whatever. Can we work on that again? I don't like feeling vulnerable," she explained, still leaning against the wall, watching him as he moved around the room tidying things.

"You're not vulnerable." His eyebrows drew together for a moment as he thought about her request. "Of course. It is what I would have you do."

"Good," she replied with a satisfied nod and triumphant smile. "But can we wait until tomorrow? I didn't know when I signed on for this how tiring it would be," she laughed weakly.

He chuckled under his breath. "Sure."

"Thanks," she replied quietly, feeling awkward again.

She didn't know what else to say, so she turned to walk back up the hallway to the door.

"Uh, Sophie?" He called.

She spun around on a heel and looked at him.

"Have you had any sort of combat training or martial arts?" He asked carefully.

She dropped her eyes. "Self-defense classes. When I was a teenager."

"I thought as much," he replied, his eyes watched her carefully. "Why did you take them?"

"I don't want to talk about it," she answered briskly.

"That's fine," he replied.

She nodded at him and then she was gone.

# Chapter 13

"Hello," called a quiet voice.

Her heart thumped against her ribcage. She closed her eyes; she would know that voice in a sea of voices. She turned away from the view of the sunset and looked up at him.

"Hi," she replied.

Alexander draped his suit jacket over the arm of the couch next to her and sank into it.

"How was work?" she asked. *Am I really trying to make small talk?*

He smiled. "It went well, thank you."

He unbuttoned one of the sleeves of his Oxford shirt and began to roll it up. He didn't look at her, but she watched him as each fold of the fabric revealed more of his sinewy forearm. The light of the setting sun caught the fine golden hairs that dusted his skin. The tendons moved under his skin; his strength was overwhelmingly obvious. He switched hands to roll the other sleeve up and she looked away.

"So, um, what's up?" she asked awkwardly, staring at her hands.

"It occurred to me today that we have not discussed the nature of our enemy at length. I feel that I'm doing you a disservice by not telling you everything we know about them," he replied. Studying her face, he added, "They seem to be inordinately preoccupied with you."

She shivered at the thought.

"The most important thing to remember, here at the house, is that you must never invite anyone inside the house that one of us does not already know. A vampire cannot enter a home unless he is invited, but that does not mean he will not try."

She nodded again.

"Also, as you are well aware, they *can* come out during the day. They are not quite as powerful as at night, but the sun does not keep them indoors. And it doesn't burn them up, unfortunately. You've been lucky so far, and we try to make sure that anyone new is inside before the sun goes down...," he hesitated and looked at her warily. "And, we also make sure all of the females of our kind are accounted for before nightfall."

Sophie opened her mouth, and was about to object when he stopped her with a look.

"Wait. Before you say anything, listen to what I am trying to tell you. It's not sexism on our part," he responded, holding his hands up to show that he meant no harm. "The women of our kind tend to be more psychically gifted than the men, making them— well, *you*—a much larger threat to them than say, myself. Like many of our attributes, we don't know why this is; perhaps it is simply a fluke, perhaps it is part of some grander design. Either way, a coven will attack the females of our kind first, to eliminate the most gifted enemies at the start of a fight."

She felt a shiver run up her spine at the thought of something coming for her, just before her mind shifted to Laney. The others seemed to be able to take care of themselves, but Sophie was inexplicably worried for the younger girl. She swallowed her anxiety and watched Alexander carefully.

He was looking off into space, deep in thought.

"What is it?" she asked, shifting closer to him.

"Actually, have you read *Dracula?*" he asked suddenly, as if an idea had just dawned on him.

She eyed him incredulously and shook her head no.

"Wait here." He rose in one graceful motion and vanished. Moments later, he was there again, handing a book to her. "Take care of it for me," he said.

She took the book from him. It was a copy of *Dracula,* by Bram Stoker. *Are you kidding me?*

"Bram actually had it right," he said as he sat beside her again, musing.

"*Bram?*"

"Stoker."

"Yeah, I know who he is," she laughed through the words, "And you're on a first name basis with him then, huh?" she joked.

"I *was*."

"What?"

He shrugged.

"You're serious," she deduced. "I thought you said you were born at the turn of the century. Stoker wrote this sometime in the mid-1800s, right?" She waved the book in the air between them.

"1897, actually," he answered, "and I *was* born at the turn of the century. You just guessed the wrong one," he replied with a mischievous smile.

She shook her head at him. "So, tell me about '*Bram*'."

"He exaggerated a few points, but generally speaking, his vampires are fairly accurate," he answered matter-of-factly.

"Was he a vampire?" Sophie figured that anything was possible at this point.

"He was Van Helsing," he replied quickly. She would have laughed in disbelief, if he hadn't been so solemn. "Read it. It is really quite informative," he added, pointing to it.

She nodded and set the book on the cushion between them. He picked it back up and shoved it into her hands.

"Trust your instincts. If something doesn't feel right, then you're probably right. Just *promise* me that you will be careful."

"I promise."

He sighed and gazed into her eyes. He leaned towards her and tucked a piece of her hair behind her ear.

"Please be safe," he begged. The sad look that came into his eyes occasionally when he looked at her was suddenly there again.

"Alexander," she gasped. "What is it?"

He shook his head and touched her cheek with the back of his hand. He stared into her eyes with a pained expression that seemed to transfix her. He seemed so sad, so wistful. Her heart pounded against her ribs.

"Tell me," she begged in a whisper. "What's behind that look?"

"Ahem!" They heard from the doorway, but ignored. "Hello?"

Sophie forced her eyes away from Alexander's and turned to see Jim standing in the doorway.

"What is it?" Alexander asked briskly. He stood and turned his back to Sophie. The air suddenly cleared.

"Scouting time!" Jim replied, grinning from ear to ear, rubbing his hands together.

Alexander looked down at Sophie. "We'll be back. Read while we are gone."

"Will there be a test, professor?" She asked sarcastically.

"Not a bad idea at all," he replied, shooting her a smile before starting for the door.

"So, when do I get to come along?" Sophie called.

Alexander opened his mouth to object, but Jim quickly assured her with, "Soon!" before heading out. Alexander stared at Jim before following him out the front door; he looked like he was going to argue but couldn't find the reason to do so.

Sophie reclined back on the couch and let out a long, slow breath. She opened the volume and started, glancing at the portrait of Stoker on the inside cover.

"She'll be fine, y' know," she heard Jim say from the front porch.

"I know. She is stronger than either of us; she just does not know it yet," Alexander replied quietly.

"Just watch it when she figures that one out. It'll be all over but the shootin'."

Alexander said something in return, but she didn't hear what he said. She turned their words over and over in her mind. What did Jim mean about it being all over but the shooting? Could she really be considered a threat to the vampire race? Could they actually be considered a race, now that she thought about it? Maybe most importantly: would her questions ever stop?

Again she looked to the book in her hands. It was time to speed read, if she could concentrate well enough to get anything from it.

"Here goes nothing," she muttered to herself before beginning.

*

It was well after midnight by the time Alexander and Jim returned. Sophie used to wonder how she could run on only a handful of hours of sleep each night, until she'd gotten her answer a few weeks ago. Insomnia was just another "perk" of their state of being, she'd recently found out. They didn't need much sleep, which was convenient when it came to fighting vampires in the dead of night.

She was sitting on the couch just finishing *Dracula* when he sauntered into the room. She didn't have to look up to know it was him.

"I did not expect you to be awake still," he commented quietly. Everyone else was already in bed.

Jim waved at her, but kept walking up stairs on his way to bed, no doubt. Sophie waved back at him, before she replied to Alexander.

"I don't sleep," she confessed.

He grinned and sat beside her. "That makes two of us." He glanced at the book in her lap. "What have you been doing?"

"Learning about the Undead," she answered, holding the book up as proof.

He glanced over at the notebook on the couch beside her and chuckled under his breath. "Did you take notes?"

She scowled. "Are you laughing at me?"

He shrugged and grasped the notebook, on which she'd composed a lengthy list of vampire characteristics:

*"Vampires can/do/are/have: strength of 20 men; no reflection; immortal; survive on blood; appear as mist or fog; appear as wolf or bat; cast no shadow; turn victims into vampires; have hypnotic powers*

*"Vampires are limited by: garlic, holy symbols; can't enter house w/out invite; killed by stake thru heart and decapitation; must sleep in homeland's soil; no supernatural powers during day; can't cross water w/out the tide"*

"Hmm. Nice work. Now," he continued, reaching for the pen that lay on the couch next to her leg and he marked through some of her notes, "*that* is what you have to worry about."

She wondered if it felt like electricity to him too, when his fingers grazed her thigh. If she hadn't known any better, she would have thought her skin was on fire under the denim of her jeans.

He handed the notebook back to her. In a quick glance, she saw that he had struck out a few things with a swift move of his

97

hand. She grimaced. He'd told her that Stoker embellished the truth, but she hadn't realized that he'd only exaggerated the lighter, less terrifying stuff.

"So they do cast a shadow and have a reflection. They can't shape-shift, but they have no limitations, as far as water and land are concerned, right?" She looked over the list again. "And no go on the garlic, huh?"

He shook his head. "Of course that makes them more difficult for humans to spot. Only the younger ones fear holy objects," he replied, touching the cross at her throat as he spoke. Did he know what it did to her when he touched her? He continued, "They are symbols of God. Think of them as stop signs. Vampires truly fear God's power, so they will usually stay away from clergymen and churches, but these symbols do little in the way of repelling any vampire more than a few months old. They *do* tend to find holy water uncomfortable." He tugged on a light chain around his own neck and showed her a hammered cross that hung there. "It doesn't mean we don't rely on them as much as possible."

"So, they're effective, but not as effective as Stoker made it sound in the book," she said, looking over her list. "And the vampires are still powerful during the day."

"Yes."

She knew that she looked worried; there was no way to hide it even if she had been a better actress in front of him—he could hear every thought that ran rampant in her head.

His eyebrows furrowed. "What is it?" he asked.

"They seem so strong," she replied contemplatively, studying the paper. *The strength of twenty men?*

"Please don't worry too much. In a fair fight, it takes two of us against one, simply based on physical capabilities alone," and then he smiled, adding "but you don't fight fair against the devil, now do you?"

"Meaning?"

"Meaning that we capitalize on our psychic talents, and we train together to learn how the others react in a fight. In this way, we present a formidable enough foe for them."

"No wonder. Laney, Catherina, and I can literally see what's coming."

He grinned. "And Zoey can send a stake through the heart of a vampire trying to attack the house before he can reach the front steps."

"That's convenient, but I've got to say: I feel a little like a sitting duck here."

He took her hand. "We'll keep you safe," he swore. He laced his fingers through hers. She sucked in a breath.

"I know. I just don't want to have to rely on others," she murmured.

"Don't worry about it," he replied, looking at her hand.

She could practically see the electricity around them. He traced his thumb along her palm, sending chills up her arm. She closed her eyes to the sensation; her heart felt like it was in her throat.

When she opened her eyes, he was just inches from her. Their heads had bent so close to each others that she could feel his breath on her cheek. She didn't move, but she felt like every nerve in her body was on fire.

"It is late. I should leave," he said, just above a whisper and moved as if to stand.

"No!" she gasped.

He looked at her with surprised eyes.

She cleared her throat. "What I *meant* to say is that I have another question."

"Yes?" he whispered.

"Will you tell me what's going on between you and Catherina? She was talking to Dante about you today, but she stopped when I walked in the room. She didn't look happy."

He took her hand in both of his, turning it palm side up and tracing the lines in the fair skin there. She sighed.

*Do you know what that does to me?* She thought but didn't ask.

The faintest resemblance of a smile tugged at the corner of his mouth. He knew.

"I first met Dante many centuries ago," he whispered, "before he and Catherina had found one another, even before the one knew the other existed. I was in Paris at the time and ran into him on the banks of the Seine. We recognized each other's nature and he quickly introduced himself to me. We developed a natural friendship which grew into a fraternal regard over the years," he explained. "In many ways, he is the brother I never had."

She nodded and waited for him to continue.

"Catherina views me...*differently* because I was associated with Dante before she met him," he went on. "She tends to be the jealous type. She bears a grudge against me for this, I know. For my part, I cannot agree with her morals. She leads this family, but I have seen her lead people to destruction. I don't want to be a part of that. But Dante was my only family for so long, how could I abandon him simply because I do not — let us say '*agree*' — with his companion?"

"So you don't like her?" she whispered.

"You could say that," he answered. "I do not sympathize with how she conducts her life. She has always been ready to sacrifice her acquaintances, her friends, and even her principles when she wants something."

"Jim and Laney think of her as their mother," Sophie stated.

"Yes, but Jim does not see Catherina in that light as much as Laney does. He has been with us longer, although not as long as Zoey. Time and experience erase all manner of ignorance," he replied bitterly.

"I don't trust her," she confessed. "And I don't know why."

"I understand."

Sophie looked down at the hand he still held. She watched him absentmindedly run his fingers from the bottom of her palm to the tips of her fingers and back again.

"Why is it," she began, "that I can hear everyone's thoughts outside, but I have such a hard time here in the house?" *I can't hear Catherina at all.*

"We can choose who may hear our thoughts. It's as simple as refusing to speak to someone aloud."

"How?"

"Simply decide that you don't want them to hear you. For instance, you may decide that you don't desire me to hear what you are thinking. In such case, you simply tell yourself that I may not hear you and I won't be able to until you decide to let me in."

*I wouldn't,* she thought automatically.

She saw a flash of relief across his face.

She smiled shyly at him, but then, despite her wishes, she was overcome by a yawn. He smiled.

"You should get some sleep," he whispered.

"You're right," she replied and reluctantly pulled her hand out of his.

She stood and started to gather the book and her notebook so that she could head upstairs. "Oh," she said, and turned back to him, "thanks for the book." She held it out for him to take.

He stood silently and took it from her. "Of course," he replied. His eyebrows furrowed for a moment as he looked at her, before his expression smoothed. "Goodnight," he said quietly.

She watched him for a moment, trying to figure out what the look on his face had meant, but then nodded; maybe she imagined it. "See you tomorrow," she whispered and closed her eyes.

She felt the air move around her body, but felt an ache in her chest, right before she opened her eyes and found herself in her room. She sighed and sank down on the bed.

\*

She slept in late the next morning, which was unlike her. Soon, she was hurriedly accompanied to school by Jim. She ended up in line for hours at the registrar's office, withdrawing from classes and her feet ached when she climbed back into his truck hours later.

He chuckled to himself and shook his head. "I don't know why you two keep trying to resist everything," he said, looking ahead at the road.

"What are you talking about?" she replied, although she could easily guess what he meant.

"You know, you two are supposed to be together. It's so obvious the rest of us can hardly stand it. The tension between you two gives me a headache."

She laughed nervously.

"I'm serious. Anyway, what's the big deal?" he asked.

"What do you mean?"

"Well, you know what happens when destined companions meet."

She snickered. "You sound ridiculous when you say 'destined,'" she interrupted.

"Maybe so, but that's what it is," he replied. "I know it doesn't make any sense, but you're supposed to be together. Why don't you just chill and let it happen?"

She looked down at the hand Alexander had been holding the night before. She stroked it with her other hand, remembering his touch. "I've had…bad luck with guys," she whispered.

"Alexander's not just any guy, and this thing is bigger than some kiddy crush," he retorted.

"I don't need you to patronize me. Everything's just been happening so fast," she replied. "Anyway, he never lets me in his head. I can't tell what he's thinking."

"Can't you?" he asked incredulously.

She shrugged.

"Give him some time. He's gone through some crap before. He's lost some people that he loved. I think that's why he's dragging his feet, but I wish y'all would just get over it."

"Does it *really* give you a headache?" she asked.

"I've been listening to that guy's thoughts about you for months," he replied with a martyred look. "Hell, I've been listening to your thoughts about *him* for months. It's annoying."

"Hey, I didn't ask you to stalk me," she joked.

He pulled into the driveway, set the parking break, and turned the engine off. He turned to look at her. "Sophie, in all honesty…" He paused and looked at her seriously, something Jim rarely did.

"Yeah?" she asked.

"In all honesty, if you want to get by in this life, you just gotta follow your heart and your gut. That goes for Alexander, too."

She nodded.

He glanced toward the house and a huge smile spread across his face. "Well, speak of the devil!"

Sophie's eyes tracked up to the back porch of the house. Zoey and Alexander stood a few feet apart from one another, deep in conversation. His hands were in his pockets, but there was a smile on his face. Zoey stood with her arms crossed, and her flame of red hair blowing in the wind. She laughed.

Jim and Sophie slid out of the truck and the other two stopped talking immediately. Zoey smiled at them both and waved a greeting, but Alexander seemed not to notice that anyone other than Sophie was around. She sent him a shy smile as she and Jim got closer.

Zoey slinked down the stairs and walked up to Sophie. "Alexander and I were talking. You need another round of practice." Zoey gestured to the training bunker.

"Right now?"

Zoey nodded.

Jim smiled. "Good a time as any."

"Okay," Sophie replied. She looked up at Jim warily.

"You're not sparring with me," Jim said.

"No," Zoey interjected. "With me."

The room was the same as Sophie remembered it. She'd thought that maybe her memory had enhanced the way it looked, but the stainless steel racks and overhead lights reminded her of something she saw in a movie once.

She glanced around the room for objects Zoey might use against her.

Zoey shot her a reproachful look. "I'm not going to hurt you," she said to Sophie before looking at Alexander and Jim. "Just keep her from hurting *me*."

"Tell me why we're doing this again?" Sophie asked.

"Jim and I need to observe you without having to worry about you trying to kill us," Alexander replied as if it were the most simple and logical explanation in the world.

"Right," she replied, but she didn't feel completely comfortable. She'd seen what Zoey could do against a vampire; she was well aware of the other woman's abilities. There was something a little wilder about Zoey, too. Alexander was refined, in control, and Jim was playful. Zoey on the other hand did everything with stealth. She rarely spoke unless she had to, and she possessed a feline grace that was mildly unsettling.

"No weapons," Zoey instructed. "Attack me."

"What?"

"You heard: attack."

"Yeah, right," Sophie mumbled, staring at the redhead as if she were crazy.

Suddenly Sophie was staring at a blank wall. Zoey had disappeared. She was about to turn around when something hit her in the back of the head with a pop.

"Ow!" Sophie yelped.

She turned around on a heel and found Zoey there, laughing at her. Sophie glared at her.

"You were right, Alexander," Zoey said. "You have to get her mad."

"Don't get her too mad," he warned, before whispering something to Jim.

Jim nodded, his eyes fixed on Sophie.

"I'm not sure I believe that," Zoey replied, circling Sophie. "I think someone could easily take advantage of her." She grabbed Sophie's arms and jerked her closer with a maniacal look in her eyes. "I think I could make her do anything I wanted."

"Like hell," Sophie growled through gritted teeth, but she still didn't attack.

Zoey's smile faded. She leaned forward until her face was inches from Sophie's. "Prove it," she challenged.

Sophie shoved her back. "You talk too much."

Zoey stood her ground. "That's a first. Of course, I sometimes feel compelled to tell the truth," she replied.

"What are you saying?" Sophie asked, taking a step forward. Zoey's attitude was really starting to piss her off.

"That there's a weakness in you," Zoey replied, drawing the words out. "That someone could have their way with you and there's nothing you could do to stop it. I mean, you're not fighting back."

"Shut up!" Sophie yelled, swinging for Zoey.

Zoey jumped out of the way and was behind her. "Missed me."

Sophie swung her arm behind her. Her fist connected with Zoey's ribs, but the redhead danced out of her way, cackling. Sophie bit her lip and tasted blood.

Zoey was harder to gain an advantage over; she had to change her tactics. Even in her rage, she was thinking clearly enough to realize that. She became very still and closed her eyes.

"What are you waiting for?" Zoey taunted.

Sophie listened to her footsteps. They sounded like light brushings on the concrete. Zoey was walking counterclockwise around Sophie. She stopped, changed direction and starting walking clockwise in another circle.

"I don't know, Alexander," Zoey started to say, switching direction again in her circle around Sophie. "I don't think she's going to fight."

Sophie lunged. Her right shoulder caught Zoey in the side and sent her to the ground. They fell like two snarling cats. Zoey tried to shove her off, but Sophie was just as strong as she was.

Zoey struggled harder and pushed off the ground and was suddenly on top of Sophie. Jim leaned over to say something to Alexander, but the latter waved him a way. Zoey was on her feet, but Sophie tackled her again, pressing her forearm into the redhead's neck.

Zoey's hand shot out and suddenly Sophie was being lifted off of her. Sophie tried to struggle against the arms that held her, but Jim was too strong when for. He pinned her arms behind her back, but she tried kicking at him when she couldn't free her hands.

"I've gotcha," Jim whispered in her ear.

Sophie relaxed at the sound of his voice.

Zoey was quickly on her feet, and Alexander stepped between the two women as Jim continued to drag Sophie backwards.

"I told you not to make her too mad," Alexander said to Zoey.

The redhead chuckled and wiped her busted lip with the back of her hand. She inhaled a whistling breath through her clenched teeth. "Thanks. 'I told you so' never gets old."

Alexander turned to Sophie. "And I have seen her angrier."

Sophie leaned against Jim. She didn't want to hurt anyone, but she'd already bloodied Zoey's face and now Alexander stood between her and the redhead. Sophie watched Alexander.

"You are doing well," he said. "Just calm down a bit and Jim will let you go."

"I'm calm," Sophie replied grimly. "I'm just pissed."

"Sorry about that," Zoey replied genuinely. "I hope I didn't strike a nerve."

Zoey's words had been too accurate for comfort, but she shut that thought out of her mind. "It's fine," she said. "I'm fine."

Alexander nodded to Jim, who loosened his grip on Sophie. She pulled her arms forward and rotated her shoulders a bit.

"You okay?" Jim asked.

"Yeah," she replied. "Thanks."

"That was very good, changing your tactics like that," Alexander observed.

"She'll be ready to get out there soon," Zoey said to him. Alexander nodded.

"So, I passed?" Sophie asked incredulously.

"*This* test," Jim answered, elbowing her in the side. "Let's go. I'm starved."

She started to follow him, but someone grasped her arm from behind. She turned and was face to face with Alexander. She looked over his shoulder, but Zoey was already gone.

"Are you alright?" he asked.

"Yeah, I'm good," she replied.

"You are doing very well. Your control is impressive."

She shrugged. "I don't *want* to hurt any of you."

He nodded. "It's your instinct to fight back. We all understand."

"So, am I going to be able to hunt vampires with you soon?" she asked, a grin spreading across her face.

His eyebrows furrowed into that expression she didn't quite understand, but he nodded. "I have another test for you first, but it can wait for another day."

"Good," she replied with a sigh as her stomach growled. "Because I think Jim was on to something. I'm pretty hungry myself."

"Let's go then," he replied.

He switched the light off along the way, and they were plunged into darkness. Sophie felt like a live wire. She could practically feel the energy radiating off of him as they stepped into the light.

# Chapter 14

Sophie and Alexander stood across the room from one another as Jim looked on, a few days after their first experiment at her combat instincts.

"Do you recall what happened when the vampire attacked you on campus?" Alexander asked.

Sophie shuddered, but nodded firmly in response.

"He was able to exact such power over you because one of their abilities is hypnotic control of their victims."

"Really?" Sophie asked, surprised.

"Yes," Alexander answered. "If he had attacked you without the benefit of the psychological assault, you could have easily fought against him."

"Okay…"

"So, Jim is going to help us," he went on. "He is going to distract your mind, similar to how a vampire would distract it, while you and I practice."

"Alright."

Jim grinned almost maliciously at her.

"You said you wanted to learn," he reminded her with a shrug. "This is the best way to teach you. You need to learn to take us on before we let you out to face our enemy. *We* won't kill you; they will try to."

She nodded and looked him directly in the eye, waiting for his first move.

*You're getting very sleepy.* Jim silently taunted her in an eerie old-Hollywood thought.

Sophie snickered and looked at him with humored disbelief just as something hard slammed into her chest, knocking the breath out of her. By the time her head swung around to see what hit her, Alexander had propelled her into the far back wall with the force of one hand to her ribcage.

*What the hell?!* She thought. She pushed off of the wall and charged toward him.

*You don't want to do that,* Jim suggested with a soft thought. Suddenly, Sophie lost some of the motivation that propelled her toward Alexander.

She shook her head to try and clear it while she felt the rage start to boil up in her chest. More resolutely, Sophie ducked her head and crouched down, waiting for Alexander to attack her once more.

*Come on,* he challenged her.

He mirrored her crouch and a subtle growl crawled its way up his throat. He rocked back on his heels and hurled himself at her, charging towards.

*Hey, over here!* Jim silently called, pulling her attention away from her attacker at a critical moment.

As soon as her head turned toward Jim, Alexander's shoulder slammed into her chest, momentarily bruising her ribs.

She hissed in reply and ducked out of his grasp at the last minute. She dove for Jim's knees and knocked her unsuspecting brother off of his feet.

Alexander turned as Jim hit the ground with a flurry of curses before Sophie turned back on him.

Sophie ran towards Alexander. She would no longer be distracted by Jim's vain attempts to call her attention away from Alexander who jumped just out of her reach at the last minute. She turned on a heel. She swept her foot under his, attempting to knock him to the floor as she'd done with Jim. Alexander was quicker than his brother, though. He jumped quickly, just to reappear behind her.

He grasped her from behind, his arm tightly around her neck as she kicked and screamed. He dragged her backwards away from Jim. She twisted, sinking her elbow into his ribs, knocking the breath out of him and returning the favor of an aching bruise. She pulled out of his grasp and turned once more so that she was facing Alexander. She kicked his knees so that he landed with a resounding crash on his back underneath her.

She pressed her hard forearm into his neck as she pinned him there, panting violently through her teeth with the effort.

He kept calm and showed no surprise as he looked her sternly in the eye. "Let me up, Sophie," he commanded.

She growled at him once more, but suddenly leapt backwards and off of him and landed in a defensive crouch, waiting for his next move. She glanced maniacally over her shoulder at Jim who had just stood up.

"Satisfied?" She asked, in control of herself, but still on the defensive.

Jim began to laugh at himself. "Man, I quit," he said, swatting at the air between them.

Alexander nodded, straightening his shirt. "That was unexpected, but you've done well," he said. "Have you got control of yourself?"

Sophie slowly stood and exhaled. She smiled quickly at his compliment and nodded her head. "Yeah, I'm good," she replied. "Wait! What do you mean, 'that was unexpected'?"

"He means nobody's ever done that before," Jim explained, stretching his arm across his chest.

Sophie shrugged at him. "Sorry, Jim," she replied.

He shook his head. "That's not what I mean."

"What he means to say," Alexander interrupted, "is that we have never met someone able to resist a simultaneous mental and physical assault on the first try."

"Yeah it usually takes practice," Jim said, "and nobody's ever attacked both of us at once like that. You're somethin' else, girl."

"I'll take that as a compliment, I guess," she said with a grin.

"Good," Jim replied. "I'm gonna go now, though; before he gets you riled up again." He winked at her and the heat spread across her cheeks.

"Thanks for that," Alexander replied reluctantly.

Jim had disappeared.

"Is he okay?" She asked, looking away from where Jim had been standing.

"You've just bruised his ego," Alexander replied with a chuckle.

She snickered and looked around.

"I think you will do well against a vampire or two. You are learning very quickly."

"Thanks," she replied with a smile.

Her eye fell on the bow Alexander had used in training against her.

He followed her gaze. "Would you like me to show you how to use it?"

Her eyes widened. "Would you?"

He nodded. "Of course."

She grinned. "Sure," she replied.

"Follow me," he said, gathering the bow and several arrows and stepping through a doorway she'd somehow not noticed before.

As she stepped across the threshold, Alexander flipped on the light and Sophie found herself in an indoor firing range.

She froze. "Wow," she whispered, looking around. "How big *is* this place?"

"Come here," he said and she followed him to the far end of the underground room.

At the end of one of the firing alleys, there stood a wooden target board ready to receive arrows. He held the bow out for Sophie to take. She reached up with her left hand to take the grip.

"Hold it like this," he said, adjusting her hand so that it properly griped the bow.

He stepped behind her, taking her right hand in his own and positioning it properly on the bow string.

"This is the nocking point," he said, caressing the string and her hand. She tried not to notice. "This is where you place the nock—the end—of the bow."

She nodded and tried to keep her thoughts to herself as she felt the heat of his body against her back. He placed his hands on her hips to rotate her into the proper position. He moved his hands back up to hers where they were placed on the bow. She drew in a shaky breath and waited. She felt his chest rise with each breath as he stood behind her.

He cleared his throat. "Now, pull the string back…like this," he said, pulling her right hand backwards with his so that the back of his thumb gently grazed her cheek.

He slowly guided her hand back to the start position so as not to dry fire the bow, and picked up an arrow.

"Place it here," he instructed, making minor adjustments to her hands and fingers.

The space between them became tenser and the silence of the rest of the room fell like a heavy cloak.

"Now," he instructed, pulling her right hand back with his own, "I am going to let go. Inhale and release your right hand when you are ready."

She nodded, the gesture causing her hair to move so that it tickled his cheek. He took a step back from her and after two deep breaths she inhaled and released the bow string.

The arrow whistled its way through the air and plunged into the wooden target at the end of the lane, a little high and to the right of the bulls' eye.

"Still a lethal shot," he commended.

She looked over her shoulder at him and smiled tentatively. It sounded like a compliment to her.

"It *is* a compliment," he replied.

"Thanks," she said.

"You're welcome," he said. "Now, let's try again."

He stepped up behind her once more and he ran his fingers along her right arm, positioning it correctly. She closed her eyes at the touch; the sensation was more distracting than she thought it should be. She chastened herself to focus as his palm pressed against her hand and left a warm sensation there when he let her go.

"Fire when ready," he instructed.

She nodded and concentrated on the target within her sights. She inhaled and released the bow string and watched the arrow fly towards the target and land between the bulls' eye and her first shot. She was getting better…not that she had been bad to start with.

She turned to reflexively look for his approval. Instead, she found a pained and distracted expression there, as he gazed at the target.

She dropped her hands and turned to face him completely.

"What is it?" she asked, quietly.

His eyes shifted to hers and he stared at her for what could have been two seconds or two hours, she wasn't sure for how long. She knew it felt like an eternity. He stepped towards her and looked like he was about to say something to her. Instead, he shut his mouth once more and turned away to look at the target that now held two of her arrows.

She sighed, exasperated.

"Look!" she exclaimed, suddenly angry at him, and surprising even herself with her response. "If you won't let me in there," she pointed a violent finger toward his head, "then at least have to courtesy to let me know what the hell you're thinking when you look at me like that!" She exclaimed. She threw her free hand up in the air, exasperated. "I can't...I can't *stand* it anymore, Alexander! We've gone months, sharing the same hallways, the same school buildings...there've been months of watching you watch *me* and I *never* know what you're thinking. Now we're living together, and everyone else is letting me in their head – well, except Catherina, but you know what I mean, and you're still silent to me. And it...it..." she trailed off, feeling defeated.

She sighed and shook her head. He reached down and silently took the bow from her hand and placed it on the table beside them.

"I can't...I mean, I don't know what to think," she mumbled. "I'm sorry."

"Forgive me," he said quietly, and all of the frustration and irritation melted from her instantly.

She shook her head not understanding him, about to speak, when he held a finger up to stop her. She inhaled steadily and watched him.

And then the flood gates were wrenched open as his thoughts suddenly rushed over her. She gasped as she recognized her feelings and her emotions in his.

He stepped towards her. He took her right hand, tracing his fingers along the inside of her arm as he stepped closer.

"What?" she asked.

*I cannot pretend any longer,* he thought in the same instant that he pulled her into his arms.

His free hand suddenly grasped the back of her neck and his lips crushed down on hers and the invisible wall that had been built between them disappeared. She kissed him back with as much passion as she'd felt when she was trying to kill him earlier. She stepped into him and his back was suddenly against the wall.

He held tightly, like a man drowning and she lost herself in his kisses. His kissed her neck as she turned her head and without thinking about it, sighed into his ear. He growled somewhere from deep in his chest and his lips were suddenly, almost violently, on hers again. She returned his force with her own unbreakable assault.

Suddenly, he pulled away from her to look into her eyes. He released her arm and wrapped his own around her waist. They were both breathless.

"What?" she asked again, looking into his eyes, panting. "I don't...understand."

"What is there to understand?" he asked, running his fingers through her hair, sending distracting shivers down her neck.

She smiled at the chills he gave her. She shook her head. "I don't know," she admitted, wrapping her arms tighter around his neck. "I don't even know what I'm talking about," she whispered. "This is happening so fast."

"I know," he whispered, resting his forehead against hers. A warmer smile than she'd ever seen grace his face spread across his lips as she reached up and kissed him again.

He sighed under her kiss and their mutual thoughts entwined themselves around each other. The effect was electric and a relief all at once. Everything seemed to fall into place as the façade was finally torn down between them.

She pulled away from him then and smiled.

"Shall we go inside?" he asked quietly.

She blushed. *They're going to be able to tell.*

*They already know,* he thought back and smiled at her, stroking her cheek. *They are going to be relieved.*

She grinned sheepishly at him and nodded. "Sure," she whispered and took his hand.

He glanced down at her hand in his and both marveled at the naturalness of the action. Hers was soft and strong in his as they turned to go back to the house the "old fashioned" way: strolling at a casual pace.

They started towards the door, flipping off lights along the way.

When the last light was turned out, she turned to him. Her half-human, half-vampire eyes could see him perfectly in the dim light.

"Come here," she murmured.

Sophie leaned against the wall and pulled him towards herself. He pressed his body against hers and she was overcome with emotions and foreign thoughts as their lips met again.

The heat rose between them in the confined, dark underground passageway before he smiled against her lips.

"What?" She asked.

"They are waiting for us," he replied. "Can't you hear them?"

"I was trying not to," she admitted. *Fine...if we have to.*

*For now, we must,* was his silent reply.

He took her hand again and led her to the door where he pushed a button to open it. They were assaulted by the fading sunset that shone directly into the path of the doorway.

They stepped out and with a quick turn and swift fingers, Alexander typed a code into the keypad and the door shut inaudibly. He looked down at her and smiled contently before they began again for the house.

"Wow," Sophie whispered in amazement.

"What?" Alexander asked.

She stopped in her tracks and looked at him. He watched her calmly, waiting for her to speak.

"I've never been so aware of my surroundings. I feel the, oh how do I explain it? I feel the *urge* to look around me and to check my surroundings. I don't ever do that," she explained, compelled to check the shadows with a quick sweep of her eye.

He chuckled under his breath.

"Is that you?" she asked.

He nodded. "Yes."

"Wow," she said to herself again. "So *that's* what Catherina was talking about."

"When was she talking about this?"

Sophie shook her head dismissively. "I misspoke. She didn't *talk* about it; I was reading her memoirs, or diary, or whatever, in the library the other day. She wrote about the exchange of thoughts between her and Dante."

"Ah," he replied and then gently pulled her towards the house.

"That's wild," she whispered to herself, marveling at her new discovery and following him inside.

# Chapter 15

Present Day—Romania

The queen sat on her tall throne, her thick black robes flowing like water down the sides of the golden seat, with a hint of her royal blue gowns peaking from underneath.

"I await your reports," her frigid voice called to no one and everyone at once.

There was no need for introductions; they knew their place and knew the order which the queen would have them respond. They did her bidding automatically and without question.

"From Eastern Europe, my queen," a male in a gruff but faintly metallic Russian accent responded with a bow, "we have no news to report. Two of the covens have grown in size: Vladimir's in the Ukraine and Annika's in Germany. There is no activity of the *others* within our jurisdiction, my queen, and the situation seems peaceful within our borders." He bowed once more.

"Thank you, Konstantin. That is a relief," the queen replied and looked to his cohorts who flanked him.

With a bow, the male to Konstantin's right began, "Business reports are well." He informed her of their recent acquisition of a fifty-one percent shareholding majority in a popular German automotive company, adding significantly to the Council's monetary funds and sphere of influence.

The queen's Machiavellian smile spread at Varro's report. Wilhelm subsequently stepped forward to report that the Council now had the ear of two members of the German Bundestag. The queen's pleasure multiplied at the news.

Dismissing them with a pleased air, she turned to her next group of sycophants and one by one, the twelve groups of three reported the progress, the acquisitions, the deaths, and the battles of their regions. The Middle Eastern Councilors were busy stirring unrest in the desert and the South American representatives were spreading the ideals of socialism in efforts to exact more control over the irritating human population; Adonis and his cohorts were peacefully reigning over the Mediterranean. There had been some unrest in Asia: Daisuke reported that the challenge with the *others*—the hybrid kind, who are not human, but not quite vampire—had been subdued in northern Japan without much effort and very few losses.

"So, it seems we have trouble only with our American enemies," the queen concluded at the meeting's end, turning her harsh glare at the final three.

An unsettled quiet fell over the room as Cusick, Sloane, and Bennett held their breath.

"Let us hope that your Jacques rids us of this irritant," she replied in warning before standing swiftly and floating out of the room.

The eyes of the other Councilors looked on their American associates with wariness and scorn.

# Chapter 16

Present Day—Texas

Sophie chewed on her thumbnail as she gazed out the front window, basking in the early morning sunlight. She was the first one awake. Her eyes were drawn to the tree which the vampire had been pinned to when Zoey and Jim had killed him; the vampire that had asked her if she wanted to know where her mother was.

"Penny for your thoughts," Zoey murmured.

Sophie turned and found Zoey sitting on one of the couches behind her, still in her pajamas, her red hair wild around her face.

"I'm just thinking about the vampire who attacked here the other day."

"Yes?"

Sophie sighed. "I feel like all I do is ask questions around here."

"But if you don't know something, it's wise to ask those who do," Zoey observed and gestured towards the open seat next to her.

Sophie plopped down on the couch and looked at the other girl incredulously. "How did you do that to the vampire?" she asked. "You weren't even outside yet."

Zoey smiled. "Do you remember when I said that my gift is different?"

"Yes."

"Laney is able to move anything she wishes, with just a thought. She catches glimpses of the future; she's useful in a psychic circle, just as you are."

Sophie nodded and waited.

"I can't move just anything, but I do have the ability to manipulate natural objects."

"And she's damn good at it, too," Jim interjected, suddenly appearing across the room from them, on his way to the kitchen.

"Yeah, I gathered," Sophie replied.

"He flatters his sister," Zoey said reproachfully.

"It's not flattery, it's the truth," he rebutted. "Laney's good and she's getting better, but give Zoey a wooden stake, and there's not a vampire who stands a chance."

Sophie looked at Zoey. "Is it just wood that you can control?"

"No," Zoey replied. "I can manipulate several elements: water, fire, wood, and earth. Anything that is natural to this world, I can move."

"She's trying to get wind figured out," Jim added with a smile. "Then she'll really give 'em a run for their money."

A smile played at the corner of Zoey's mouth.

"Oh!" Sophie exclaimed. "Is that why there are piles of wood around the house outside – so you have plenty of things to throw around if you have to?"

Zoey nodded.

"Huh," Sophie mused. "But you're not good at the whole seeing the future thing we did, right?"

"That's right. I can manipulate parts of the physical world only."

"You smelled the vampire," Sophie said, the realization dawning on her.

"Yes, but I didn't *sense* him."

"Hmm."

Zoey watched her for a few minutes, allowing her to stare off into space.

"What else is on your mind?" Zoey asked.

"He said something about my mother," Sophie replied quietly.

"Yes, he did," Zoey replied.

"I wonder what happened to her."

Jim grimaced. "Probably nothin' good, kiddo. He probably mentioned her because he knows where she is. You're here, so we know she didn't die during the transformation; she's a vampire. But, she's not your mother anymore."

"I wonder where she is," Sophie whispered.

Zoey reached over and grasped Sophie's hand. "No good can come from those thoughts."

Sophie sighed. "You're right. I know you're right." *But still...*

The room fell silent. Sophie stared down at Zoey's hand where it held her own.

Sophie ran her finger over the band of gold that encircled the ring finger on Zoey's left hand. "That's pretty," she said quietly. The band was etched with a swirling design that looked like it was from the 1920s.

Zoey pulled her hand away. She spun the ring around her finger and pulled it off. She handed it to Sophie.

Sophie glanced up to where Jim had been standing, but he had disappeared. She looked back at the ring. There was an inscription on the inside.

"What does this say?" Sophie asked to herself, holding it up in the sunlight. "To my sunshine; my Hazel. Love always, Jack." She cocked her head to the side and looked at Zoey questioningly.

The redhead reached out and gently took the ring back from Sophie. She pinched it between her fingers and read the inscription. The sunlight reflected off of the shinning surface, and when the light hit Zoey's eyes, they were sad.

"Who's Hazel?" Sophie asked, feeling the sadness emanate off of her newly-adopted sister.

Zoey looked at her meaningfully.

"Oh," Sophie whispered.

"I changed my name," Zoey replied. She slipped the ring back on her finger and tugged on a chain at her neck. Sophie had seen the small cross at her throat, but she hadn't noticed the long chain tucked into Zoey's shirt.

Zoey slipped the chain off over her head and handed the locket to Sophie.

Sophie hesitantly took it from her. Zoey nodded. Sophie carefully opened the locket to find a dashing face smiling back at her in black and white.

"That's Jack," Zoey whispered sadly. "I couldn't bear hearing anyone else speak my name if he wasn't around to say it."

"What happened?" Sophie gasped.

Zoey took the locket back and tucked it safely back into her shirt, close to her heart. She smiled wistfully. "We were attacked. A small coven came after us. They didn't know what we were; they thought we were human. We fought back, but there were too many for us. We'd killed most of them, but there were still two. Jack took them on. He killed them, but not before they killed him first." She dabbed at her eye with a shaking hand. "He died in my arms."

Sophie didn't know what to say. "I'm so sorry," she whispered and pulled Zoey into her arms.

The older woman sank against her, and Sophie stroked her hair. Zoey didn't cry, but she trembled in Sophie's arms. Sophie sighed, holding her there.

Suddenly, something in the air had changed. She didn't know what it was until Alexander suddenly appeared. Sophie's eyes met his and held them there. She tried to smile at him, but she was struggling to hold back tears, and the look came out wrong.

He nodded, bowed his head slightly and disappeared out of the room.

Zoey exhaled heavily and leaned back from Sophie's arms. "Thank you," she whispered. "I don't mean to get upset."

Sophie shook her head. "It's okay. Don't worry about it."

Zoey nodded. "Sometimes I wish our memories didn't stay with us as well as they do." She sighed. "I'm going to go get ready for the day."

"Okay," Sophie replied, and watched Zoey disappear out of the room.

She shook her head and walked to the window, running her fingers through her hair. She closed her eyes and let out a long, steady exhale through pursed lips. When she inhaled, the scent of coffee filled her nose, and it beckoned her to the kitchen.

It was occupied only by Alexander. She found herself feeling awkward around him; she didn't really know how to act. Everyone else seemed to think the change in their relationship was normal and expected, but for Sophie it was something entirely foreign.

Everything had been wonderful the day before. She and Alexander had emerged from the weapons room, and when they'd walked into the house, everyone acted like nothing had changed.

122

He held her hand, but no one noticed. They spent the evening talking quietly, their heads bent towards each other and not one person commented on the change in the pair.

Being together hadn't seemed awkward the day before, but now that it was a new day, it was almost like Sophie didn't know how to act.

"Good morning," he greeted. "Did you sleep well?"

"Yeah," she whispered. "Thanks."

"Would you like some coffee?" he asked.

"Please," she replied and walked closer to him.

He walked over to the cupboard and pulled two coffee mugs out.

"Zoey was up early," he commented. "It's usually just me awake this early. Mornings will not be lonely any longer, now that you are here."

"I think she wanted to talk to me."

He nodded as he poured two mugs of coffee. "She needed to tell you her story."

"It explains why she's so quiet," Sophie said. *And why she's not afraid of anything. She's got nothing left to lose.*

He nodded as he poured the perfect amount of cream into one, stirred it with a spoon and then pushed it towards Sophie.

"So what are you doing today?" she asked.

"Just a few things to wrap up at work. We'll be leaving soon."

"That's right," she replied quietly. "It'll be weird leaving this town."

"Good morning!" Laney exclaimed, suddenly appearing in the room.

Sophie jumped and Alexander took a step backwards from her and picked up his mug of forgotten coffee.

A fully-dressed Zoey silently appeared in one of the chairs at the table.

As if someone had thrown a switch, the room was suddenly filling up. Alexander meandered over to the table with a newspaper under his arm as Catherina and Dante walked in the doorway. Sophie wiggled up onto one of the barstools beside the long countertop and blew on her coffee as she watched everyone mill about.

Zoey picked an apple up out of the bowl on the table and bit into it. Dante set a cup of coffee in front of her and another in front of Catherina. The latter looked up and smiled at him, and then scowled at Alexander when she realized he wasn't paying any attention to the pair. Jim and Laney were bickering over the cereal and milk, which ended in Jim tousling her hair and Laney punching him in the arm.

Alexander sat forward in his chair and laid the folded paper in front of Zoey with a serious look on his face. She snatched it up, biting her lip. Sophie pulled her cup away from her lips.

"What's up?" Sophie asked.

Alexander grinned. "Shoe sale."

Zoey tossed the paper at his head, which he easily ducked.

"I've got to go," he said. He stood up and kissed Sophie on the forehead before disappearing from the room.

She and Zoey exchanged a look; Zoey smiled.

*

"How did it all begin? I mean us. How did our kind come to be?"

"Well," Alexander answered, "that story is one in which Catherina was uncharacteristically useful. Many decades ago, she was determined to find the answer to that question herself. From his own research, Dante believed that our kind had originated in Mesopotamia. He gathered stories of Kahala, the first vampire there and her daughter—I mean to say her biological daughter—Ishta. Kahala was a beautiful young woman in life and—as you would guess—with child when she was attacked and transformed.

"Legend holds that when Kahala traveled to the underworld, the creature at the gate did not allow her entry. She returned to the Earth with an insatiable thirst. And of course, her daughter had sprung from her womb at her death.

"According to the stories, Kahala was the epitome of evil and Ishta carried an inner light. It is a legend which has been handed down verbally through many generations of humans and of our kind.

"Catherina eventually found Ishta. At the time, Catherina was truly remorseful of the lives she had taken. Ishta believed she

124

was good. She saw that Catherina was a creature like herself and not a blood-thirsty vampire like her own mother. The two spoke with one another for a time, but Ishta had no answers for Catherina except to say that she believed that we are created for the sole purpose of balancing out the evils brought into the world by our mothers and fathers.

"She said something to Catherina that I shall always remember. To Catherina's question of what we are, Ishta replied that ancient India had named us untouchables—those cast out of society, but she added, 'Never forget that we are more immortal than the vampires; virtually untouchable by the angel of death'."

"But not immune to it."

He nodded. "That is true. We may dodge death for centuries, but it does not mean that we will dodge it forever," he responded. *Then again, we may.*

"Well…," she began, but stopped.

"What is it?" he asked softly, taking her hand in his own, stroking the palm with his fingertips.

"How did you find out…you know: that you're…?"

"Different?" he added, to which they both snickered; the word didn't do them justice.

"Yeah."

"I shall tell you that story some other day, when I have more time," he replied and glanced toward the door. "In short, I learned it from an enemy, but I suppose that goes without saying."

\*

*Everything is in black and white. I walk down a gray path that is overhung with arching trees, their black limbs creating a canopy over me and blocking out the moon, though light from its fullness is evident on the path. I wear a luxurious red ball gown with heavy taffeta skirts. I look down at my left hand and recognize that something is missing there, but I don't know what.*

*The path winds around in a switchback so I can look to my left and see, through the trees, the part I have already walked upon. I know my goal is through the archway created by the trees up ahead, but I don't know what I'm looking for.*

*A white wolf watches me from the misty forest which surrounds me. He is not threatening and I'm not scared. He stares at me for a moment and then turning, he walks away from me back into the trees. His movements draw my eye back to the path to my left, before it winds around the corner.*

*Walking up the path towards me is a teenage boy, with black spiky hair and bangs that cover one eye. He wears a red and black striped hoodie and I'm more nervous about his presence than the lone wolf's. He turns the corner and passes me though, in his own world, without even looking at me before he suddenly disappears before my eyes.*

*I gather up my large skirts and notice just now that my hair is incredibly long—and golden—and it dawns on me that my hair is very strange. I look back up the path and continue in the same direction, along the soft soil. I stop suddenly as another wolf crosses in front of me. He is already through the archway and he stops to look at me. He is beckoning me to follow him. Grasping my dress, I fearlessly start up the path toward him, walking quickly.*

*As I step through the archway, I'm suddenly in a different place. I look down and my pretty dress is gone. In its place, I wear jeans and a tight black t-shirt. My hair is my own and pulled back into a ponytail. I look around and I remember this. I am in the nursing home where I'd first—and last—met my grandmother.*

*There she is, lying in her bed.*

*'She was a little hussy, your mama!' she says. 'Runnin' off with that boy and gettin' herself in trouble with you!'*

*Right. My mom had left home when she'd gotten pregnant with me, or at least that was the story. Who knows what stories are true anymore?*

*'Little ungrateful hussy!'*

*Does anyone actually say hussy anymore? I look down at my grandmother, who is more than half crazy by this point anyway.*

*'Grandma, what was she like?' I ask.*

*'A little spoiled thing!' she exclaims. 'Always wantin' the world on a silver platter. Thought she deserved it all too!'*

*Okay, this is going nowhere, fast. Just like when the visit had happened in real life. I know I'm dreaming.*

'Did you ever see her after I was born?' I ask.

'Yeah, once,' she answers and is silent.

'What was she like?'

'Darlin' I can't remember what she was like, but I do remember she looked sick. She was all pale in the face and her eyes just didn't look right.'

Her description hadn't made any sense when I'd heard it the first time, but now it did. Of course my mother looked pale and her eyes were all wrong. She probably smelled different and spoke differently, too.

Of course her mother would not have known why the change had occurred, but reliving the conversation, I knew this time around that my mother had become a vampire.

'Grandma,' I say, deviating from the memory. I am dreaming, I reminded myself. 'Grandma, she's lost.'

'Of course she's lost, darlin'. Your mama was a lost soul all her life.'

'No, Grandma, I mean she's not your daughter anymore. She's a monster.' Why am I telling this frail old woman all of this?

I hear a sound and I freeze in my place. A woman walks in. She doesn't acknowledge me; she must not be able to see me.

'Hello, Mother,' she says and I recognize instinctually that the voice is my mother's.

'Leslie! What the hell are you doin' here?' my grandmother demands; she is panicking and I can't do anything to help her. I reach out to my grandmother, but I'm as effective as thin air.

My mother creeps to the bedside and I can smell the sickening scent of her vampire self as she stirs the air around her body. Why is this happening? This is so different than what had been a relatively benign visit in reality.

I try to move; I try to yell, but I can do neither. I can simply watch as my mother deliberately hovers over my grandmother. She watches her daughter with fear in her eyes.

'I've owed you a visit for a while, Mother,' she says.

'You been busy. I understand,' my grandmother says softly with fear in her voice.

I turn away. I can't watch, because I know what's next. I can hear my grandmother gasp as my mother sinks her teeth into

127

*her papery thin elderly skin. I feel the change in the room when my grandmother's life is ended and I look up to see my mother stand at the bedside.*

*'Better than you deserve,' she says bitterly, crudely wiping her mouth with the back of her hand.*

*I am horrified and begin to cry...*

And the tears were real when Sophie woke up, even if her grandmother's death hadn't happened that way. She *had* passed away soon after Sophie had met her; from a stroke, not a vampire. But, it didn't make the dream any easier to bear.

She blinked at the sunlight that streamed into the window. She must have fallen asleep while studying and slept through the night. She sighed. Her breath was shaky.

She was used to having weird dreams, it was true, but the merging of her grandmother's memory and the image of her mother as a vampire together didn't make any sense.

*What do they have in common?* She thought. She wiped the tears from the corner of her eyes and sat up on the edge of the bed, still shaking a little, but quickly coming back to reality. *Probably nothing.*

There was a soft knock at the door and she knew it was Alexander. She looked up as he opened it and peeked inside.

"Are you alright?" he asked, very concerned. He'd probably seen the dream.

"Yeah, I'm fine," she replied with a weak smile before adding, "thanks." She wiped a tear that lingered on her cheek.

He nodded and quietly, albeit reluctantly, closed the door.

She sighed and ran her hands through her hair, before diving into her closet to get dressed so that she could join him as quickly as possible.

# Chapter 17

Alexander sorted through some papers for work and let his mind drift to Sophie, listening to the conversation she was having – not because he wanted to necessarily, but because he was so connected to her that he couldn't help it.

"Laney?" He overheard Sophie ask.

"Yeah?" Laney asked.

"I've been thinking about something. Alexander told me that vampires are twice as strong as we are…so, how was he able to get that one off of me so fast a few weeks ago?"

Alexander stopped what he was doing and listened.

"Daylight," replied Laney matter-of-factly.

"Oh, right."

"That, and he's in love with you. He'd die before he'd let anything bad happen to you."

There was a long pause and Alexander held his breath as he listened.

"I know."

"Pizza dude!" Jim called out, so that the whole house heard.

Alexander stepped into the hallway and looked over the railing into the foyer below. Jim reached the door before the delivery boy could manage to get up to the patio with the twelve pizzas he had ordered.

"Come on, y'all!" Jim called. "Time to eat."

"Holy crap!" Sophie exclaimed at the sight and fell into gales of laughter.

Alexander walked into the room to see her perched on one of the barstools, watching Jim stack a whole pizza on his plate in a mountain of mozzarella and pepperoni, as Laney danced around the room. Sophie looked up when she realized Alexander was there and held her hand out to him for him to take. He walked to her.

Wrapping his arm around her waist, he kissed her on the top of the head.

"Hi Alex," she whispered contentedly.

"Yeah, *Alex*," mocked Jim.

Alexander picked an apple up off of the counter and hurled it at his head. Jim caught it and he hurled it back at Alexander who snatched it out of the air before it reached him; he hadn't even looked up.

"That was *really* fast," Sophie said, frozen over a slice of pizza, her eyes wide and her mouth hanging open.

Jim looked at her and smiled. "You have no clue what this guy can do. Trust me sis, you ain't seen nothin' yet!"

"Is *that* right?" She asked, looking at Alexander with an interested but flirty look, a delicate eyebrow rising in response to a sudden thought that ran through her mind.

Zoey smirked at the pair.

"Oh, *yuck!*" exclaimed Laney from the other room. "Ew! Blech! Would you two keep your thoughts to yourself?"

"Stop listening!" Sophie called back before Alexander kissed her lightly on the lips. "So…," she prompted after a moment.

"Yes?" Alexander asked, suspecting something.

She looked like she was preparing for a fight. "I need some hands-on experience. I don't want to have to rely on you or Jim to come save the day all the time, and it's going to get worse."

Alexander groaned.

"And," she continued before he could argue, "I want to go out with you and Jim tonight."

He grimaced and she held a hand up to keep him from saying no.

She looked at him almost reproachfully. "I need you to teach me how to find them."

Alexander shook his head in response. "Sophie, you are not ready for…"

"I *am*, actually, Alex," she interrupted firmly, becoming more committed to her goal. "You're not ready for this, but I am."

He opened his mouth to argue as his grip around her waist tightened.

She shook her head. "I know I'm a lot newer at this than you are, but I've relied on myself my whole life. If I decide I can handle it, please let me try. I'm not as fragile as you think I am—I think we've proven I can get an advantage over *you* if I try hard enough. Besides, I need to be prepared. Isn't it better that I see what this is all about when it's on *our* terms and when we're fully prepared for what could happen instead of waiting for them to hit me first? I mean, it doesn't look like they're going to cut me slack anytime soon."

He studied her face for a minute. Her logic was solid and he really couldn't argue. "Alright," he finally consented, "but under one condition."

"What's that?" Sophie asked.

"You do *exactly* what I say when we are out there. I will not have you getting hurt."

She nodded in agreement. "That's what I'm trying to prevent." She strutted out of the room.

She grinned at Jim as he walked into the room for his second helping. He turned in a circle, watching her walk away and then settling his eyes on Alexander. "What'd I miss?"

"She's going with you tonight," Zoey replied.

"Awesome!" Jim exclaimed, clapping his hands together and ignoring Alexander's grimace. He looked at Zoey. "You going too?"

The redhead shrugged. "Might as well. It's been a while and it looks like we'll have a lot to deal with soon."

"Nice."

Zoey's eyes settled on Alexander's. "She'll be okay."

"She needs to learn this stuff sooner or later, you know," Jim added. "She may be really good at it, who knows?"

"She will be *very* good at it," Alexander corrected him, before leaving the kitchen and disappearing on the way to his own room. *She must be.*

# Chapter 18

Jim groaned. *Typical.* He was the first one ready. He paced at the foot of the stairs; he wanted to get out there tonight so badly he could taste it. Something in his bones told him that it would be a good night.

"Ready?" Alexander asked, suddenly appearing at his side.

*You really have to ask?*

Alexander shrugged seconds before they looked up to see Sophie and Zoey coming down the stairs. Jim muffled a snicker when he heard what ran through Alexander's head. *Good luck, man.*

Alexander raised an eyebrow at his brother.

*Good luck keepin' your mind in the game with her lookin' like that.*

Sophie shot Jim a smug smile.

"Alright! Let's go," Jim said, leading the way out the back door.

"Have fun!" Laney called from in front of the T.V.

"Thanks!"

Jim held the door open for the others and led them back to the storm cellar out back.

"What's first?" Sophie asked.

"Gettin' a few things, just in case," Jim answered, typing the code in at the door. "After the increase of activity the past couple of weeks, I'd put money on seeing one or two out and about."

"Dante mentioned that their migration pattern has changed," Alexander added, quietly, "Perhaps it is due to the fact that we are here and growing in numbers, although it has taken them a while to catch on."

"They're a little slow, huh?" Sophie asked.

Jim shrugged and swung the doors open and walked down the descending pathway into the dark hole, not bothering to turn on the light. They could all see as well in the dark as the day, so what was the point?

Sophie watched as the other three went immediately to work. Zoey strapped a belt—full of wooden stakes—around her waist. Jim slung his gun belt around his waist and checked the magazine in the Desert Eagle .50 AE he preferred to carry, before sliding it into the holster, while Alexander examined his Smith and Wesson revolver, spinning the cylinder with a quick touch of his thumb.

Sophie watched them with wide eyes. "What are those for?" she asked quietly.

"Pretty much anything shot through the heart slows one of those suckers down long enough for us to get them," Jim answered, slipping a knife and a couple of stakes in his belt. He pulled a leather jacket on, concealing his weapons. "Silver's the best, but these'll do."

"Oh," Sophie replied, sounding unsure about the situation.

Alexander leveled his eyes at her. "You wanted in on this, Sophie, and this is how we do things."

"No, it's not that," she retorted. "It's just…I've never shot a gun before. I don't know what to do, or *how* to do it."

"Well, we'll remedy that soon," Jim promised as he reached for a belt that held six stakes. "Here," he tossed it to her, "you can use these. No point in taking you out there with no self-defense."

She fastened the belt around her waist, the stakes concealed on the inside of it, against her body.

"You will not need them," Alexander assured her.

Jim nodded in agreement. "We'll take care of whatever's out there. You're not gonna be in any danger."

Zoey patted Sophie on the shoulder reassuringly.

Sophie shrugged; she wasn't scared. "Let's do it," she replied.

Alexander nodded before he led the way out of the cellar, threading his arms through the sleeves of his jacket as he walked. Jim reached down to secure the door after them all.

"We're not driving?" She asked as they bypassed the cars.

"No," Alexander replied. "We can be more mobile if we don't have to concern ourselves with vehicles. We'll go to the square first."

Jim nodded and Sophie shot him a questioning glance.

"It is a heavily populated area at night. The bars especially draw them out," Alexander explained.

Sophie restrained a shiver as she recalled the nights she'd spent on the downtown square before she knew what the real world was actually like. Those images ran through her head as they walked in silence into the approaching dusk.

*So why aren't we jumping there?* Sophie asked in a thought.

*The threat of exposure is too great to jump in. We could appear right before someone's eyes and that could be...bad,* Alexander replied.

*Oh, right.*

The square was full of people and the trees around the courthouse were full of white lights and it made it feel festive. Safe.

Jim and Zoey fell behind Sophie and Alexander. Jim stopped on the corner of Elm and Oak, taking a seat on a bench there, and Zoey went to peer into shop windows nearby. The other two continued on ahead of them, watching everything as they walked along.

Alexander looked around, and when his eyes settled on a good observation spot, he led Sophie to it. *Let's sit here for a while and see if you can spot anything out of place.*

Alexander and Sophie sat so the building's wall was to their back. He looked at her seriously for a split second. *You have spent the past twenty years trying not to* hear *anyone. Now, you must listen.*

Passersby walked in a wide arch around their table, giving them a wide berth. The two didn't intend to look threatening, but there was something about them that made people want to steer clear.

*We're lookin' for anyone who doesn't seem normal,* Jim commented silently.

*Shouldn't be too hard,* Sophie replied sarcastically.

From the other side of the square, Zoey laughed silently.

Sophie was right; they *were* in a college town, but of course she knew what he meant. She'd been able to pick Jim and Alexander out of a crowd of hundreds in that town; she figured it wouldn't be too hard for her to find what they were looking for.

*So, not all of us hunt vampires like this, right?* She asked.

*Correct,* Alexander replied without looking at her.

*Then why do you—we—do it?*

Alexander sighed. *Because it's the right thing to do,* he answered too casually, not meeting her eye.

She wasn't buying it. *Is that all?*

*No,* was all he would answer.

*What else are we going do with all that time?* Jim interjected quickly.

*I could think of a few things to do with my time.*

*Damn girl, get your head out of the gutter.*

*Okay, you two,* Alexander warned with a faint smile on his face.

*Sorry,* she replied, a smile spreading across her own face. And then they were silent for a while.

*Does it ever bother you?* She asked all of a sudden, still staring across the street towards the courthouse.

*Does what, ever bother us?* Alexander asked.

*Killing someone like that?*

*You mustn't think of them as individuals, as human beings. They are not human any longer, but they* do *take human lives. Oftentimes, we are all who stand between them and the humans they would kill. Besides,* his thoughts hesitated, *each of us has the innate capacity to kill, whether we recognize that characteristic or not. Must I remind you of your reaction when one of us has 'attacked' you? It is simply our nature.*

*I don't believe that.*

He chuckled. *Alright,* he countered, watching her with humor in his eyes, *without thinking about it, how would you kill Jim?*

Jim laughed.

*Easy,* she replied automatically, *I'd run up behind him, stab him in the back and then go for his...* "Oh!" She exclaimed out loud, covering her mouth with her hand, horror spreading across her face. *Oh, Jim, I'm so sorry,* she thought frantically, *I didn't mean it! I can't believe…*

*It's okay, Sophie,* Jim interrupted her, *Don't worry about it.*

*But that's horrible. I'm SO sorry, Jim!*

*Sophie—seriously—get over it.*

She smiled meekly in response, but didn't quite believe that she hadn't insulted him.

*Do you see now?* Alexander asked. *Now imagine how easily and naturally it would be to end the life—if you wish to call it that—of something that is trying to kill you or your family. There would simply be no hesitation.*

*Hmm…I see your point, but I'm still not…* Her thought trailed off as something caught her eye. She froze.

*What is it?* Alexander asked.

*Jim, Zoey, can you guys see the guy on the opposite corner there, by that statue?* She asked.

Jim's eyes shot across the street, scanning the crowd. *What's he look like?*

She shot an image to Jim of the guy she'd seen.

*Oh, okay, yeah I see him,* Jim thought.

*Just watch him for a minute,* she thought back.

*The one in the gray hoodie?* Zoey asked.

*Um hmm.*

The four surreptitiously watched him for a few moments.

*He's moving a little too fast, don't you think?* Zoey thought.

*Good eye, Sophie,* Alexander thought. *Let's get ready to follow him if he moves.*

*Told you she was a natural,* Jim said.

*Thanks, Jim.*

*You betcha, sis. Whoa, he's moving.*

*Come along,* Alexander instructed Sophie, rising from his chair. *Slowly.*

She rose silently. He reached back and grabbed her hand, taking the time to appear casual.

Jim crossed the street to be closer to the vampire and pretended to talk on his phone. Zoey remained a few yards behind him.

They began slowly following the vampire as he moved south on Elm, exiting the square.

*He doesn't know we're following him,* Sophie thought idly.

*Is that an assumption?* Alexander asked firmly.

*No,* she shrugged again, confused. *That's what he's thinking.*

Jim and Zoey came to a halt. They exchanged looks, shocked by the revelation. *Whoa!* Jim exclaimed. *That's crazy, Soph.*

*What's crazy?* She asked.

*No one's been able to do that before,* he answered.

*Let's keep up with him. We will follow him and see where he leads us,* Alexander pulled Sophie along with him.

*And then?* She asked.

*And then, we'll take care of him,* Zoey answered. *And we'll see if you can pick up on all of their thoughts.*

Jim's heart rate quickened. He could see the vampire perfectly. He started walking faster. *I can't wait to get him alone in a dark alley. Dirty, stinking, evil piece of...*

*Language,* Sophie jokingly warned. *There's a lady present.*

*Please, I've been in your head, girl,* he replied. *"Lady" is questionable.*

*Now, Jim,* Alexander warned.

Sophie snickered. *I was talking about Zoey.*

Zoey laughed quietly.

They were slowly gaining on the vampire as he turned the corner and headed down a dark alley.

*Surprise, surprise,* Jim thought. *A dark alley.*

*Quite the cliché,* Sophie agreed.

The four of them came together a few feet from the vampire's turn. Zoey stepped away from Jim. Alexander stood with his hands in his pockets and Sophie, a couple steps behind him, had a hand behind her back, her fingers just touching one of the stakes concealed there. She didn't stop to think how instinctual the action was, but she felt the familiar boil of aggression in her gut when she saw the vampire up close for the first time; her first reaction was to have a weapon in her hand.

Alexander whistled and the vampire spun around to face them. The vampire hissed in their direction and Sophie stiffened as his stench wafted toward them through the stirred air. She shifted her right foot forward ever so slightly in anticipation and sunk subtly closer to the ground. She never took her eyes off the vampire.

"Easy, Soph," Jim whispered.

Alexander smiled darkly at the vampire. "Where are *you* going?"

"None of your damn business," the vampire hissed as something in the shadows moved behind him.

"Oh, damn it," Jim whispered, "do you *feel* that?"

"I smell it," Zoey murmured.

Three other vampires slithered out of the shadows

*Do* not *let Sophie out of your sight,* Alexander warned Jim.

*Don't worry about me,* Sophie immediately replied.

*Yeah, right,* Jim thought back.

*They're scared,* Sophie thought.

*They're young,* Jim answered.

The vampires crouched, waiting to see who would spring first. Their black eyes shifted back and forth between the other four as they watched them nervously. One of them rocked back on his heels and sprang forward.

"Damn it," Jim grunted.

He drew his handgun from his belt. Two rounds went into the vampire's chest through the silencer which muted the sound of the bullets. Buckling under the wounds, the vampire fell to the ground. He landed in a ball at Jim's feet, clutching his chest. The other vampires charged.

Alexander gripped a knife with one hand, his revolver with the other. He barreled towards the vampire closest to him. He shot him in the chest at point-blank range; the bullet made a hissing sound. He crashed into his enemy. He struck in one swift movement, and took off the vampire's head. It fell to the ground with a thud and rolled a few feet away. He pulled a stake from his boot and plunged it into the vampire's heart.

Another vampire backhanded Zoey. The redhead spun around on a heel and plunged a wooden stake into the vampire's spine. The vampire's back arched against the pain and he wiggled trying to reach around and pull it from his back. Jim took the vampire's head off and the body was still.

Sophie's eyes moved to the vampire in front of her. He was the one they'd followed into the alleyway. He must have sneaked around the others, because he seemed to appear out of nowhere. Sophie was too far away from the rest of her family. The vampire walked in an arch around Sophie, between her and the others, and they wouldn't be able to get to her; two other vampires slinked out of the shadows. Alexander realized it first.

*NO!!* His thoughts screamed.

Sophie stood perfectly still, both hands behind her back, watching her attacker. Her breath was calm and even. Her eyes were fixed squarely on the vampire's.

*Can you get a read on her?* Jim asked; he couldn't tell what his new little sister was thinking. Only half paying attention to what he was doing, he sent two bullets into the heart of a vampire moments before Zoey decapitated him.

*SOPHIE!* Alexander's panicked thoughts yelled as he fought another vampire off of himself. It landed in a heap of dead flesh at his feet.

Zoey and Alexander traded a look. The vampire paced from the right to the left in front of Sophie, like a dog, deciding how to attack his prey. She moved her right leg to the side to crouch in front of the vampire, pulling her hands slowly out from behind her back, a gleaming stake in each hand.

*I'll take him on his left,* Alexander was thinking.

Jim and Zoey inched forward on the right. The vampire continued to stalk Sophie before suddenly freezing in his tracks. He was about to attack; Alexander saw it before any of them. He and Jim took off. But the vampire was on her, spinning around and grabbing her from behind. He dug his claw-like fingers into her neck. She gasped against the pain.

"Nobody move!" the vampire yelled.

Small trickles of blood ran from beneath his fingernails where they cut into the white skin of her throat. Her eyes were wide with shock.

Alexander skidded to a stop.

Jim looked at Zoey meaningfully. She nodded.

"No!" Alexander roared at his sister, throwing a hand up in warning towards Zoey.

The vampire looked at them, his eyes shifting from one to the other as his lips pulled into a maniacal grin. He pulled Sophie backwards toward the mouth of the alleyway. She shuffled her feet to keep up with him.

The vampire laughed. "Pathetic!" he spat.

Alexander rocked forward, wanting to spring. His fear for Sophie held him back.

She shot him a warning glance that he didn't understand, and then she closed her eyes. Her hands tightened around the stakes that she held in each hand.

She forced her mind to probe the vampire's brain; it was wired differently from a human being's. It was harder for her to tell what he was thinking, harder still that she had to concentrate on surviving the situation. Still, if she could just predict what he would do...

"Sophie?" Alexander asked.

There was a tremble in his voice that Sophie didn't expect. Her eyes shot open and stared at him. The faintest smile tugged at her lips.

The vampire licked at the blood on her neck. "You're mine now," he hissed.

Sophie let out a burst of angry laughter. "Not tonight."

The piercing grip at her neck relaxed infinitesimally and the vampire staggered backwards. His hand slipped from her throat and went to his own. Sophie spun on her heel and faced the vampire. He stared at her with his wide, soulless eyes. His mouth gaped open, looking for air.

She felt the heat of her anger course down her arms, through her fingers. She gestured toward the staggering figure. The stakes shot out from her hands and plunged into the vampire who stood several feet away. He stumbled backwards from the force, watching her with terrified eyes.

She tore another stake from the belt around her waist and stalked toward him. Her eyes were wild and a feral growl boiled in her chest. She jumped toward him, suddenly appearing inches from his face. In one hand she gripped the stake, in another she tore at the hair on his scalp.

Comprehension momentarily washed over the vampire's face. She plunged the stake into the side of his neck and tore through the flesh. She tossed the head to the side and wiped the back of her hand on her pants, staining them with black, sticky blood.

She turned to face her family. Her hair had been torn out of its ponytail and hung wildly around her shoulders. Her neck ached from its wounds.

Jim and Zoey stared at her wide-eyed; she saw them over Alexander's shoulder. She dropped the bloody stake to the ground and threw her arms around his neck.

"Sophie," he whispered against her cheek.

He reached up and tenderly touched the wounds at her neck. She winced against the pain. He frowned at her.

"I'll be okay," she promised.

"How did you do that?" Zoey breathed.

She shook her head. "I wanted him to die."

"But you *choked* him," Zoey said. "With your *mind*."

Alexander stroked Sophie's neck, wanting to take the pain away. He looked at Jim and Zoey. "We need to burn these things; the police will be here soon." He handed Sophie a handkerchief, which she immediately placed at her neck.

Jim gathered the bodies and tossed them in a nearby Dumpster. Alexander struck a match and tossed it in on the bodies. Zoey watched Sophie approvingly.

"Back to the house," Alexander commanded, walking back to Sophie and pulled her protectively into his arms.

They made it back within seconds of each other, but Alexander didn't waste any time with pleasantries.

"Let's get you cleaned up," he said. He pulled Sophie gently into a bathroom on the first floor.

"What happened?" Dante asked, following them around the corner. Laney and Catherina were on his heels.

Alexander positioned Sophie against the marble countertop and proceeded to dig through the contents under the sink. He pulled alcohol, gauze, and myriad other medical supplies out and spread them on the countertop. He didn't seem to hear anyone.

"She's hurt, but she killed a vampire with her own hands," Zoey offered quietly. She looked meaningfully at Dante. "She used her mind to choke him when he attacked. Then she all but tore his head off."

From the corner of her eye, Sophie spotted Catherina as she looked on, an unreadable expression in her cold, hard eyes.

"Excuse us," Alexander said gruffly and closed the bathroom door in their faces.

Sophie watched him carefully. He frantically doused a cotton pad with alcohol and finally looked at her. He brought the piece of cotton within inches of her neck. She grasped his wrist and looked into his eyes.

"I'm okay," she promised.

He nodded and sighed. "This will hurt a bit, I'm afraid."

She chuckled in a whisper. "I've had worse."

He tried to smile and hesitantly dabbed at her neck. She sucked air in through her teeth and winced against the sting. He dabbed at the cut gently and blew on the injury, taking the burn away and giving her chills all at once. He moved to the next cut; dabbed at it carefully and then blew on the wound. He stepped closer to her and repeated the process with another cut. Backed against the sink, she couldn't have moved away from him if she'd wanted to.

She closed her eyes to the simultaneous pain and desire that coursed up her neck. Every hair felt as if it were standing on end. His body was pressed against hers as he doctored her wounds. She slipped her arms around his waist and held him.

He moved to the other side, where the vampire had dug his thumb into her flesh.

"This one is deep," he whispered in warning, "but I need to clean it."

He pressed the cold piece of cotton against her tender neck. She gritted her teeth against the icy burn. He pulled it away from the skin and blew on the crescent shaped cut that was already healing. His nose grazed her jaw line. Her breath quickened.

"I thought I was going to lose you," he breathed.

She sighed. "I know."

He dropped the cotton pad into the sink. He gently held the back of her neck and brought his lips to rest on hers. She sighed into him and pulled him closer. She clawed at his back and crushed her lips against his. They lost themselves in the feel of each other, until she suddenly pulled away.

"I promise I'm not going anywhere. There was no way that vampire was taking me out tonight."

He rested his forehead against hers and looked into her eyes. "I don't know if you realize how amazing you are."

She tried to argue with him, but he silenced her with another kiss.

# Chapter 19

He screamed. It was a bone-chilling, terrifying, guttural scream. He scratched down the sides of his face, his nails tearing the skin away from his ancient bones. Almost as soon as the black blood started to trickle from the wounds, the skin began to heal itself, stitching the dead--yet somehow alive--fibers back together.

"Jacques," a soft voice said.

He turned his crazed eyes towards the speaker.

"What is it?" she asked.

"Matthew is dead!" Jacques exclaimed. "My brother! They've killed him."

"Who has done this thing?" she asked.

Another slid out of the shadow. "Elizabeth, it is our enemies to the west who are responsible."

Upon seeing the speaker's face, Elizabeth fell into a sweeping bow. "My lord Cusick," she said.

He stepped closer to her and placed a hand on her cheek. The room started to fill with others of their family, watching what was happening in the center of the room. He ran his fingers down the side of their face. "Would you like to know how they killed him?" he asked.

"Yes, Councilor," she replied, looking up at him reverently.

His eyes met hers and bore into her inner self. The look in her eyes changed in response. They widened in shock and she grasped at her throat, stumbling away from him. He continued staring at her, his head cocked to the side, as if he were looking at her with mild curiosity.

She clawed at the invisible force around her neck, gasping in shock. Her nails tore at the noose that was not there, the one that cut off the air and burned her throat. The skin peeled back like a

145

ripe orange, and black blood spilled from the gashes until she was kneeling in a pool of her own putrid fluids. What little dead light exists in a vampire's eyes was extinguished with her last breath.

And the room was silent.

"That," said Cusick, "that is what the new one is capable of. Let that be a lesson to you all." He turned to Jacques who had composed himself and seemed possessed with a fire of hatred. "Take care that you do not meet the same fate at their hands."

"I will have vengeance at their death," Jacques vowed.

"Take care of it. If not..." Cusick's eyes narrowed "You will have more problems than you can possibly imagine. And I can promise that you will not like the outcome, if you live through it."

# Chapter 20

Dante opened the door before they could reach it and Alexander stood just behind him. The rest of the family was perched strategically on the staircase between the new arrivals and Catherina, who waited on the landing above them. Sophie sank down to sit on the stairs, still in view of the front door.

Celia arrived at the door first. She was tall, thin, dressed in a form-fitting black long-sleeved shirt and tight jeans. She wore combat boots, black sunglasses and her slightly curled blonde hair cascaded to the middle of her back. She exuded confidence. She looked like she could conquer the world.

*I'd like to look like her,* Sophie thought reflexively.

*You do,* Alexander thought back.

Sophie's eyes flashed to him and she smiled.

Celia slowly removed her sunglasses, taking her time not to make any sudden movements as they all waited in anticipation.

"You must be Dante," she said in her perfectly husky voice. Her eyes glanced from him to Alexander and rested there. "It's been a while." Her lips curled into a smile.

"Indeed," he replied stiffly.

Celia smirked and then turned back to Dante.

Dante stepped to the side. "Please come in. We have been expecting you."

The trio flowed into the entryway. Sophie held her breath, watching and waiting. Masumi and Chaz looked around the room defensively, surveying the faces of the others, the house, everything. Celia's eyes settled on Sophie's, unblinking. Sophie didn't look away.

"Would you please be seated?" Dante asked.

"Of course," Celia replied, her eyes never leaving Sophie's. "Thank you." Her stare did not release Sophie until Masumi gently touched the back of her arm. The connection was instantly broken and Celia turned to enter into the front room.

Dante and Alexander followed the trio into the room and sat on the opposing couch. Jim leaned against the door frame at the back of the room, just a couple of feet behind the other two men. Laney stood behind his shoulder in the wide doorway; gatekeepers between them and their matriarch. Zoey slinked down the stairs and leaned against the banister at the bottom. Sophie stepped forward to join the group, but Catherina stopped her with a touch.

Celia glanced around the room, her eyes continually shifting back to where Sophie stood.

Dante spoke first. "Celia, we expected you; however, what we do not know is *why* you have come."

"We're just passing through," she replied casually. "We thought it'd be nice to come pay our respects to the Leone coven."

"*Family*," Jim articulated menacingly from the doorway.

She chuckled. "*Family*. My mistake."

The room fell silent for many minutes, but no one gave the other party a glimpse into their thoughts, as they stared each other down.

Alexander's eyes narrowed. "What are you really doing here?"

"Just passing through," Celia insisted, her frigid eyes leveled at him.

Chaz looked up. "There's been talk that something's about to go down," he said. "We wanted to see if it's true."

Dante nodded.

Alexander's eyes never left Celia's—as if he were waiting for her next move. She in turn didn't look away from him.

Sophie silently drifted down the stairs and wandered towards the group. She stopped a few steps behind where Alexander stood. The tension in the room was nearly palpable.

Dante finally broke the silence: "The rumors are true. An old enemy of my wife's is coming."

The trio did a double take at the mention of the word "wife." Celia glanced away from Alexander for half a second in surprise, but then leveled her gaze back at him quickly.

Masumi looked to Dante. "Is it true he spoke to the Council about it?" She asked in a light, accented voice.

"It is."

The trio glanced at each other meaningfully.

"Do you know when he's going to be here?" Celia asked quickly, shifting her gaze to Dante.

"No one has seen him yet, but his cohorts are quite active in the area."

"Well, in that case, we were wondering if we might stay here tonight. We'll be on our way tomorrow, going back home to Austin. We'd prefer not to be out at night. You know how it is," Celia said. "Especially with the entire ruckus you all seem to be so good as to stir up."

Jim smirked at her in response. *You've got no idea.*

Dante turned to Catherina. She nodded slightly to him before he looked back at Celia. "You are welcome here for tonight."

Celia's eyes flicked back to Sophie before looking back at Dante. "Thank you," was all she replied.

Sophie's eyes shifted quickly to the window. The sun was just beginning to set.

Dante rose and looked down at Celia and her little group. "Please make yourselves comfortable. We have extra rooms upstairs which you are welcome to utilize. Jim will show them to you," he said before walking to the kitchen.

"Come on," Jim said to the three as he walked towards the stairs.

They stood together in one sweeping movement. Sophie watched Celia and the others go up the stairs. Celia looked back over her shoulder at Sophie after she'd passed; her mind unreadable.

"You could cut that tension with a knife!" Laney exclaimed in a whisper once their visitors were upstairs with Jim.

"That's an understatement," Sophie replied quietly.

"Sophie, may I have your arm?" Catherina asked gently.

Sophie walked to her and offered her arm to Catherina. She took it and Sophie could feel Catherina's weight shift onto her. Even so, Catherina was as light as a feather and Sophie tried to keep herself from thinking that some of the weakness might be an act. It all seemed just a bit too good, too convincing; perhaps contrived. Sophie couldn't believe her.

She glanced at Catherina and flinched. The older woman truly *looked* at Sophie for the first time in the few weeks they'd known each other, but it spoke volumes. Her look was a defiant glare, and the chill in her eyes was penetrating as a shiver ran up Sophie's spine.

She cleared her mind of her suspicions and helped Catherina down the stairs and into the kitchen. Laney followed them there, and took a seat beside Catherina as they watched Dante begin dinner; a man who, clearly, thoroughly understood the joy of cooking. Zoey wandered over to the window.

Alexander walked to Sophie, silently took her hand and led her out of the room. They walked into the library on the opposite side of the house. He closed the door behind them.

"Are you alright?" he asked, concerned. He held both of her hands to his chest.

She looked at him, confused. "Yeah, I'm fine. What was that all about? Why did Celia keep staring at me like that?"

"She can tell that you are very powerful," he replied simply.

"What is it with everybody?"

"Sophie, you have no idea," he replied.

"You're right, I don't. Could you clear that up for me?" She asked, feeling the irritation build into something more ominous.

She knew her frustration was misguided even as the words erupted from her throat, but she could do little to stop them.

"I'm sorry," she said.

He shook his head and ignored her anger.

"Sophie, what you did when you were searching for Celia and the others was extraordinary in itself. No one reacts as you have in a psychic circle; to the intensity that you have," he began. "And then there is your uncanny ability to access your instincts," he ran a hand through his hair, a wild look of excitement in his eyes. "I have *never* seen someone accept their abilities as well, and as *quickly* as you have. Add to that what happened last night..."

"You mean the fight?" She interrupted. "It was pretty crazy; you guys are amazing, but I still didn't understand what exactly that had to do with me and why *I'm* getting all the attention."

"There are so many things about vampires that you haven't learned yet," he sighed, collecting his thoughts.

He dropped her hands and crossed his arms, staring at the floor in concentration. His thoughts were a confusing web of excitement, frustration, and near anger, which Sophie couldn't even begin to decipher. After a moment, he looked back at her.

"How do I explain?" he wondered out loud. "Vampires are psychically connected with one another, and they are organized into a highly-intricate infrastructure, or a government one might say. They would have *physically felt* when the group we vanquished last night was killed; when they were no longer part of the collective, I suppose you could say. They function as if they were on a spider's web: if one section is pulled or destroyed, the others feel and react to it. And they would also have seen what those six or so saw before we ended them."

She nodded, though she wasn't entirely sure where he was going with it. He continued patiently.

"The Council is organized in such a manner so that they know what is occurring at all times. The chances of another vampire knowing what you have done and what you are capable of is *extremely* likely. In fact, there are probably a very large number who know already, and news travels fast. I would be willing to bet Celia heard about this on the street."

Sophie stared at him in disbelief. "You're kidding me. But I didn't really do anything. You guys were awesome...I mean, you both were so fast and...And Zoey was just as good." Her mind raced for an answer.

"Yes, we were, but we were only acting *physically*. Remember what you said when Jim asked how you had killed the vampire?"

Sophie shrugged. "Yeah, that I just wanted..." she stopped mid-sentence, and looked at him with wide eyes. "Oh. I just wanted it. I only had to *want* it."

"Your psychic ability is something that we have never seen before. You crippled him *with your mind*. Do you see how significant that is?" he asked, searching her face. "You envisioned it, and it came to pass. You need to look within yourself and find the strength that is there," he said, shaking his head back and forth slightly. "You have no idea how much potential you have, but

Celia can tell; we all can. That is why she watched you so cautiously. You make her nervous."

"She seemed to like baiting you, regardless."

"Yes, but that's ancient history. She is wary of you."

She smiled a bit, but still didn't believe him.

"Alright," he replied with determination, "I shall prove it to you."

"What are you doing?"

He didn't answer, but he stepped over to one of the shelves and pulled a heavy book down from the towering piece of furniture. The spine had to be five inches thick. It was old and sturdy, dusty with lack of use.

"Stand up," he commanded.

She slowly rose from the chair she hadn't realized she had sunk down into as they had been talking.

"Now," he said turning to face her. "Protect yourself," he said causally before violently hurling the heavy tome directly at her head.

She panicked; she couldn't believe what he was doing. She saw the book coming at her, flying through the air, and before she had time to think, she instinctively sent the book flying into the wall where it crashed and then fell in disarray onto the floor. It left a dent in the wall.

Her eyes were like liquid fire. "What the hell?" She shrieked at him. *Are you trying to kill me?! Are you crazy?*

He was before her in an instant, grasping her face between his hands.

"Don't you see?" he asked. "*That* is the power you have, Sophie." His intensity was so fierce that his hands were trembling.

She started to shake her head no. "I don't know what you're talking about."

He dropped his hands and nodded. "Here, make the paperweight move," he said, gesturing to the heavy glass orb sitting on the table beside him. He watched her with almost frenzied eyes.

"You're crazy, you know?"

She looked at the paperweight, skeptical. *Move the paperweight, huh?* She thought, and it moved a couple of inches across the tabletop. Her mouth fell open.

"Are you *kidding* me?" She asked.

He shook his head as a crooked smile crept across his face.

Sophie looked back at the paperweight and willed it to float. Her breath caught as she watched it hover effortlessly over the table; her hands were at her sides.

She stared wide-eyed at the weight. "Oh, this is going to be *cool*." But then her smile faded and the paperweight fell to the floor. "I don't know if I can choke one again like that, though. That took some crazy concentration."

"We'll work on it," he promised.

Jim suddenly burst into the room with Laney fast on his heels. "What's going on in here? We heard a crash."

"Watch this!" Sophie said.

She looked at the paperweight that was lying on the floor and moved it back up to the top of the table, allowing it to rest gently in its place, all with the power of her mind only.

Laney started clapping her hands and jumping up and down. "Do it again!"

Sophie looked behind her at the book Alexander had thrown at her, laying in a disheveled heap. It was suddenly righting itself and gliding gracefully back to its spot on the high shelf—all at Sophie's command. She looked below the shelf to where Alexander was standing and watched a proud smile spread across his face.

"It's so easy," Sophie muttered to herself. "I had no idea."

"I do it all the time," Laney chimed in smugly.

"Yeah, but *I* don't," Sophie replied.

"True," Laney conceded, but Sophie wasn't even thinking of her.

She looked at Alexander. "Thank you for believing in me," she whispered.

He shook his head. "You are so quick to place your faith in others, but not yourself."

"It's just really hard to believe that it's been inside *me* all this time," she tried to explain, her smile fading into something a little sadder. *Just think what I could have...*

He narrowed his eyes at her, hearing the thoughts as they ran through her head, before she suddenly halted them in their tracks. His eyebrows furrowed in frustration, trying to grasp onto the image that flashed through her head.

Jim clapped his hands together. "Come on! Let's go show everybody else!"

"Go," Alexander whispered encouragingly to her, but watching her warily, still thinking of the images she'd so quickly concealed.

Sophie gave him a small smile, turned on a heel and followed Jim out the door, disappearing before she was halfway across the room, leaving Laney behind with Alexander.

# Chapter 21

Alexander turned to Laney once Sophie and Jim had left the room. "Have you seen anything in the future that I should know about?"

"You mean about Sophie?"

"Yes."

Laney thought a moment and then shook her head. "No, I haven't seen anything. Is everything okay?"

"It seems that way," he replied.

"She's really getting the hang of things, isn't she?"

"Indeed."

"Well, I'll let you know if I see anything," she offered with a shrug.

"Thank you."

She smiled. "I'm going to go see what everyone else is up to."

He followed her out of the room and past the staircase where Celia, Chaz, and Masumi were coming into the room. Virtually ignoring them, Alexander turned the corner to walk into the dining room but stopped short, finding Sophie juggling pieces of fruit with her mind before an audience of their family members.

Zoey was laughing at Sophie in amazement. "Here's another one," she said. With a flick of her wrist, Zoey sent another orange over to Sophie, who moved the additional piece of fruit into orbit with the others.

A smile crept across Alexander's face. The image would have been comical except for the implications of what it would mean later—when something deadlier than citrus fruits would be subjected to Sophie's power.

"I suggested she practice," Dante said.

Alexander nodded. "Good idea."

"Catch," Sophie said, hurling an orange to him without touching it.

He reflexively snatched it from the air just as Celia turned the corner. She let out a scoff as she came to a surprised halt, and looked quickly between Alexander and Sophie.

Sophie met her gaze with more confidence now, steadier than before. When her eyes traveled to Celia's, they changed; they became something dark, as something almost black boiled behind them.

Without looking away, Sophie moved her hand and the pieces of fruit settled back into their bowl on the table. She suddenly spun on a heel and headed towards the back door, but then stopped short.

"What is it?" Dante asked.

"Nothing," Sophie replied. "I thought I heard something." She looked to Zoey for affirmation.

Zoey shook her head. *I don't hear anything.*

"That was impressive," Celia quietly commented from behind Alexander.

"You have *no* idea," he responded, without turning to look at her.

"I'm sure I don't," she replied incredulously.

Alexander glanced over to the corner where Catherina sat on a stool, humming tunelessly to herself. He'd known her for long enough to realize the change that seemed to have abruptly taken hold of her over the past few weeks. She seemed half-crazed, but focused, maniacally driven by unseen forces as she rocked back and forth on the stool. Perhaps it was fear which motivated her, or perhaps it was the feelings of inadequacy that Sophie was likely imposing on the older woman that changed her, but he couldn't know for sure. Catherina was unreadable.

*Laney?* Thought Dante.

She smiled and responded by flittering into the kitchen, opening cabinets and pulling dishes out to swiftly set the table, which would be full tonight. Alexander silently watched her dance around it, placing items gently on the table. Sophie slipped her willowy arm under Alexander's to wrap it around his waist; his lips grazed her forehead. She sighed as she leaned against him. And just as quickly as she had grasped him, she was pulling away. He never seemed ready to let her go.

Catherina sat at the head of the table as always, Dante to her right. Alexander assumed his customary seat at the table's foot and Sophie next to him. The rest of the table was filled and Celia slowly lowered herself into the chair directly across from Sophie who stared relentlessly at her.

Celia was the first to look away this time. Zoey and Jim exchanged a look, and Laney watched Celia carefully.

Sophie sat back in her chair. "So, why are you really here, Celia?"

All other sound abruptly stopped and everyone else sat as still as statues, watching the two women on either side of Alexander.

A slow smile crept across Celia's face. She shrugged. "We were just passing through and wanted to know if the rumors of a vampire war were legit."

Sophie's eyebrow shot up in response.

"And...I had to see for myself."

"*What* did you have to see for yourself?"

"I had to see who Alexander *the Great*," her voice dripping with sarcasm, "finally chose."

Alexander stiffened at the tone of her voice and turned to glare at her, a subtle rumbling deep within his chest.

"Ah! *There* it is," Sophie replied, slapping the table with her hand and laughing.

"News travels fast," Jim interjected.

Alexander watched Sophie. Her laughter diminished to a disgusted smile. "Is that all?" she asked, a hint of surprise behind her words. *Pretty lame, if you ask me.*

Alexander disguised a chuckle as a cough.

Celia wasn't giving an inch. "We want to inform you that *we* have no quarrel with Jacques and the others. We'll not take part in whatever it is you all have going on here. Austin is uncomfortably close to the region this family regularly frequents. We have no desire to be dragged into *this* conflict," she added, gesturing to them swiftly with her fork.

"Satisfied?" There was no malice in Sophie's solid eyes, but most of the diners would have thought twice before crossing her.

Celia nodded once more.

"Good," finished Sophie with the smile.

*

Sophie knocked on the doorframe to Alexander's office as he sat reading. He looked up to find her standing in the doorway and smiled. He could hear Jim and Chaz talking downstairs, Masumi and Celia interjecting occasionally. They were talking sports.

*Jim likes everyone, the fool,* Alexander thought to himself.

Sophie nodded. Her eyes drifted to the book in his hands. "Clausewitz?"

"Some human theories are also useful against vampires," he replied and watched her from his chair as she walked over to his bed to sit.

"'*Know thy enemy, know thy self?* '"

"That's Sun Tzu, but the idea's the same."

"It makes sense." As if she couldn't sit still, she stood and looked out the window; the nervous energy radiated off of her. He closed the book and studied her face for a minute as she gazed out the window. To him, her face was the most precious in the world, and as the moonlight hit her eyes, even in the dim light, they shone.

He took a deep breath. "What's bothering you?"

"You said something earlier…about the Council and their organization. What exactly did you mean by that?"

He cleared his throat. "It's an intricate system. At the very core of the vampire world is a queen."

She raised her eyebrows in surprise, but didn't interrupt him.

"Hero is quite ancient, perhaps several thousand years old. There once was a king as well, though he was killed. Some believe that it was Hero herself who murdered her husband, but no one in the vampire world has attempted to pursue the accusations to the point of any sort of investigation. It's a good way to get killed.

"Initially, around the king and queen, there was a council— the *Consilium Strigis:* Council of the Vampires. It was a time of monarchs, and they strove to be like their human counterparts. Hero retained the officers and expanded the Council to include ministers from all parts of the world. There are twelve minister sets of three each."

She shook her head.

"The regions are split into countries or large sections of the globe. There are miniature councils in Brazil, the remainder of South America, Western and Eastern Europe, Asia, India, Africa together with the Middle East, the Mediterranean, Australia, Canada, Mexico and of course, the United States."

She looked at him. "So, there are three members of the Council in charge of the U.S.?"

"Yes and each have many contacts and coven leaders throughout their regions who report to them, creating a sort of network. The three Councilors for the United States are Cusick, Sloane, and Bennett. Bennett is relatively new to the Council, and she has recently accepted the charge of the western part of the United States. Sloane maintains the traditional north; Cusick monitors the south."

She sank down to sit on the edge of his bed. He went on.

"One reason Jacques is a *significant* challenge, aside from the obvious, is that he is one of the coven heads who reports directly to Cusick, therefore possessing a direct line of communication with the Council as a whole."

"*Great*, so anything we do that involves him…"

"…will be known almost immediately by the entire Council."

"Fantastic," she breathed.

She chewed on her thumbnail and was lost in thought. She didn't look at anything in particular, and Alexander didn't try to listen to her thoughts. Suddenly, she looked at him.

"Not to *totally* change the subject, and I don't want to come off sounding jealous or anything, because I'm not. I mean, you could hear that if you really wanted to," she began nervously, which was unlike her. "But, what's with Celia? I mean, she's found her companion in Chaz, so what gives? Why does she care so much about you? There's got to be a back story there."

"Well," he deliberately rose and walked over to the bed, taking a seat facing her. "I must agree that *you* are not the jealous type, but Celia always has been. She is also excessively competitive. I met her many years ago and we did not get along

159

then. She saw me as a challenge at the time, because I did not care for her in the way she believed I should. It is a very long and sad story, and it is one that ended in the death of a dear friend of mine."

Sophie shook her head.

"She intentionally put herself in the middle of a foolish and life-threatening situation. Another of her family attempted to come to her rescue, but he was killed by the vampire who had been poised to attack her. She wanted me to be the one to save her life. She believed that had I done so, it would change how I felt about her."

"How stupid is that?"

"Quite," he answered. "I walked away from the family after that. I did not bother to tell her I was leaving. I have not seen her from that day to this. Obviously she hasn't changed. She still accomplishes nothing but the spread of contention wherever she goes."

"What a waste."

He looked at her cautiously. "Her concern about Jacques was genuine though; she will be of no help to us," he added. "In fact, she would likely tell him where we are if it benefited herself in any way."

"You pissed her off that bad, huh?" Sophie asked with a laugh behind her words.

He shook his head and didn't smile in return. Hers faded quickly in light of his serious tone.

"No. That is simply her way. She is entirely concerned for herself only—a true narcissist to the end. She always has been—and always will be—her own highest priority," he answered simply.

*Sounds like someone else we know,* Sophie thought.

He nodded solemnly. Still thinking about Celia, Sophie walked to his bookshelf. He listened to her as she silently read through some of the titles.

"We'll be going to New Orleans soon, now," she said.

"Yes," he replied, still watching at her. "Dante mentioned flying out on Friday."

"I guess I should pack," she said.

"They'll be gone soon."

She nodded wisely. "I know."

She stepped lightly to his bedside and kissed him on the cheek before she glided out of the room with a quiet smile.

# Chapter 22

"Come in!" Laney called through her closed door.

"Hey," Sophie replied, suddenly appearing on the other side of the still-closed door.

"Hi! What's up?" Laney asked.

Sophie shrugged. "Just thought I'd see what you were up to."

Laney smiled knowingly, but gestured to the piles of things around her; the mounds of clothes and stacks of magazines, DVDs, and literal piles of jewelry. She giggled.

"I'm trying to get organized," she admitted to Sophie, and then the rest of her thoughts came out in a quick, fluid stream of words. "I can't believe we're going to be in New Orleans next week! We're going to have so much fun! I really, seriously, totally *cannot* wait! I've always wanted to go there. It's gonna be amazing!"

Sophie nodded, fingering a long strand of fake pearls on the dresser. "Yeah, I know. It's going to be kind of hard to say goodbye to this place, though."

"We'll be back."

*But when?*

"Does it matter?"

Sophie didn't answer and the room fell silent. Her eyes became glazed over, and her face unreadable as she listened to the conversation below. In the quiet of Laney's room, they could easily hear the discussions going on downstairs between Celia's group and their family members.

*You okay?* Laney asked in a thought.

"I'll be back," Sophie replied distractedly and disappeared.

When she opened her eyes, she was in the living room where Dante was discussing with Celia and Masumi the research

163

he'd been compiling. He was showing them the results of his their migration. The data looked like weather maps.

Sophie stepped up to the little group and looked at him. "How'd you put all this together, Dante?" she asked.

He turned to her, pleased at her interest. "We have several friends throughout the United States with whom we share information: where vampires have been seen, how many were sighted, that sort of thing. I also take it upon myself to track missing persons lists. Taken together, we gain the data of a fairly accurate pattern trace for vampires throughout the nation."

Sophie nodded and looked down at the map in his hand. "May I?" She asked. He handed it to her in silence. She ignored the weight of Celia's and Masumi's eyes on her.

Dante pointed to the map. "You can see that there has been an increase in the travel patterns in the southwest, towards Texas," he explained.

"They're heading this way," she stated grimly.

"Yes. They will likely branch off into two separate paths. Here," his finger traced northward to the Tennessee and Kentucky area, "and here," he said, pointing to New Orleans, right where they would soon be heading.

"Hmm," Sophie sighed. "Why do you think they're going north like that?"

Celia looked at her. "There haven't been many things happening in Tennessee for a long time." Sophie looked at her questioningly. Celia shrugged. "We all keep track of this stuff."

Sophie felt a sudden brush of air behind her. Alexander was suddenly standing behind her.

"Vampires typically attempt to attract as little attention to themselves as possible," Alexander explained quietly, "doing so ensures their survival, and in this way, they are virtually untraceable by humans." He placed his hand on the small of her back.

"We have been tracking their patterns for quite some time. We are very familiar with their habits," Dante explained.

"Hmm," Sophie replied and handed the map back to Dante before she walked over to the couch and sat down, absentmindedly chewing on her thumbnail.

Masumi followed Sophie. "What are you thinking?"

"What? Oh, uh…nothing," Sophie lied. She'd really been thinking about the patterns researched by Dante and how surprising they were. The whole thing went deeper than she'd thought.

"Yes, it does," Alexander said, coming to sit beside her.

*There's a whole network of us out there, then?* Sophie asked as she struggled not to get lost in his intense green eyes.

*Yes.*

*And the vampires are traveling this way.*

*Yes. They will be on our heels as we travel east.*

*Not sure I like that idea.*

*Nor I, but we shall be at an advantage in New Orleans.*

*How?*

*Home field advantage.*

Sophie smiled.

Masumi watched the exchange between the pair in unobtrusive silence. She took a seat adjacent to them.

"Let us not worry about such things tonight, with friends under our roof," Dante suggested.

Sophie looked up at Dante's words and raised an eyebrow in response. "Friends" was a loose definition for their guests, but she wasn't going to argue. She glanced over to Chaz who sat talking with Jim on the opposite couch.

"So, what takes you to Austin?" Sophie asked him.

"I have a home there, near downtown actually," Chaz answered in a quiet voice.

"Why do you care?" Celia asked shrilly, appearing out of nowhere. She stood menacingly over Sophie.

Sophie looked up at her from the corner of her eye and smiled. "Just curious," she answered simply with a shrug.

"Nosey bitch," Celia grumbled.

*Alright, that's it!* Sophie stood up quickly to face her. She'd had enough. "Celia," she growled, "what's your problem?"

"I have no problem with you," Celia replied dismissively, while staring brazenly into Sophie's eyes.

"Then who *do* you have a problem with?" Sophie demanded.

"Some wounds leave scars," she replied grimly with a quick glance at Alexander.

The room fell silent in the presence of their little exchange. Jim stood up and Zoey suddenly appeared from around the corner, silently slinking back into the room. Alexander watched Sophie carefully from his seat.

"What the hell *is it* with eternity?" Sophie demanded. "Does it turn people into petty children?"

Celia slinked down into a defensive crouch. A quiet growl erupted from her often sarcastic lips. Sophie paid her aggression no mind; she would take anything Celia threw at her with glee. Alexander slowly stood; ready to strike Celia if she made a move against Sophie.

"We're running from a vampire who has held a—what—*two hundred* year grudge? And now, you!" Sophie declared, taking a step toward the other woman, heedless of the fact that Chaz now flanked his companion. "You 'just drop by' to pick a fight with a man who not only has no interest in you, but is also ten times better than you have *ever* thought about being, and who you attempted to lure—*unsuccessfully*, by the way—into a trap that left a mutual friend dead? Get *over* yourself already!" Sophie declared, glaring at the other woman, "or get the hell out," she finished firmly, not caring that it was technically Catherina's house she was volunteering to throw Celia and her friends out of.

Celia cautiously straightened out of the partial crouch she'd sunken into, as Alexander mirrored her movements just behind Sophie. Jim visibly relaxed. He stood closer to Celia than the others; just waiting for the moment to spring. Catherina watched on from her chair, her eyes unreadable. Zoey watched Celia carefully and Laney stood at the top of the stairs. She held her hands up as if to try and keep the peace.

"It appears we've worn out our welcome," Celia growled.

"So it appears," Dante replied, the only calm one in the room.

"I'll call a cab," Masumi volunteered quietly and was on her cell phone in a moment.

Jim still hadn't relaxed from his tense pose and Sophie's eyes locked on Celia's. Alexander stood so closely to her that she wasn't sure who would get to Celia first if she had decided to charge in their direction. Chaz looked warily between the fighters who had effectively backed him and Celia up against a wall.

166

Masumi must have worked wonders with the cab company; they left a few moments later. Sophie wasn't sorry to see them leave; only Masumi seemed to regret the sudden parting. The tension quietly melted away with the departure of their guests.

Alexander looked at her once they were alone. "Why don't we go for a walk?" he suggested.

Her eyes darted to the dark windows. It was nighttime. He smiled again and took her hand, leading her to the back door. He led her to the remodeled storm cellar out back and collected a few weapons, just in case. They weren't going out to actively look for anything, but it was quickly becoming apparent to her that they were magnets for vampires, whether they meant to be or not.

"Not always," he replied to her thought.

"Really?"

"Some of the time, everything is quite peaceful. There is simply a sudden influx of their kind lately, with the actions of Jacques and their present migration. It's not always like this."

"That's kind of a relief."

"Who knows but that we may have a peaceful walk?" he mused, while picking up his revolver. He spun the cylinder and it clicked resoundingly back into place in the silent concrete room. "But, just in case we have," he said, cocking his head in the direction of the gun with a faint smile.

"You *like* hunting them."

"I like protecting human beings," he clarified, "and my family," he added, looking so meaningfully at her that it made her self-conscious.

She looked away.

"Here you are," he said. He handed her the same belt she'd worn last time she was out after the sun went down—the one with the stakes shoved into little loops on the inside. She wound it around her waist and buckled it there. "You probably won't need it," he said and then smiled. "But, you're quite good with them, so you might as well take some."

She smiled. "Thanks."

"Shall we?" he asked.

"Sure, let's go."

He led her back outside and the cold air of the night swirled around them, but not uncomfortably. She smiled to herself as he pulled her arm gently through the bend in his, just like in an old movie. He was irresistibly old-fashioned; one of the many traits of his that she found endearing.

"We're going toward campus?" she asked incredulously.

"I thought you might enjoy a walk this way, since we are leaving soon," he explained softly.

He knew her so well...*already*.

He squeezed her hand. "Not really, but I'm learning."

She smiled. "Thanks. It'll be hard to say goodbye to this place. It's really become home for me." But, now her home was with him and the rest of her new-found family.

"Are you relieved at all to be done with this place?" he asked, casually.

She let out a little amazed laugh. Were they really having a normal, everyday conversation...one that didn't involve vampires or grudges or the supernatural in any way?

"It does feel nice, doesn't it?" he asked.

She shrugged and leaned against his arm, enjoying the contact and the warmth of his body beside her own. "In a way. I mean, it's not like I ever fit into the college lifestyle," she admitted.

"No, I don't think you did."

It seemed so strange to her, to be thinking about something as mundane as college life while looking down the barrel of inevitability as it was pointed directly between her eyes; her new life seemed so overwhelming.

"It will not always seem that way," he promised.

"Okay, I have a question that's totally off-subject," she said.

He chuckled under his breath at her instantaneous change. "Yes?"

"Um..." she began, "I don't know how to say it, how to put this into words."

"Just tell me in any way that works best for you."

"I get so mad," she admitted. *I never used to have a temper, well not as bad a temper.*

"Ah," he replied, stroking her hand with his reassuringly. "Think about it for a moment. You're half vampire. They're emotional, lustful, and violent in the extreme. They are quick to

168

anger; quicker than even you or I. They embrace their tempers and desires without thought or concern for the ramifications—they are like animals in that way. A vampire's only goal is the satisfaction of some craving or desire. This is why they are particularly good at holding grudges, and why some of *our* kind, like Celia for instance, are particularly prone at doing the same thing."

"But, this has always been inside me…"

"Yes," he agreed, "but my dear, we have been provoking you *quite a bit* lately. Think of your life before you came here. It was fairly solitary and mostly void of confrontation. I took you to be quite a loner. Is this incorrect?"

Sophie sighed and let out a sad chuckle. "No, you're right."

"The anger and the instincts…well, it is simply how we are," he explained.

"*You're* never like that," she replied.

"I've been doing this much longer. I simply hide it better than you do." He grew silent for a moment, sorting through his thoughts while Sophie waited. He shrugged. "You *are* unique, however," he said.

"Yeah, whatever," she replied with a roll of her eyes.

"No indeed, your abilities are quite extensive, and your temper is impressive."

She playfully slapped his arm. He chuckled.

"Actually, we have found that a strong hybrid comes from an exceptionally strong maker."

"So…?" she led.

"The vampire that turned your mother must have been *incredibly* strong," he said.

"Heh." She shook her head.

"Believe it. About twenty to thirty years ago, key members of the Council and several coven leaders—who incidentally are the strongest and smartest in their world—were deployed around the United States for the specific purpose of creating a large population of vampires."

"And you think that my mother's creator was one of them?"

"It is possible. That is why there are so many of us around your age. A woman with child usually has richer blood. Nowadays, this is especially true as doctors regularly place expectant mothers on iron supplements and vitamins. They are extremely difficult to resist for vampires, and while our kind is despised by theirs, they often suppose that the babies will simply die when a woman is changed or killed."

She shook her head in disgust.

"Most of them do expire," he added. "But most are very reluctant to bite any woman carrying a child—they do not want more of us in the world than this."

"Why did they set out to create a slew of new vampires?" she asked. "What's their plan?"

He looked grim. "I don't know."

She shivered, but it wasn't from the cold, and she found herself wanting to change the subject.

"Why don't you tell me more about yourself?" She asked drawing closer to him as the wind whipped sharply around the buildings.

"What would you like to know?"

She giggled. "Everything."

"Humph."

"Like...*I don't know*...maybe you could start with *which* turn of *which* century you were actually born in...?"

"I was born in 1693," he said simply.

1693. She ran through all the random facts stored in her nearly photographic memory that came to light with the mention of that date. The year that America's second oldest college, William and Mary was founded; when John Locke wrote his treatise on education; the year that the National Palace in Mexico City was rebuilt; the year Pope Clement XIII was born, and New York City had its first printing press, back when it was part of a colony...

And the year Alexander Jones was born.

"Alexander Carleton, actually," he corrected.

She stopped in her tracks and stared at him. "What?"

"My name at birth was Alexander Carleton. I have only been Alexander Jones for the past, oh, sixty years or so. It's getting to be about time to change the name again, actually."

"Um...why?"

"Well," he explained, pulling her back into the walk with him, "it's only wise for us to change names every human lifespan or so, especially in this day and age. I have had several different last names, not to mention a few differing Social Security numbers."

"Oh, well, no biggie," she replied sarcastically.

He laughed silently. "Sophie, why do you think we have such common names? Alexander Jones, Jim Cooper, Laney Roberts, Zoey Martin…they are all names which we have chosen; the kind of inconspicuous names which help us to 'blend in,' from the government's point of view," he said.

"What about Dante and Catherina?"

"Ah, well, neither of the pair feels the need to find employment, nor do they generally participate in society on a regular basis, so it has not been as necessary for them to assume other names."

"Oh, so he's *always* been Dante Leone?"

"Yes, and at one time, he and Catherina were legally wed, so she is as well."

"Hmm," she thought aloud. "Okay, so Alexander Carleton. 1693."

He looked down at her with a peculiar smile on his face, trying to listen to her thoughts, but they were all of him, and all waiting in anticipation for the next fact he was going to throw her way. He chuckled under his breath and shrugged.

"Yes, 1693. I was born in the Virginia colony," he replied.

"Wow," was all she could say. "I can't even imagine what all you've seen. You've seen so much history. I mean, the stuff I've only just read about in books…*you've experienced firsthand.*"

"I have always been an American; although once, many, many years ago, I traveled to Europe for an extended period of time." He looked off into the distance, in a way that told her that he wasn't seeing the sidewalk or the buildings in front of them. He was remembering something a hundred years ago or probably *hundreds* of years ago. His thoughts were too confusing for Sophie to try and keep up. He looked wistfully into the past as the brisk winter breeze played in his hair.

"I love this nation," he explained softly, "and I have fought, and tried to die for it, in every major conflict that she has had. Until recently."

"*Tried to die?*" She asked, stopping in her tracks once again.

"Well, yes," he admitted frankly, in a voice barely above a whisper. "There were many years of my life that I wished to bring it to an end."

She stared at him in horror. "And now?" She demanded. *Great, the last thing I need is a suicidal boyfriend.*

"And *now…*" he smiled, "I do not wish to end my life. It has *only just now* becoming worth living," he answered, pulling her along with him once more.

She walked at his side, mulling over everything he said. He stroked her hand as her thoughts were the confusing torrent.

He abruptly stopped in his tracks and looked smugly down at her. "Your boyfriend?"

She laughed at the look on his face. *What else would I call you?*

"You make a good point," he conceded with a shrug as they continued on their path and rounded the corner.

*So I guess all of your experience kind of gives you an unfair advantage in the academic world, huh?* She asked in a thought.

It really all made sense now: why he would pose as a history grad student to follow her around.

He chuckled under his breath again. *I have been in quite a few arguments regarding certain subjects, as you may well imagine.*

She snorted in response. *I bet.*

They continued walking along the gravel pebbled sidewalk. They were in the part of campus that was her favorite. It was so green and lush, large oaks leaning protectively over the little park areas. Even in the dark, the trees overhead were beautiful.

"I wonder what they look like to human eyes," she mused, nodding towards to swaying leaves. Though it was dark, she made out the different shades of green, even the veins in the tender flesh of each leaf.

"I don't know," he replied with a smile.

They passed the large statue of Don Quixote, prancing along on his steed. It stood in front of the ultra-modern general studies building, its boxy splendor a strange contrast to the 1950s-era Colonial-style chemistry building. The construction of the university's campus was very appealing to her; the juxtaposition of differing styles creating a discordant, yet cohesive atmosphere of learning.

They turned another corner and were suddenly heading back in the direction of the house. She sighed.

*You're not ready to go home?*

"Oh, no, it's not that. I think I'm just now finally starting to calm down after today," she confessed.

"It has been a very eventful day, has it not?"

She agreed silently, thinking it all over. They walked in silence the rest of the way home and before they reached the front porch, he turned to her.

"Do you see, my dear, that not *every* night is full of blood and violence?"

She breathed a deep breath, the cold hurting her nose, but she didn't care; it was the burning breath of freedom.

"It's really nice, just being with you, not dodging fangs," she answered.

He smiled down at her as they turned for the door and headed inside before it got too late.

# Chapter 23

Sophie sat on the black leather seat, looking at her family as the black limousine sped down the highway. They all looked like fashion models. Despite her best efforts, Sophie's clothes from The Gap didn't really compare to Armani, Calvin Klein, Yves Saint Laurent, Versace, and Chanel. She would really have to do some shopping in New Orleans, because if they all dressed like this on a regular basis, Sophie was screwed.

The limousine pulled up to the terminal, making it to the airport in record time, and other passengers stared at them as one by one, they piled out of the massive car. There were nudges and whispers as their driver piled the luggage on a cart and pushed it inside after them, while the family followed.

*Who are they?*

*Is she a movie star?*

*Body guards?*

The thoughts were endless, and exceedingly humorous.

"Mr. Jones, Miss Page," the lady behind the counter addressed them as they approached.

*Did they know we were coming?* Sophie thought.

*Yes,* Alexander answered silently and smiled at the airline employee.

Amazingly, there were no questions asked as Sophie and Alexander were handed their boarding passes. They had boarded the plane ahead of all of the other passengers before Sophie knew what happened.

"You will get used to it," Alexander whispered into her ear.

She smiled to herself but didn't say anything. She tried to relax for the short flight as she settled back into her seat. Granted, her anxiety over flying was eased a bit now that she knew how virtually indestructible she was—but old habits die hard and she was hugely inexperienced with air travel. Laney was listening to her MP3 player and Jim typed away on his laptop. Catherina and Dante huddled closely together, whispering privately to one another, and Zoey was gazing out the window nearby. Sophie turned to Alexander.

"So tell me about New Orleans," Sophie said.

"What would you like to know?" he asked.

"What's it like?"

"Different. There's much activity there, and there are many people. It's unlike anywhere you've visited," he mused. "There's an undercurrent of things otherworldly in New Orleans."

"Meaning…?"

"Well, there is a large amount of voodoo and occult activity in the city, and there are also many *other* beings there," he answered enigmatically.

*Vampires,* she thought.

*Yes.*

*And…others of…us?*

*Yes.*

"Ah," she replied to herself.

"We will be meeting up with some very old friends of Catherina's," he said in a whisper so soft that even she could barely hear, "a group of sisters who are at least as old as she, and who are especially unique among our people."

Sophie was admittedly nervous about meeting more of their kind, after the iffy situation with Celia, but Alexander's peace of mind helped reassure her. He was quiet for a several moments as they pretended to listen to the flight attendant and the best way to survive a crash over land and sea. They would probably be able to swim away from an ocean crash.

"What makes them so unique?" Sophie asked.

Alexander's eyes narrowed as he continued to look forward, deliberating. "They are companions," he finally answered.

"So they're…?"

"They're called sisters because their relationship is much like that between Jim, Laney, and yourself. However, it is stronger than that; like the relationship which you and I share. They've each had their share of male companionship, but it is their sisterly bond which is paramount in their lives. Because of their link, they are exceptionally strong and intuitive. Just suppose what you, Catherina, and Laney could accomplish if you were linked as companions are."

"Wow," she replied. She sat back, mulling over what he'd told her. Suddenly, Alexander turned in his seat and looked at her seriously.

"What is it?" she asked.

"I've just realized something," he answered enigmatically.

"What's that?" She asked.

"Well, while you've all but cornered me for story of my life, you have not told me about your own history."

She looked away quickly. *There's not much to tell,* she replied silently and somberly. She looked down at her hands and folded them together, not wanting to meet his eye. And she knew he hadn't just thought of that; it was something that he'd been thinking about for weeks.

*I would like to know,* he thought, and turned in his seat to face forward. He reached down to grasp her hand, rubbing the back of it with his thumb.

She continued to look at the floor and he glanced out the window periodically.

She sighed. *What do you want to know?* She concentrated on the tiny electric pulses that seemed to radiate through her skin where he touched her hand – that was a safer thing to think about.

*I believe you wanted to know everything about me, though I would be satisfied with far less. I understand if you don't want to tell me; if some of those memories are too painful—I suspect they may be.* He could hear her thoughts and feel her emotions as if they were his own, but he rarely delved into her memories and she didn't think about them much in any case.

She chuckled under her breath at the irony and looked casually across the aisle, glancing at the other passengers. *You're one to talk, you know? You're not exactly forthcoming with your story,* she thought kindly.

*That is true. Memories can be our enemies.*

*Yeah,* she thought and then sighing, gave in. *I was raised in the foster care system. I jumped around to different homes, one every few months or so until I was a teenager and figured out that if I just kept my mouth shut about hearing everyone else's thoughts, I wouldn't be branded a troublemaker and could gain some permanency.*

*I guess I was fifteen or sixteen when I finally made it to my last foster home. My foster parents were really nice. They were an older couple and couldn't ever have kids, so they fostered a whole slew of us.*

*I finally met my maternal grandmother once I was of legal age. She was in a nursing home and I don't know who paid to keep her there, but she was beyond crazy when I met her...literally crazy. I asked her about my mom, because I didn't know about her then. She just kept calling her a hussy and bemoaned the fact that she'd run away when she got "in trouble,"—you know, with me.*

Her features turned into a look that struck him straight to the heart. The pain overwhelmed him and he turned to face her. He cupped her chin in his hand to turn her face toward his. Alexander's eyes searched hers frantically as her mind cleared of the previous train of thought. The dewy vulnerability in her eyes wrenched his heart.

"What is it?" he whispered.

She dipped her face down and looked away from him, toward the window over his shoulder.

"I don't want to talk about it anymore," she whispered in return.

He nodded, looking straight ahead. "We don't have to," he promised.

There wasn't much to say about her childhood, or her life in general before she'd joined her new family. She had usually been on her own, and it never bothered her; she didn't know any other way to be. There were things about that part of her life she'd rather leave in the past; instead of bringing them all back to the surface. It wasn't lost on her that some of the really bad ones had almost gotten out this time.

She'd fallen into the habit of drifting through life, minding her own business, trying desperately to not hear anyone else's thoughts, and to be as normal as possible. Ironically, Sophie had never felt as normal as she did with her new family—she could be herself, answer silent questions aloud, and tell others about the flashes of the future she occasionally received, without being considered a freak. She was finally home. Dredging up bad memories wasn't something she wanted to do—now or ever—but especially not now.

*

They landed at Louis Armstrong International after about an hour long flight. After claiming their baggage, they were greeted by another black stretch limo. People around them universally thought they were part of the mafia, which made Sophie wary of the new city she found herself in. It seemed to be the knee-jerk assumption from those around them, and she wasn't sure that was the best thing.

But she quickly forgot her anxiety with the thoughts of the suspicious humans around her. If some of those people had realized that they could all hear what they were thinking…well, it made Sophie laugh.

"We shall be meeting with some old friends of mine very soon," Catherina said once they were all situated in the limo.

Sophie sat between Alexander and Laney. Laney laid her head on Sophie's shoulder and closed her eyes as she held her hand.

Alexander looked at Catherina. "The sisters?" He asked quickly.

"Yes," Catherina replied. "I am hoping that they will offer to assist us, although perhaps they will not. Regardless, we owe it to them to make sure they understand the serious nature of our situation."

Laney sank against Sophie and began to breathe slower and heavier. Sophie knew from the images in her head that Laney was asleep. She slowly lowered her sister so that her head rested in her lap and smiled at Alexander as he watched her. Laney's dreams were incredibly light and airy, but had no plot or real meaning to them. She was so innocent at times; she seemed so young, and eternally happy.

*What I'd give for such peace!* Sophie thought wistfully.

Alexander squeezed her hand.

She looked out the window and watched the city zooming past them as they sped along.

*I guess speed limits mean nothing to the Leone family,* Sophie thought.

Alexander chuckled under his breath. He laid his hand on her crossed knee, stroking it absentmindedly and looked out his own window, seemingly oblivious to the physical impact such a move had on her. A shiver ran up her leg where he'd touched her, but he was distracted by his own thoughts: It had been years since he had been back. It was obvious that he was happy to be returning, even if it was under dangerous conditions. Those thoughts occupied his mind for the time being, as he absentmindedly stroked her knee.

She inhaled heavily, trying to wrestle her blood pressure into submission. He looked at her quickly and winked.

She narrowed her eyes at him; he knew what he was doing to her.

*Of course,* he thought with a conspiratorial smile, before turning swiftly back to the window.

The limo drifted down streets lined with various beautiful homes before coming to stop before a pale grey two-story home on the corner of two intersecting streets. It peeked out from behind the giant oaks that stood like sentinels in the yard, just beyond the intricate and swirling wrought-iron fence. Stately columns lined both the stories, floor to ceiling windows looked out onto the street below.

Catherina sighed. She was home.

Sophie gently touched Laney's cheek where she lay on her lap, and the younger girl immediately woke.

"Oh, sorry, Sophie," she apologized sleepily, looking ashamed.

Sophie tucked a stray piece of hair behind her ear and said, "No, it's okay. Really."

She nodded toward the open door and after a moment, Laney caught on to what was going on. She stepped out, and Sophie followed her. Alexander was immediately, and eagerly, leading the way inside. Sophie smiled as she watched him. Walking inside, the beautiful hardwood floors and light silk draperies greeted them. It was obvious that the rooms had been freshly cleaned.

"Downstairs," Alexander began as Dante and Catherina disappeared off to the left. Sophie looked around, taking it all in. "Dante and Catherina's room is there," he said, gesturing in their direction.

Jim and Zoey disappeared in an instant; they'd lived there before, too. Alexander turned on a heel and led the way through the downstairs part of the house, showing Sophie and Laney the paneled library; the pale grey dining room with its white silk curtains and antique table; the kitchen with state-of-the-art stainless appliances and its wall of wide windows; the two sitting rooms, one with a Baby Grand in the corner. He was inspecting it all.

"Follow me," he commanded to Sophie and Laney, leading the way up the stairs to the second floor.

Laney giggled at his formality behind his back and Sophie shook her head in disapproval. Laney's smile faded as quickly as it appeared. She looked at her sister apologetically. Sophie wrapped her arm around her shoulders and hugged her as they continued on after Alexander.

Time passed as everyone got settled in. They each explored the house, unpacked, but predictably Sophie soon found herself at Alexander's door.

"Enter," he replied to her knock.

She opened the door and found him sorting through the books and papers he had brought along with him from Texas. He glanced up and smiled at her.

"May I help you?" he asked with a gleam in his eye. He turned back to the desk in the corner.

She slowly approached him and gently slid herself between the piece of furniture and his body. She sat on the desk and grasped his shirt, slightly rumpled from their trip. She pulled him closer. He set the books in his hands down on the desk and grasped her by the waist, pulling her forward.

"I don't know," she replied playfully, her face inches from his, "maybe you can."

She pulled him closer and kissed him, feeling the desire rise in her core as her heart accelerated. It was something she'd wanted to do in the airport, when he called every woman they'd encountered "ma'am;" when he held the door open for her; when they had been inches from one another on the plane, when he nearly drove her crazy in the car, the electricity between them impossible to ignore.

He kissed her neck as she ran her fingers through his hair and sighed.

"Ahem," Jim interrupted.

"Ah!" She exclaimed, dropping her hands in frustration. "Damn it."

Alexander chuckled softly in her ear, sending more chills down her spine, and pulled her still closer.

Jim snickered. "Get a room," he said.

"Hello!" Sophie replied, gesturing to the room they were in.

"You *know* what I mean," Jim replied.

"What can we do for you, Jim?" Alexander asked with a sarcastic smile, still refusing to remove himself from between her legs.

Jim rolled his eyes. "I need the key to the garage."

"The garage?" Sophie asked incredulously, looking to Alexander for an explanation.

"Do you remember your thought on the way in about our 'preoccupation' with speed?" Alexander asked her enigmatically.

"Yeah...?"

He took her hand and smiled as he pulled her down from the desktop and into his arms. "Come with me."

They were there before she knew what had happened. She was used to jumping, but not when he suddenly grabbed her hand without warning and she instantaneously found herself in a new place. It would take some getting used to. Jim appeared almost immediately after them.

"You could warn me before you do that next time," Jim grumbled.

"Ha!" Sophie exclaimed sarcastically.

Alexander turned his head. He looked over his shoulder replied, "Yes, but tell me: where is the fun in that?"

Jim rolled his eyes.

Sophie looked around and suddenly realized that they were in the garage, a cavernous building with gleaming vehicles lined side-by-side along its length. It had obviously been added onto the back of the house much later.

Jim clapped his hands and rubbed his palms against one another. "You got it!" was all he said before lumbering over to a huge red Hummer H2 truck.

"It is *literally* bulletproofed," Alexander said.

Jim climbed into the cab. Sophie chuckled in disbelief. Alexander turned to her to explain.

"Our enemies are far more real here; bulletproofing makes sense." Then he shrugged. "And he drives like a madman."

Sophie released a mirthful laugh, and turned to look around as her eyes rested on a shining gun metal silver sedan. *That has to be yours*, she thought.

"It is," Alexander replied softly, smiling at her.

It was sleek, undoubtedly expensive, and hinted at excessive horsepower. He smiled at her as Jim let out a long, slow whistle.

Sophie turned and looked at Jim with one eyebrow raised.

"That's a *nice* car," he said, admiringly, walking over to stroke the hood gently.

Sophie grinned and shook her head. *Men and their cars, I'll never understand.*

"It's a *customized* Audi A8! *What* is there to understand?" Jim asked.

She shook her head and laughed quietly at her new big brother. 'Nice' was an understatement. Of course she knew what it was.

"How?" Jim asked quickly.

Her smile disappeared. "Uh…" she stammered, caught off guard, "um…a…foster brother was into cars," she answered awkwardly.

She swiftly looked away. She tried never to think about Danny, and forced her thoughts away from her memories of him entirely, though his face stubbornly broke through the barriers she defensively threw up in her mind.

Alexander watched her, his eyebrows furrowed in worry; he saw the pain behind the memory that flashed in her brain. The heat of shame, embarrassment, and fear coursed through his mind as they swam through her veins, but he didn't push the issue.

She blinked quickly. *Now's not the time.*

Alexander cleared his throat. "Sophie, here is yours," he said, gesturing to another car and changing the subject all at once. "I believe you know how to drive a standard transmission?"

"Are you kidding me? I love driving stick," she whispered, but this was too much. She wasn't expecting to turn around and find a midnight blue, tinted windowed Mercedes convertible staring back at her.

"You won't be able to walk everywhere any longer. You need some wheels under you."

"I can't accept this," she replied and then grimaced through a smile. "But...argh! I *want* to! It's *so* pretty!" She crooned, lovingly stroked the hood.

"Of course you can accept it," he said. "It's a gift. I thought you would like it."

"Like it?" She replied, "It's just...so...*wow!* Thank you."

He smiled and caught her as she propelled herself into his arms, hugging him tightly around the neck. He laughed in his sensual way, right beside her ear, making the hair on the back of her neck stand on end.

"It is a selfish gift," he admitted. "Our family is getting large enough to necessitate more transportation. We can't all fit into one car and this makes it easier."

She pulled back and looked deeply into his eyes. "Thank you," she whispered. "It's not selfish at all."

Laney suddenly popped into the garage, and feeding off of the excitability in the room, she began bouncing up and down.

"Wow!" Laney exclaimed. "Is that yours, Sophie?"

"Apparently," she replied still a little shocked, as Alexander dropped the keys into her hand.

"Nice wheels, Jim," Laney continued and bounded over to inspect his new ride. "Where's mine?"

Jim chuckled. "You can borrow mine until you get to pick something out."

She clapped her hands gleefully.

Zoey strode into the room gracefully. Alexander nodded at her in greeting.

"Thanks for arranging it," Zoey said quietly and sauntered over to a Ducati motorcycle that looked like it was made of quicksilver. Sophie watched the graceful, old-fashioned redhead incredulously, but then figured to each her own.

Alexander looked down at Sophie and smile. "It is *a bit faster*, perhaps, than what you are used to," he warned, only half-seriously.

She laughed. Well, she'd been traveling on foot of late, so yeah, this was sure to be something quite different…

"Let's take it for a test drive," she replied, walking over to the driver's side and sliding inside.

"We will be back after awhile. Lock up for us, Jim, if you please," he said before climbing into the passenger side, ignoring Jim's smirk.

He pointed to a button on the console before her. Pressing it, the garage door lifted suddenly.

"Oh," she gasped, "cool."

She pushed the clutch in, and pressing on the gas; the car lunged forward.

"Easy, tiger," Alexander said with a laugh behind his words.

"Sorry," she replied. "It's been a while since I've handled a clutch."

It all came back to her quickly enough, and they were soon speeding through the streets of New Orleans, heading for the freeway as she followed his directions. The top was down and the wind was blowing her hair out behind her. She felt like Grace Kelly as she drove along. Shifting smoothly between gears, she felt the engine surge well beyond the speed limit. It didn't take long before she heard the sounds of sirens behind her.

*Oh, hell,* she thought.

Alexander chuckled as she gently brought the car to a stop on the right shoulder of the freeway. She watched in the rearview mirror as the police car parked behind her.

*Get out of it,* Alexander thought quickly, touching her hand that rested on the steering wheel.

*Huh?*

*The ticket: Get out of it,* he repeated with a devilish smile.

*Money and morals, huh?* She thought sarcastically. He grinned.

"Miss? License, registration, and insurance," he officer requested without looking at her.

*Here goes nothing.* "Here you are, officer," she replied, handing him the paperwork and pulling her sunglasses off of her face, leveling her eyes at him in an attempt to look alluring. She bit her bottom lip coyly.

"Uh…um," he stammered, having locked eyes with her. "Do, uh…um…do you know how fa…fast you were going?"

"Oh, I'm so sorry," she replied in her best coy voice, "I just wasn't paying any attention." She shamelessly gripped the stick shift as Alexander repressed a chuckle. "I guess I'm just not used to the power," she added innocently. "It's brand new," she shrugged innocently. "My first time out."

She smiled at his unspoken response and Alexander pretended not to notice. *Don't overdo it,* he thought.

"Uh…" the officer stuttered, handing her paperwork back to her slowly, "um…yeah…uh, just…uh…watch it next time, okay miss?"

"Of course officer," she replied. *I'm actually getting away with this?* "I'm *so* sorry." Another smile.

He turned abruptly to walk back to his cruiser and nearly stumbled as he tried to look at her over his shoulder without her noticing. Sophie put her sunglasses back on before looking over at Alexander.

"I told you," he said smugly.

"You did," she agreed with a shrug. She started the engine and pulled gingerly away from the cruiser, hoping not to attract more of the officer's attention. She still didn't know how it'd worked, but it had.

Alexander laughed at her. "There are several reasons why that worked, the two most important being that you are gorgeous and you're psychic. You can convince anyone—well, *humans*—of anything. Aside from his conscious thoughts—which you used to your advantage quite well if I may say so—you are also aware of his subconscious thoughts even if you were not actively listening to them," he answered.

"You think I'm gorgeous?" She asked coyly.

He smiled in answer as she took the first exit ramp, heading back home.

"You also have a lot to learn," he reminded her.
She certainly couldn't argue with that.

*

The sun began to sink below the horizon. The breeze started to stir the leaves as the air cooled for the night. Sophie was lost in her thoughts, but she was still aware enough of her surroundings to tell when he walked in the room.

"I have a question for you—if you don't mind."

She nodded.

He hesitated, before drawing in a breath. "The young man you thought about in the garage, who is he? Today was not the first time I've seen him in your thoughts."

She sighed and felt her heart drop. She'd known she wouldn't be able to dodge this question for long, not with the intimacy she shared with him which guaranteed their synced minds…She sank into one of the chairs in the living room. He followed her lead and crouched down in front of her, holding her gaze even as she looked down, trying to avoid it. He watched her with pleading eyes.

She didn't speak and she didn't tell him out loud; she simply let herself remember. It was easier, somehow, than putting it all into words. She knew he'd get the full story that way, without any editing.

The face flashed into her head again; it wasn't a menacing face. Danny was kind of baby-faced…which was a large part of his danger. You didn't know *not* to trust him, and she'd only been thirteen or so—just a couple of years younger than Laney.

He had dark hair on top of his sweet looking face, but if the second you looked into his eyes you'd know that he couldn't be trusted; there was a coldness there that seemed out of place with the rest of his face, as if he lacked feelings, as if he lacked a soul.

Sophie remembered the time she'd been out in the garage at one of the numerous foster homes she'd stayed at: they lived on a small farm. She was looking for something high up on a shelf, but she couldn't reach it.

She watched Alexander's face as his expression changed, effected by her emotions, but suddenly, she didn't see him any longer. It was as if he wasn't there anymore. She looked beyond him and back into the past.

*The door creaks open. I am on my tip toes, reaching for something, and Danny comes in, his hands in his pockets. He wears an amused and condescending look on his face. He is seventeen and makes me a little nervous, but he's always been nice—he likes to tell me about cars. His thoughts have never betrayed anything malicious towards me, though. I don't know to be afraid of him, but there's something about him that makes me nervous.*

Maybe that was the most traumatic part of the whole thing: it hadn't been premeditated. What he'd done was absolutely spur-of-the-moment there in that dark, hot garage.

*He comes up behind me and presses himself against my back.*

*"Lemme get that for you," he says, too close to me, his breath on my neck.*

*He reaches up and grasps whatever it is that I've been reaching for. I can't remember what it was. I try to turn around, but he is pressing so close to me, towering over me, that it is nearly impossible to move. I finally turn around and his thoughts flood me with disgusting images and desires…things thirteen-year-old girls should never know about. He pushed me to the ground and pushed himself on top of me.*

Sophie shuddered, coming back to reality for a minute. Alexander's hands were clinched in fists before her; the veins on his neck bulging in his fury. His eyes were black. She'd never seen him like that. She slowly reached down and placed her hand on one of his and he exhaled heavily.

"What happened?" he managed to ask through clinched teeth.

"Nothing good," she replied with a resigned shrug.

She didn't want to go back there anymore than she already had, but she had to. He had to know.

"My foster mother found me out there, a few hours later, in the shed. My clothes were all torn up. She had to throw a tarp around my shoulders to get me in the house," she explained. "I'll

188

always remember how scratchy it was, and how ashamed I was. The blood had run down my legs, but of course by the time I'd made it to a doctor, they couldn't tell where the trauma had been. He didn't leave any physical scars."

She remembered everything, of course, and as her mind ran through the memories, she watched his face become grimmer, his eyes become darker.

"My foster mother was absolutely mortified. *Thankfully,* she believed me when I told her it was Danny who'd left me there like that...who'd done those...*horrible*...things to me," she sighed. "I'll always remember his thoughts; when he'd decided to attack me," she said quietly, to herself as much as to Alexander, "...and I'll always remember when he decided *not* to kill me."

She cautiously glanced back at Alexander's face. His jaw was like iron, clamped shut; his eyes were burning. For the first time, she saw something terrifying in his face, something that made her believe that he was part vampire, something that would have made her back away from him if it hadn't been *his* face etched with such fury.

She stared at him and reached for his hand. "It's in the past," she whispered, trying to be soothing. "It's painful, but it's done."

He stood and walked away from her. He suddenly turned, walked back towards her and then turned away again. He was pacing, and deep in rage. She watched him warily as he growled under his breath, pacing towards her and away, stewing and plotting.

"What happened to him?" he demanded in a roar, giving her a glimpse of the violent anger she'd thought only she was capable of before then.

Sophie shook her head. "I didn't know; he ran away afterwards," she answered. "I was moved to another home and the one I'd been in was closed. I went to a therapist for a while."

Alexander looked back at her—*glared* at her, actually—and an absolutely lethal thought crossed his mind.

"Oh, no you don't, Alexander!" She declared, standing immediately after hearing what he was thinking. "Just leave it alone."

He exhaled roughly and crossed his arms, not pleased.

*Seriously, Alex, leave it alone. It's in the past,* she thought firmly, glaring back at him. She stepped forward, which caused him to take a step back.

"But he *hurt* you!" He roared back, the mirror on the wall behind him shaking with the sound. He moved a step forward as she stepped back. "He *raped* you!"

"And I lived through it," she yelled back. "Just...*leave* it."

Jim was suddenly in the room. "What's going on?" He demanded.

The room quickly filled with the rest of her family. Sophie held her hands up as she watched the rage churn inside Alexander.

"Stay back," she ordered. Laney backed slowly away and Catherina stood silently in the corner looking on.

"Why *shouldn't* I?" Alexander demanded through violently clinched teeth, glaring at her. "Give me *one* good reason why I shouldn't hunt him down, choke the life out of him, and make him regret every last disgusting thought that's entered his head and every horrid thing he has *ever* done!"

"Because, there's no point!" She yelled back. "So much for superior self-control...Get a hold of yourself, Alex!"

His nostrils flared and his mind ran at breakneck speed through the possibilities in a thought stream that only Sophie could hear. *It wouldn't be difficult to find him. No one would know. I have done it before...*

Sophie snarled and pushed him back with a mighty shove delivered to his chest. Jim and Zoey exchanged a worried look while Dante stepped forward as if to intervene.

"That's enough. Drop it!" Sophie ordered. "Get a grip, Alex. It doesn't do any of us any good to go that route. Leave. It. Alone!"

She pushed him back again when another determined look came into his eyes. She shook her head in warning and kept him at an arm's length. She could feel his heart beating under her hand where it rested on his chest.

He glanced over at Catherina who still stood like a specter in the corner. Sophie followed the glare in Alexander's eye to the other woman. Catherina looked warily at Sophie; as if she had something to fear from her. She bowed her head, and instantly

Alexander and Sophie were alone in the room as the others quickly followed Catherina's lead.

Alexander sighed and closed his eyes. He rested his head on the wall behind and took a slow, deep breath.

"Are you okay?" She asked briskly, still too keyed up to sound calm.

"Hmm," he replied, nodding his head, but not opening his eyes.

Sophie took a step back from him.

He finally opened his eyes and looked at her questioningly. "You think about him often."

"No," she replied. "Just lately, and *remembering* is the better word. Something about dredging up personal histories and all the talk about violence has done it."

"And..." he began, studying her, his eyes narrowing. "When *I* touch you? Does that conjure up demons?"

She sighed and smiled gently. She felt suddenly deflated.

"No. Not at all," she promised him, reaching for his hand. "It's *completely* different, Alex. Being with you is nothing like that day, nothing at all. And I don't even think about all that when I'm with you."

She looked deeply into his eyes in a needless effort to convince him of her honesty; he knew she was telling the truth.

"Are *you* alright?" he asked.

She nodded. "Yeah. I think it's actually easier now that you know."

"I can appreciate that," he said and silently pulled her against his chest and simply held her there. "I am so sorry that you had to endure that," he finally said.

She shook her head quickly to chase the thoughts away, hopefully for a very long time. She looked up at him with a reserved smile.

"It's okay now," she replied. "*I'm* okay now."

He nodded as Laney bounded back into the room, pulling their attention from painful memories and to the more important present. She said nothing, but quietly took her place at the piano, trying her best to distract them with a melody.

# Chapter 24

Jim and Alexander strode down the wide stairway to find Dante waiting with Catherina and the others in the front living room. Laney was sitting at the piano again, her fingers lightly dancing over the keys, a tentative tune coming out of the instrument. Sophie looked up when she sensed Alexander entering the room.

Dante immediately rose and met them in the entryway. They spoke in hushed tones. Sophie watched curiously, the book in her hands forgotten.

"Head west on St. Charles," he said. "Begin searching in the Quarter. It is very populated. Catherina believes that you may find something or someone useful there."

Alexander nodded.

Dante clapped him on the back *"Respice finem,"* he said: *Look to the end.*

Alexander shrugged. *"Audaces fortuna iuvat,"* he replied: *Fortune favors the bold.*

"God willing."

Alexander chuckled under his breath.

Sophie stood and began walking towards them. "Mind if I come along?"

Alexander abruptly turned to look at her. "Yes, I do actually," he answered briskly.

She rocked back on a heel as if he'd physically struck her. Her lip curled in anger, but she said nothing. Alexander grimaced; he regretted his words the moment they escaped his lips.

Jim looked warily from one to the other. "Uh, we're gonna be out really late and we don't really know what to expect," he interjected quickly, trying unsuccessfully to salvage the situation.

Alexander quickly walked over to Sophie. He grasped her by the arms. "Please understand that I want you to be safe. Remain here with everyone else. You'll go with us soon, I promise."

"Fine," she replied curtly, her eyes on fire. She turned on a heel and took her place in the oversized chair next to the piano. She picked up the book she'd abandoned a moment before without another word, and she didn't look up at Alexander.

Alexander frowned at her, but didn't say anything.

Jim clapped him on the shoulder. "Come on."

They closed their eyes and were in the garage when they opened them.

"I'll drive," Alexander said quickly.

"Aw!" Jim grumbled, disappointed. "Alright man."

They slid into the Audi and were on the road in moments. He headed north on First to St. Charles, and then headed northwest towards the French Quarter.

"Geez, how long's it been?" Jim quietly asked after a minute, looking around at the scene outside of the windows.

"A little more than five years," Alexander replied.

"Really? It seems a lot longer."

"It does."

The city was typically festive, just as any other Crescent City evening. This time of year, with the approaching holidays, it seemed to have an added undercurrent of excitement. Alexander was reminded that he would need to find a Christmas gift for Sophie.

"Yeah you do," Jim agreed.

Alexander nodded. He steered the car to a metered parking place where he and Jim slid out to continue their search on foot.

"Let's go this way," Alexander suggested.

They swiftly passed bars, nightclubs, and restaurants. The smells of Cajun food and alcohol saturated the air as they scanned the crowd. They walked perhaps a bit too fast for humans, perhaps a little too quietly, but in the highly-congested streets they were still able to go largely unnoticed. They were dressed as inconspicuously as possible and nothing about the two revealed that they were not what they appeared to be.

"Hey man!" A youthful voice called out.

Alexander and Jim froze mid-step and turned at the exact same time. The youth who had called out to them jumped back at their synchronized movement.

Alexander glared at the group through focused eyes. "May we help you?" He asked, coolly.

"Yeah, man! Come here a sec," he said, gesturing to them.

Alexander and Jim looked at each other. They surveyed the group before them, clustered unnaturally in an alley. They were dressed in black, with pale makeup and black eyeliner distorting their facial features.

*More damn vamp kids,* Jim thought dismissively.

*Wait,* Alexander replied.

*What is it?* Jim thought back, scrutinizing the group.

*They're not all human.*

*What?*

*Third from the left.*

*You've gotta be kidding me.*

*Unfortunately not.*

*Wonder how long he's been hanging with them?*

*It is anyone's guess. We need to get him away from them.*

*How?*

*Just follow my lead.*

The swift mental exchange, taking less than two seconds, was followed by the uncertain shuffle among the group waiting at the back of the alley. The vampire in the group leered at them, a nearly imperceptible tension rippling down his limbs. He recognized Alexander and Jim moments after they'd figured out what he was.

In truth, the vampire was not conspicuous in his little band, and most humans would not have guessed that he was different. Yet he was there in their midst, hidden in plain sight.

*Such foolish humans,* Alexander thought. *Other animals shy from their hunters, yet here the prey wrap their arms around their killer and find him mysterious.* He shook his head in disgust.

*If they only knew,* Jim thought.

The vampire's scent was too subtle for human senses to find repulsive. Alexander and Jim weren't immune to it however, and the putrid scent of sugar-coated death brushed off of him and churned up Alexander's and Jim's noses in the same instant. Its rancidity flowed into their lungs and threatened a natural wave of nausea.

*Who are they?* A girl with hot pink hair asked in her mind. *How does Trent know them?* A boy in all black wondered. *Aren't they the guys with the drugs?* Another thought to himself.

Jim smiled at Alexander. *Follow my lead.*

"What do y' think you kids are doing?" Jim asked sternly, puffing his chest out.

Each individual panicked as they exchanged glances between themselves again.

*Ah, the good cop, bad cop routine,* Alexander thought. *Well done.* "New Orleans P.D.," he suddenly lied, knowing of course that none would have the presence of mind to ask for his non-existent identification.

The crowd scattered, leaving the vampire alone facing the two "police officers". He slowly backed himself against the wall as his lips stretched over his gleaming teeth. Alexander reached him before he had taken two steps, grasping him around the neck, and pinning him against the same wall.

"What do you want?" The vampire hissed.

"Aw, what's wrong?" Jim mocked over Alexander's shoulder. "Did we spoil your fun and chase dinner away?"

The vampire hissed at him. Jim rolled his eyes.

"Where is Jacques?" Alexander asked in an eerily calm voice.

"I don't know what you're talkin' about," he replied, his black eyes flat.

Alexander gripped his neck tighter and knocked his head against the wall. The vampire hissed and spit in his direction.

"Oh, come now...*Trent* is it? Surely you know *what* we are and you probably even know *who* we are. Do spare us the theatrics and tell us where Jacques's coven is hiding," Alexander said.

Recognition flashed in the vampire's eyes before they narrowed into deadly slits.

"You can go to hell," hissed the vampire in response and he lunged forward, attempting to strike at his throat.

"Not today," Alexander replied, before his hand shoved a stake through the vampire's chest so hard that the bricks in the wall behind him cracked with the force.

The vampire gasped as realization hit, right before he slumped over the stake. Alexander stepped back and Jim tore the head off with the knife he carried in his belt.

"Good riddance," Jim said.

Alexander flipped the top of his silver lighter back, ignited a scrap of wood and set the body ablaze. They slipped out of the alleyway unnoticed.

"Well, so much for *that*," Jim said, disappointed.

"It was productive," replied Alexander. He shrugged, pleased with how it had gone.

"How's that?"

"He would have honestly claimed innocence if Jacques were really not here, of that I am sure. Instead he cursed us, confirming that Jacques and his coven are indeed here in New Orleans," Alexander quickly explained.

"So what now?"

Alexander's jaw clinched, but he didn't answer.

"We need Sophie," Jim said.

"Yes," Alexander replied grimly. "As much as I want to keep her from this, it can't be avoided."

Jim patted him on the back. "It'll be okay, you know."

"Always the optimist."

Jim laughed. "Well…we could always wait for them to come to us."

Alexander raised an eyebrow at him. "You know the best defense is in taking the offensive."

"Yeah, I know. I just thought I'd try."

"Let's look around some more," Alexander said.

"And then?" Jim asked, for he detected hesitation in Alexander's voice.

"And then I am afraid we'll need Sophie."

*

Dante, Zoey, and Sophie greeted them when they walked through the door. It was a few hours past midnight, but they had been strategizing while Alexander and Jim were gone.

"Well," said Jim, "if they didn't know we were here yesterday, they do now!"

"What happened?" asked Sophie.

"Let's just say we deprived the city of New Orleans of a few of their more *menacing* citizens," Jim answered with a grin.

"How many?" Dante asked.

"Three," Alexander replied; they had encountered two others before returning home.

Dante exchanged a look with Zoey and Sophie before he turned back to Alexander. "Were you able to glean any information from them before dispatching them to the devil?" asked Dante.

Alexander nodded with a smirk. "From one female: we learned that Jacques's coven typically congregates in the warehouse district near the waterfront."

"Anything else?" Zoey asked.

"They're planning to come after us, but not yet. 'Course, we already knew that," Jim explained. "Looks like Jacques's crew is already here, but without him."

Sophie raised an eyebrow.

"He gave them explicit orders to refrain from attacking until he returns," Alexander continued.

She nodded. "He's meeting with Cusick."

"Yes," Alexander replied.

Dante nodded. "I shall inform Catherina of this news. Plan your offensive as you see fit; I leave it in your hands," Dante said to Alexander, nodding to the others. "I know that Catherina will approve of, and trust, your decisions."

He rose from his chair, closed his eyes and was gone, leaving the others in the living room facing one another.

*Right,* Sophie thought sarcastically. *As if I care.*

Alexander's eyes settled on hers, but she didn't elaborate.

"So, what's the plan?" Jim asked, looking to Alexander, knowing that he didn't care for Catherina's approval of his plan anymore than Sophie did.

"We have little choice but to confront them. We are outnumbered, but perhaps if the element of surprise is on our side, we may prevail," Alexander answered.

"We *will* prevail," corrected Sophie with confident solemnity and with so much intensity that no one dared to challenge her.

A smile slowly spread across Jim's face. "You're damn right we will!" he agreed. He sighed theatrically. "Well, kids, I'm turning in for the night." With that, he was gone.

Zoey nodded to Sophie and Alexander. "Good night," she said and disappeared.

Sophie looked at Alexander, the fire that she had contained earlier flashed in her eyes. "You *will not* leave me again," she ordered in a whisper, pointing her finger passionately at him. "I absolutely *refuse* to be left behind wondering what's going on, and being unable to help you in any way, especially for such *foolish* fears."

He nodded in response. She began pacing before him in her anger.

"I don't care what you have to do. Train me; teach me everything, whatever it takes to make *you* okay with this. I will *not* be brushed off like that again. I will not sit around here *helplessly* waiting for you to come home, when you need all the help you can get out there."

She stopped pacing and glared at him, waiting for his response. She exhaled heavily through her nose waiting for him to respond.

"You're right," he consented calmly. "You will not be left behind here again. In fact I found myself wishing that you were with me tonight. I would have liked to have your abilities at my disposal."

She nodded, exhaling sharply through her nose once more. She continued to watch him.

"And I am sorry for my earlier reaction," he apologized quietly.

She sighed. "I know," she answered. "I know you're trying to keep me safe…just don't do it again." She snickered, but her anger had already melted away.

# Chapter 25

The Audi sped towards the French Quarter, Alexander confidently gripping the steering wheel as his eyes swept over the sights outside the windshield. Laney and Jim chatted incessantly over Zoey's head in the backseat, but Sophie ignored them and their thoughts as they continued on their way. She was much too intrigued by the lights and the sounds of New Orleans to be distracted by their playful banter.

Even through the closed windows, the smell of smoky bars and spicy gumbo wafted to her hyper-sensitive nose and seemed to send excitement through every nerve ending in her body. And then they passed a movie rental store and she snorted at the posters on the windows.

"What is it?" Alexander asked quietly.

She rolled her eyes. "Just another one of those vampire movies," she replied contemptuously.

He shook his head in disgust. "Vampires seducing humans isn't anything new, but *falling in love with them?*"

Jim chimed in. "Yeah, that's something I've never even *heard* of in real life. Humans are food."

"Or assets to be traded at best," Zoey offered. "*Real* vampires don't like hanging out with their food source any more than humans like touring a slaughterhouse."

Alexander glanced at Sophie. "You can guess who is responsible for such images."

"The Council?"

He nodded.

"Great."

"Hey," Jim interrupted, "where are we going?"

"I *was* going to suggest Bacco," Alexander answered, looking at his reflection in the rearview mirror.

"That stuffy place?" Jim groaned. "Let's do Coop's instead."

Alexander sighed lightly, as Laney seconded Jim's suggestion.

"You'll love it, sis," Jim said to Sophie from the backseat.

She smiled, but looked at Alexander to judge his reaction as Jim clapped him on the shoulder.

Alexander shrugged, outnumbered. "Coop's it is, I suppose," he answered with a small smile and a consenting shake of his head. He turned the corner suddenly, the sedan handling the maneuver so well it might as well have been flying.

They drove past one of the many cemeteries of New Orleans; one of the many "Cities of the Dead." The sudden realization for Sophie that she could very easily never be a citizen of *that* kind of city hit her as they sped past its peaked roof tombs and smiling cherubim. It was a surreal revelation.

They parked around the corner from the restaurant, and stepping out of the car, she looked around herself. The cool, wet air hit her cheeks and blew through her hair, giving her a shiver. Long-abandoned Mardi Gras beads still hung in some of the trees around them, and an empty beer bottle lay in the gutter where the water from the afternoon's shower pulsed by like blood in the veins of the city.

"This way," Alexander said quietly, walking around the front of the car and holding a hand out to Sophie as the others filed out.

Coop's Place inhabited an old brick building with mortar seeping from between the red blocks, as if the air had been too laden with water to allow for proper drying time when the walls were built. A white arched doorway flanked by naked light bulbs greeted them as they entered the warm restaurant.

Opening the door, they were hit suddenly by the smell of traditional New Orleans cuisine: chili powder, cayenne pepper and rich brown roux. A huge grin spread across Jim's face and it was clear that Alexander was just as much of a fan as Jim was of the almost-literal hole in the wall. The smells of the rich Cajun recipes made Sophie's mouth water.

Jim led them to a large booth in the back corner. Sophie glanced at Alexander.

"It's not what you had in mind for tonight," she said.

"It will do," he answered with a peaceful smile and grasping her hand.

She slid into the seat and the five of them were quickly feasting on Cajun entrees, complete with cornbread. As always, they found a great deal of humor in the thoughts of those around them, but it didn't keep Jim and Alexander from reminiscing.

"So when was the last time you guys were here?" Sophie asked.

"We were talking about that the other day, and we figured it's been about five years," Jim answered.

"It does seem longer," Alexander added, glancing around the restaurant.

Laney shrugged. "This is my first time here too," she told Sophie.

"Oh," Sophie replied, a little taken aback. "I didn't realize."

She nodded, "Yeah, I guess they found me—what guys, like three years ago or something? I don't know; I don't ever think about my life before."

*Lucky,* Sophie thought to herself, and Alexander silently took her hand under the table and squeezed it in empathy.

Jim patted Laney on the top of the head, oblivious to what was going on at the other side of the table. "Yeah, we went to St. Louis for this one," he said with a grin.

Laney nodded in agreement. "I ran away from the group foster home I was in. Don't think they missed me too much though, since they didn't come looking for me," she confessed with a shrug.

"So was the family already in St. Louis?" Sophie asked.

"No," Alexander replied. "We had been in Louisville—Catherina was uncertain about Laney's location—prior to discovering where we would find her."

"Oh," Sophie replied.

Zoey smiled at her. "Catherina saw her just like Laney saw you and just like you saw Celia."

"It's all really weird, honestly, but I'm sure I'll get used to it all. Eventually," Sophie said.

"You will," Alexander assured her, stroking her knee under the table quickly, and making her jump at the touch.

"Man, this is good grub," Jim complemented when the cute waitress came up to the table. "Thank you, darlin'," he couldn't help but add with a devilish smile.

Alexander snickered and Laney had to look away so that she wouldn't laugh at the scene. The waitress, Caroline, walked off and Sophie looked at Jim reproachfully.

"You're going to give that poor girl a heart attack!" she chastised him.

"Nah," he brushed Sophie off with a wave of his hand.

He winked at the waitress when she turned around to look at him again. Zoey elbowed him the ribs.

"Uhhh," Sophie suddenly groaned, slumping back in the booth, "I'm so full."

She and Jim exchanged a smile. "Told you you'd like it," he said.

Sophie nodded. "Yeah, I ate way too much."

"Why don't we walk it off?" Laney suggested.

"Good idea," Jim replied, waving for the check which Caroline promptly brought over. She'd scribbled her name on the top.

They slid out of the booth and, dodging other patrons, eventually made their way out of the little establishment into the dark, damp street. Alexander gently pulled Sophie's arm through his, walking on the street-side of the sidewalk. She leaned against his arm as they followed the others towards the waterfront.

A lone saxophonist played a soft, slow jazz tune as boats languidly moved up and down the channel. Music and sounds floated lazily down the hill towards them as Sophie caught a chill. She shivered. Alexander wrapped his arm around her shoulders and pulled her closer to him, protecting her from the light wind coming off the water.

It was peaceful and they were quiet for several minutes. Sophie and Alexander fell behind the other three, lost in their own thoughts. They wandered away from the river and the wind changed directions.

Jim froze and looked around wildly. "Oh, *damn it!*" he cursed, suddenly spinning on a heel and pushing Laney behind him, feeling something that not even Sophie had picked up on.

Alexander wrapped an arm around Sophie's waist and reached for the revolver at his hip with the other. Jim had already drawn his own gun. Zoey pulled Laney back to stand beside her. Alexander's eyes charted the invisible line from Jim's eyes to the point of their focus, finding the source of the foul stench that wafted their direction: vampires.

Four of them slinked out of the shadows. Sophie stood behind Alexander with her hand on the small his back. She glanced at Laney and Zoey where they stood behind Jim. She nodded encouragingly at the younger girl who looked about them anxiously, fear etched on her face. With Zoey, she exchanged a more knowing look.

*There's more somewhere,* thought Jim.

Sophie held her breath. *Behind us,* she thought suddenly.

Alexander swiftly spun around. Five others slithered out of the darkness, the light of the moon shinning off of their preternatural skin and against their hollow black eyes as they cornered them in the alleyway. They were surrounded.

*Please tell me you have another gun,* Sophie begged in a thought.

*Nope,* Jim thought in response, cursing himself.

*Stakes?* She asked.

*No,* he answered again.

*Great,* Sophie thought sarcastically and sighed. They'd known better.

Zoey passed her a small vial. Sophie looked at it questioningly and then looked back at her sister.

*Holy water,* Zoey thought. *All I've got. Open it – I need both hands.*

Sophie opened the vial. She scanned the street, looking for makeshift weapons. They were surrounded. Zoey started moving her hands around the top of the vial. Sophie's eyes widened as the water began to move like a rope out of the open top. She looked at Zoey appreciatively.

Alexander and Jim slowly backed them against the wall, shielding them with their bodies.

*Give us some space,* Sophie thought. Alexander moved a step away from her in response.

A low chuckle came from one of the vampires. Sophie kept her hand securely on Alexander's back as she continued to canvass the deserted street. Laney grasped her around the waist in fear.

"What have we here?" one of the vampires asked in a deep, hollow voice. The stench of his breath reached them yards away.

He was suddenly flanked by a female. "Why Stephan, you've surely heard stories of the Leone family," she answered. Her steely voice was like fingernails on a chalkboard.

"Ah, yes, the Leone family," yet another replied, in a slightly lower feminine voice.

Sophie jerked her head around to look at the new speaker, but her attention was quickly pulled back to the first pair.

"And who do we have with us tonight?" Asked the one called Stephan, the obvious leader.

"The new warrior, Sophie, who so easily murders our kind," another male voice answered.

A shiver went up Sophie's spine.

"And the magic girl," the piercing female shrilly added.

"Laney," whispered several at once.

"And the two infamous Leone family warriors," added Stephan.

"Alexander," whispered some, while others whispered, "James."

Another whispered Zoey's name, and then Sophie's again.

*Okay, that's just creepy,* Sophie thought, watching their enemy.

The vampires continued to step slowly toward them, steadily closing the space between the parties as their whispered words swept through the air like menacing ghosts.

*You take half and I'll take half,* thought Jim.

*Sophie, Zoey, take Laney and at my word, run for the car,* Alexander instructed.

Laney got ready to run when Sophie thought: *Not a chance. We can't get out of here. We might as well fight.*

*No, Sophie, you must run,* he argued. *Jump, if you must.*

She held her breath and squeezed Laney's hand. She looked to her sister. *Listen for my thoughts,* she quickly instructed her, ignoring Alexander's admonishments. She shot a look to Zoey, who nodded in return. She handed Laney the empty vial and Zoey pushed and pulled the water into a floating, osculating ball between her hands.

*Watch 'em!* Jim warned.

*Sophie get ready,* Alexander thought. He watched their enemy approach, but then everything happened at once.

*NO TIME!!* Jim's thoughts screamed as the vampires descended in a swarm and the alleyway erupted in action.

Alexander fired at the nearest vampire. A round flew through her chest. He plunged the blade of his knife into another almost immediately.

"SOPHIE! *GO!!*" He yelled.

*They're after Laney!* She thought back in a panic, dragging the younger girl into the doorway of the building behind her, blockading her sister there, still stubbornly refusing to flee.

Zoey held the holy water mid-air with one hand. With a sweep of her fingers she shot the water towards the two nearest vampires. They collapsed to the ground, swatting at the burns on their skin.

Jim collided with another vampire and shattered her ribcage with his bare hands. Still she fought back until Jim's knife sliced through her neck, severing her head from her body.

*Laney, hold them off me!* Sophie thought.

Suddenly every object that was not attached to a wall or the ground began to levitate. Alexander shot another vampire through the heart and twisted off his head as the body stumbled towards him in a final attempt to take his life. A grating sound pulled his attention to his left. The gutter from the adjacent building began to struggle against its bolts.

Jim wrestled with one of the males as two females advanced on Sophie, where she stood between them and Laney, shielding her sister from their approach with nothing but her bare hands and her mind at her disposal.

Scattering the last of the holy water at the crowd, Zoey grabbed a piece of metal shelving that lay against the wall and drove it into the chest of another vampire. Her eyes were burning with rage.

Laney struggled to keep the vampires from reaching Sophie, holding her hands up and shaking from the effort of holding them back. She succeeded only in slowing their steps, while the vampires still continued to advance.

"Keep them off me, Alex!" Sophie yelled; determination in her voice. Her body began to tremble. *I wish I could concentrate long enough to get in their heads.*

He shot through the rest of his rounds and tossed the wasted weapon aside. Jim was already without his. Suddenly a terrible screeching was heard as the gutter was freed from its screws.

*Laney, beer bottle!* Thought Sophie. She used her mind to hurl it through the air at the younger girl.

Laney looked at it and shoved it with such force through the empty space that it burst in two, the shards embedding in the torso of one of their enemy. It did little to slow him down, simply distracting him for a moment. Sophie shot scraps of metal at the vampire, as Jim and Alexander struggled with two males and Laney held a female off as well as she could before Zoey got to her.

The metal from the gutter was suddenly ripped in two parts, producing lethal spikes of both pieces.

"Alex! Jim! *MOVE!!*" Screamed Sophie.

They dived out of her way. Sophie shot the make-shift stakes forward using just the force of her mind, and they plunged themselves into the chests of the two males who fell, twitching on the pavement. Without a word, Jim and Alexander promptly relieved them of their heads.

Sophie reached for another scrap of metal hovering in the air and grasped it with her hand so hard that it cut into her own skin. She plunged it into the still heart of one of the females, feeling the rough metal dig further into her skin. Jim grabbed another from behind and cut his head off with a swift cut of his knife. Laney stood frozen in the doorway Sophie had pushed her into. She was utterly terrified. This wasn't fun and games in the basement anymore. She looked to her sister with wide, horrified eyes.

Sophie's opponent, the shrill female, lay gasping for air at her feet. Sophie leaned over the vampire, her hand still clutching the metal scrap, her own blood running down the length of its crude blade. It distracted the ever-ravenous fiend below her, who glanced between the blood and Sophie's fiery eyes, a mix of fear and lust in her eyes.

"Who the hell sent you?" demanded Sophie in a cold tone, holding the vampire down under her foot.

The vampire spit at her. Sophie bitterly wiped her face and glared at the vampire beneath her. She turned her head to the side and concentrated on her. The vampire's eyes rolled back in her head. Her back arched as a piercing scream escaped her lips.

*It does not matter, Soph...* Alexander thought, but she interrupted him with a dismissive wave of her free hand. She didn't look away from the vampire.

"You're going to die, anyway," said Sophie. "I can make it a little less painful. Tell me. Who. Sent. You."

The vampire relaxed against the ground, panting from the pain. She garbled the response from her half-closed lips in a desperate attempt for mercy: "Jacques."

*Of course.*

Sophie quickly extracted the stake which had been trembling in its resting place of the vampire's dead heart, and cut brilliantly through the vampire's neck; the body went limp. She stood, slowly straightening herself and looked at Alexander.

"He sent them here to get Laney," she said, before suddenly looking over her shoulder at the younger girl. "You okay?"

Laney nodded, breathless, but she still couldn't speak.

"You know why they were after her?" Jim asked.

Sophie shook her head and threw the metal scrap to the ground with disgust. "They didn't even know why; they're just following orders."

Zoey looked at her. "Did you get all of that information from her?"

Sophie shook her head. She wiped her bloodied hand against the leg of her jeans, still irritated. She suddenly looked up at Alexander, with worry reflecting in her eyes. She sighed with the realization that he was alright. *That was too close.*

He nodded in response as their eyes held each other's gaze. Her breath came out in trembling exhalations as she stared at him, realizing how close they'd come to losing the fight.

"This is ridiculous!" Jim exclaimed to himself. He began piling the pieces of the vampires against the brick wall of one of the buildings. "We've got to do something to end this." *Damn it, I should have known better. I should have brought more weapons.*

"Agreed, but it's over for tonight," Alexander replied. "This cannot continue; it's intolerable. We are meeting with the sisters tomorrow. Regardless of their response to Catherina, I think we shall move forward sooner than we've planned."

Zoey set the pile of bodies on fire. They watched briefly as the limbs and torsos of their enemies were consumed by the glowing red flames before retreating to the car.

They rode in silence, although their thoughts were anything but quiet; Sophie grasped Alexander's hand as he steered them towards home, her other hand bandaged in his handkerchief. Jim's thoughts were angry, inflamed. Laney's were grateful and melancholy, more subdued than ever. Sophie's were a mixture of uneasiness and the strange relief felt after a near tragedy is avoided. Zoey's was the only mind that was blank, devoid of emotion.

And Alexander's thoughts, as he held the hand of his beloved, were determined.

The silence was deafening as they backed into the garage. When he'd turned the car off, Alexander looked over to Sophie who sat staring distractedly out the windshield. Her mouth was pursed in worry; her eyes scanned the dark manically.

He and Jim exchanged a look. "What's wrong?" they asked her at the same time.

A tremor of fear ran through Laney's frame. Zoey sniffed at the air. Her eyes widened as she watched Sophie.

"I don't know yet," Sophie replied in a flat voice, her eyes shifting quickly about, listening. She shook her head after a few moments, though, and said, "I thought I heard something."

Without a word, they were out of the car. Jim stepped out first and turned in a movement so quick that the change was nearly indistinguishable. He and Sophie locked eyes in the same instant over the roof of the car as a stream of expletives burst out of his mouth.

"They are here?" Alexander demanded.

"Get her in the house," Sophie told Jim who already had Laney by the arm.

Jim looked to Alexander.

"Do it," he said.

Jim and Laney suddenly disappeared.

Sophie jumped to her car where a rolled up piece of cloth was stowed under the front seat. She heard Alexander load a clip into one of the pistols left in the garage for such emergencies and spin a silencer on the barrel, as she unrolled the cloth and drew out the concealed silver and wooden stakes, the cloth creating a faint ringing sound as it brushed against the surface of the silver. She handed some of the wooden stakes to Zoey and took one of the silver stakes in each hand.

Alexander was already at the door, waiting for her with his gun ready.

*Where are they?* He asked

*I don't know. What should we do?*

*Let's walk to the house. Stay right with me.*

Zoey and Sophie nodded. He crouched down and let the firearm lead his trail. Every shift in the leaves directed it upward in response.

Sophie crept out of the garage, turned away from Alexander, so that her back was more to him than anywhere else. Zoey slinked at her side, her eyes roving through the darkness.

*I don't see anything,* he thought.

*Me either. I can't even hear anything. Maybe they're gone.*

He stopped and reached back with his free hand to grasp her upper arm. *Let's go,* he thought before they were suddenly moving and were abruptly in the house again.

"What is happening?" Dante asked, panic in his eyes.

Zoey went to the front door and made sure it was locked. Jim was standing at the front window, pistol in hand, watching for any movement outside it.

Alexander placed a hand on Dante's shoulder as he walked past him. "We were followed."

Catherina's already sallow face seemed to drain of even more blood. Her dark eyes looked from Alexander to Sophie and back again. None of them spoke.

"How many?" Jim asked.

Sophie shook her head, joining him at the window. "Three, I think," she said. "They were watching, and followed us back here."

Sophie's eyes tracked a subtle movement in the dark a hundred paces from the front window. "Right there, you see?" she asked Jim in a whisper.

In the same instant, Zoey and Dante leapt away from the window as a black-eyed vampire lunged at them on the other side. His fingernails scratched gratingly against the pane and Laney screamed from where she cowered in a crouch on the stairs.

Another vampire crept at the adjacent window and Sophie looked to Alexander.

*The other one's out back,* she told him.

Alexander nodded and looked at Jim. *Are you ready?*

*As I'll ever be,* Jim replied and nodded at Sophie.

She looked at the others, her eyes lingering on Laney's. "Stay here," she said and then they were gone.

Laney slowly walked over to Catherina who had jumped to the second floor in an effort to protect herself. Laney felt unsafe without Sophie, Alexander, and Jim in the room with her. She reached out to take the older woman's hand, but Catherina just stared blankly at her and pulled away to retreat into her corner. Laney's lower lip trembled at the rejection and she blinked back tears.

Dante walked to her and placed a gentle hand on her shoulder. She looked up to see him looking tenderly down at her. Without a thought, she threw herself into his fatherly embrace. Zoey patted her back.

"It will be alright," he whispered.

Laney quickly looked up from where she'd buried her face in Dante's shoulder. She walked towards the window where she saw Jim stealthily creep past.

"We got 'em," Sophie suddenly said from behind her, and Laney turned on a heel to see her standing next to Dante. "The guys are just making sure everything's okay."

Laney's heart pounded.

"Are you okay?" Sophie asked, taking three long strides towards her.

"Yeah," Laney whispered uncertainly.

Sophie hugged her quickly around the shoulders and turned a half second before Alexander and Jim reappeared.

She and Alexander exchanged a look and a thought that the others didn't hear. Sophie sighed.

"I had no idea it would be like this…" Laney trailed off.

Sophie nodded at her in agreement. Texas had been child's play. This was an entirely different game, one in which the stakes were lethally high.

# Chapter 26

*I walk down the dark, damp street. My feet barely sound on the concrete as I step through puddles and stumble on old bricks. The night is still and dark. The air is heavy and I am alone.*

*From the mist that suddenly appears in my peripheral vision steps Alex, at my right hand. A gust of wind sweeps over me from the left, and with the wind, comes the scent of them: the metallic sickly sweet smell of blood and death.*

*Materializing from the darkness, as they always seem to, they stand, poised to attack. One drags a young girl by the arm, mercilessly pulling her along despite her vain protests.*

*She cries my name but she cannot free herself, no matter how hard she struggles. Still, the mist obscures my view of her. They are stronger than she, especially now, at night. My heart pounds and I want to spring. I can't get to her in time; I know this with a certainty. The panic builds in my chest and I can't catch my breath as I watch. I know I don't have enough time to react, to strike or to free her from their grasp, whoever she might be.*

*She is going to die.*

*We are going to die.*

*I call to Alex, but he doesn't hear me. The female who holds the girl's arm snarls and hisses as if she were some beast of Hell. I can't see her face through the fog, but I know it's a woman who keeps the prisoner.*

*And with sudden, crystal clarity, I hear the girl again and recognize the voice.*

*"SOPHIE!!" she screams in a blood-curdling timbre. "Help me! Please!" She frantically begs me.*

*The realization hits me like a kick in the chest. LANEY! She is trapped.*

*I gather my strength, knowing I'll die in this fight; Alex with me, because he won't let me go in alone. And my little sister, but I have to try. I can't let them take her.*

*The wind stirs before I can take a step and the fog lifts suddenly. My eyes fall on Laney's captor. Fear and hatred rise in me, cold and burning, as I behold her with my own eyes, not believing—but unable to deny—who holds Laney in her deadly grasp, her eyes boiling black, her preternatural lips spread in a ruby red and pearl white smile...*

"CATHERINA!" Sophie yelled, sitting straight up in bed, her nightgown stuck to her skin from all the sweat.

She gasped for breath and quickly controlled her thoughts, hoping that Catherina hadn't heard her, telling herself that it was just a dream—a dream that seemed so real. *Too real.*

And then, without giving it a second thought, she did something that she'd considered weeks before they'd come to New Orleans. In that moment, Catherina no longer had permission to hear her thoughts. Sophie didn't know why she'd decided to do such a thing, or if she had even actually *decided* it, but she instinctually knew that she couldn't trust Catherina; couldn't allow her in her head anymore.

She swung her legs around and rose from the bed, her feet landing silently on the wooden floorboards. The sun was just beginning to set and night was quickly approaching. She must have slept all day, exhausted from the night before. It had taken them hours to finally calm down well enough to allow anything close to sleep to come. She clenched and reopened her injured hand, stiff but virtually healed from the night before.

She dragged her other, uninjured palm across her clammy forehead and closed her eyes, taking several deep breaths. She composed herself and walked slowly down the stairs; cicadas were still singing in the approaching nightfall. It was comfortable, even in December, as the sun set on the day. Alexander stood at one of the front windows, leaning on his arm, surveying the street below. She approached him without a word, laying her hand softly on his back.

"Bad dream?" He asked quietly, without turning to look at her.

"Something like that," she replied, equally as quiet.

He reached down with his free hand and pulled her close and kissed her on the top of the head. He inhaled deeply as he buried his nose in her hair. She pressed her hand against his chest, his heart beating against her palm through his thin shirt. She looked into his clear green eyes.

"I love you," she whispered.

His finger lightly traced her jaw line. "As I love you," he answered, his eyes sweeping over her face.

His hand slowly moved from her jaw to her throat and around to the back of neck. She wrapped her arms around the small of his back and pulled him forward, her lips instinctually finding his. Her body was pressed between his warm and solid body, and the window, hard and cool. He kissed her top lip first and then his tongue lightly traced the curve of her bottom lip as a new need began to build in her chest. The gravity of last night's combat hit her with full force as she hungrily pulled him closer and an errant tear escaped out of the corner of her eye.

He exhaled and she felt his lips move to her jaw and then to her neck. A shiver of pleasure ran up her spine, making the roots of every single hair on her head stand on end. She sighed as he kissed her shoulder, the strap of her nightgown slid down her arm slightly. She pulled him closer, her nails digging into his back; he couldn't be too close. He suddenly returned to her lips and kissed her with more passion as her hands found his hair and held him there, returning his kisses with equal vigor.

He pressed against her and a flame of desire coursed through her veins. She felt the softness of his hair beneath her fingertips, the firmness of his lips against hers, the tightness with which he held her close.

"Ahem!" someone interrupted.

Mid-kiss, Alexander turned his head to find Jim standing behind them, wearing a grin the Cheshire cat would have killed for. Sophie smiled sheepishly as she unwrapped one of her legs from around one of Alexander's hip.

"Good afternoon?" Jim asked with a taunting look in his eyes.

Sophie laughed silently at herself. "Yeah, good afternoon," she answered. She swiped at her cheek where the tear had traced an invisible line across her skin.

"Yeah, I'll just…uh…go downstairs," he said, shaking his head and chuckling as he walked away from them.

Alexander turned back to Sophie and laughed a soft, throaty laugh that nearly had her ready to jump him again, had Laney not walked into the hall. Sophie groaned when Laney came into view and slouched against the window pane.

"Oh, get a room," Laney sighed jokingly and followed Jim's lead and went downstairs.

"Their times will come," Alexander assured her. "Then we'll give them hell."

Sophie laughed and laid her forehead against his chest. He stroked her hair, running his fingers down her spine and making every single hair on her body stand on end.

"Okay," she said, sitting up and rubbing her face with her hands and then running her fingers through her hair, "I've got to get with it. This is ridiculous."

"What is ridiculous?" he asked with a smile in his eyes.

"The fact that I'm just now rolling out of bed, and the sun's going *down*."

He chuckled. "Oh, that," he replied with a smile, still not wanting to let her go.

*Catherina's going to want you guys to go with them in a few minutes. Better get ready,* they suddenly heard Laney think from downstairs.

Sophie exhaled heavily. Alexander tucked his finger under her chin and gave her a quick peck on the lips.

"What's wrong?" he asked in a whisper.

She shook her head and looked into his eyes. "It's just a lot different from what I expected," she confessed. "I didn't realize how…" she trailed off and shook her head, lost in her thoughts.

He nodded. "We haven't much time," he replied, and she hoped he just meant the present evening and not time in general.

She struggled for a smile as he kissed her forehead and jumped to his room to get ready. She reluctantly followed his example and jumped back to her own room.

She went immediately into the bathroom and yanked a brush through her tangled hair, pulling the waves into a low, loose ponytail. She pushed her legs through a pair of dark wash jeans, a black long-sleeved t-shirt, and slid her feet into sturdy motorcycle boots. She grabbed her white leather trench as she swung the door open, where she found Catherina talking to Alexander in the hallway.

Catherina stopped, and when her eyes met Sophie's, they looked puzzled. "Josephine and her sisters will be waiting for us. Shall we go?" She asked him, while still looking at Sophie.

Sophie met her gaze steadily.

"Of course," he answered grudgingly, with a sideways glance towards Sophie before they followed her downstairs.

Dante and Catherina followed Alexander and Sophie out to the garage and the four of them slid into the Audi. Catherina sat behind Sophie in the backseat, but the place may as well have been empty for all the thoughts that Sophie *didn't* get from her.

They drove without a word. Not a single thought passed between them, partly because Catherina was in the car, but her thoughts had always been silent to Sophie. Alexander steered the sleek gray car with his usual, sure confidence; only the purr of the engine was in their ears as they traveled to meet the sisters in the Quarter.

They parked a few streets away from the sisters' home. The four slowly emerged from the car, glancing around defensively.

"Four hundred eighty-five," Catherina softly commented as they neared the home of Josephine and her sisters.

Sophie and Alexander stopped short of walking up the cement stairs to the building decorated with wrought-iron balconies and hanging ferns with the number *485* above the door. Catherina mounted the stairs in front of them and came to a stop outside of the closed door.

"Josephine," Catherina called softly, barely above a whisper.

The door slowly swung open by itself, and they stepped inside. Sophie looked around with an uneasy caution that Dante and Catherina didn't seem to share. A chill ran up her spine. Again, she was aware of the influence of Alexander's thoughts mingled with her own as she looked around. She looked for exits, escape routes, and overhanging landings. She'd never been this observant before she met Alexander, but he always had been. So the habit quickly became hers as well. Her eyes trailed over an ornate railing and watched as three women floated down the staircase before their eyes. The one in front had to be Josephine.

*It is,* Alexander confirmed without looking at her.

He and Sophie stood off to the side of Catherina and Dante as the sisters approached their group. Sophie watched them with the eyes of a stranger, half-expecting something pivotal to happen.

"Hello, Catherina," Josephine greeted, her voice heavily laden with a French accent. "Hello, Dante."

"Hello, Josephine," Catherina replied, as Dante bowed slightly to her.

Josephine then turned her eyes to Alexander and Sophie.

"Ah, Alexander. It is *very* pleasant to see you once more. It has been *too* long," she greeted with a coy smile.

"Josephine," he replied shortly, nodding.

Her eyes fell on Sophie with a knowing look on her face. "And *you* must be Sophie," she surmised, looking her up and down. *La belle dame sans merci.*

Sophie nodded in response and looked quickly over to Alexander for an interpretation.

*She called you 'the beautiful lady without mercy.' I told you news spreads quickly.* He smiled at the thought, and began to translate the rest of the meeting for her. It was really quite convenient; although Sophie couldn't help except wish that she'd taken French in college when she'd had the chance.

"Alexander's new companion," Josephine stated, looking at the two. *Il est á droite,* she quickly thought: *He is on the right hand.*

The other sisters exchanged a look before turning back to their visitors.

"It is a pleasure, I am sure," Josephine continued, still looking at Sophie. "These are my sisters, Claire," she said indicating the one on the right, "and Pauline," gesturing to the woman on the left.

Josephine was the tallest of the three and graceful in the way only dancers are. Her light brown hair was cut in a bob and her dress clung to her waif-like figure, giving the impression of a 1920s flapper.

"Welcome to our home," Claire continued where her sister left off. "To what do we owe the pleasure of your company?" she inquired simply out of politeness; they knew exactly why Catherina and the others were there.

Claire was the most feminine of the three, her voice also thick with a French accent. She was voluptuous and her soft jet-black corkscrew curls were piled high on her head, wound up in a scarf. All three wore long white dresses from another era, but Claire was the only one who also wore large earrings and bright red lipstick.

"The Council has spoken, *oui?*" Pauline asked quickly in a distinctly Cajun accent, before anyone else could speak.

Pauline was the smallest of the three, barely pushing five feet tall and had an olive tone to her skin; dark eyes and red hair. Her voice had that uniquely Cajun twang to it, one which made it difficult for hearers to decide if she were from New York or North Carolina, or somewhere in between.

"Indeed," Catherina answered carefully.

"And you came back here? You brought that fiend here?" Pauline demanded in her husky, appealing voice, glaring at Catherina.

Josephine raised her hand to silence her sister, without looking back at her. "Exactly *why* have you come back here? Do you perhaps wish to secure our assistance in this matter?" she asked.

"No," Catherina replied.

"*Tout de meme*"—All the same—"What is your business here with us?" Claire asked harshly.

Apparently Sophie and Alexander weren't the only ones who had a problem with Catherina.

Pauline jerked her head in Sophie's direction quickly. *Ça va sans dire* raced through her mind: *It goes without saying.*

Sophie stared at her for a moment until she realized that of course Pauline and the others could still hear her thoughts; she'd only blocked Catherina from her mind. Pauline smiled in answer, the movement almost completely indiscernible.

"Do you wish to drag us into this fight as you have done with these two?" Josephine asked Catherina accusatorily, gesturing to Sophie and Alexander. "And the rest of your family?"

Catherina glanced quickly over her shoulder, a cold look in her eyes as they swept over Alexander and Sophie.

"No...," Catherina answered.

"Then what is your business in our city?" Claire asked.

"Our business does not concern you, apparently," Catherina answered briskly, finally pushed to anger. "Out of *courtesy* to you, our sisters, we come to warn you of the impending danger which will surely reach fruition during our stay in this fine city of my youth."

*She's lying.*

*Mais oui, Sophie; we know.* Josephine locked eyes with her for the briefest moment.

"And exactly what is it that you know?" Catherina asked aloud, having heard only Josephine's side of the silent exchange.

"We are aware of the situation, I assure you," Josephine replied cryptically.

Catherina sighed. "Then we shall leave you," she replied with an uncharacteristic bow of her head.

"Please excuse us if we refrain from meddling in affairs which do not *directly* impact us," Josephine briskly said.

"Of course," Catherina replied, her voice unable to conceal the disappointment that her behavior hid.

She turned to leave and Dante followed close behind her, his hand on the small of her back. Alexander watched Josephine's family silently for a moment before finally turning on a heel to stride out of the house once Catherina had left. He glanced at Sophie to follow.

"Please *do* feel free to visit us again Sophie," Pauline invited; a smile on her lips, "I would very much like to get to know you better."

Sophie nodded. She knew Pauline liked her, if only because they both distrusted Catherina. Sophie was grateful, for a brief moment, to have gained obviously powerful allies in such a short visit.

She nodded once more before taking her leave.

The Leone family left as silently as they had come, but this time, the atmosphere in the car seemed heavier. The approaching conflict would be fought with no help to their small family. The gravity of the situation visibly weighed on Catherina as she leaned against Dante for support in the backseat.

*

"We're crazy, you know," Sophie said, leaning against the railing that ran along the second floor's balcony.

The Deep South winter chill ran over her arms, up her neck, but she wasn't cold. She watched the light from the streetlamps dance through the leaves on the trees.

"Why do you say that?" Alexander asked quietly.

"There's seven of us and *how many* of them? We should just high-tail it out of here."

He shook his head. "I could not abandon Dante like that," he said. "Regardless of how correct you are."

"I know."

"And you would not wish to leave Laney susceptible to such a threat."

"You're right," she agreed with a grimace. "I just get the feeling we're not all going to come back from this fight."

He sighed and was quiet for a time. "I believe it is a fool's errand," he finally consented. "However, we must not think in those terms. We must end this contest with Jacques. When we do, we will live in peace for a while."

"That'd be a nice change."

"Indeed," he said. "Please do not worry. We'll scout some of the locations I suspect they occupy, keep our ear to the ground so to speak; we will be as prepared as possible for the coming engagement," he assured her.

They walked silently inside, closing the door behind them. She reached up and pulled his face to hers and kissed him hard on the lips. When he closed his eyes, she suddenly jumped them into his room. He smiled when he felt the wind blow past them, but did not stop kissing her lips.

"That was interesting," he mumbled against her lips.

"Turn-about is fair play; besides, they keep telling us to get a room…" she replied before his lips crushed hers again.

His hands moved down her back to her hips as she struggled to catch her breath. She trembled under his touch. His lips traced her collarbone, sending chills up her spine. And with the chills came the sudden realization that he could be gone tomorrow. She gently pushed him away and stumbled back a step or two. She had to catch her breath. She sank down onto the edge of his bed. She exhaled and rubbed her cheeks with her hands as the hairs on the back of her neck stood on end and her heart raced in anxiety.

He walked towards her and pulled her to a standing position again. She stepped forward and wrapped her arms around his waist. She rested her head against his chest and felt his heart race beneath it.

He shook his head and buried his nose in her hair. "I don't want to lose you," he said.

Her expression softened when she looked at him. "I'm not going anywhere," she promised. She closed her eyes a little too long as she gazed at him.

"I should let you get some sleep," he said against her neck.

A shiver ran up her spine and she smiled. "Okay," she whispered.

She stepped back from him and smiled. "Goodnight," she whispered.

"Goodnight, my love," he replied quietly as she closed her eyes and was suddenly back in her own room.

She sleepily prepared for bed, suddenly and uncharacteristically overwhelmed with fatigue. She smiled and wondered how he'd known she was so tired; she hadn't even realized it herself. The stress of their situation seemed to be working a number on her. She turned off the light and laid back on her pillow, closing her eyes to the night. But before she fell quickly asleep, she heard her name.

*Sophie,* he simply thought, and without question or hesitation, she was suddenly in his room.

She stepped carefully to his bedside as the light from the streetlamp filtered in through the window and danced off of her bare arms.

He didn't say a word, but tugged her down onto the bed beside him, and pulled her body against his. He cradled her there as he buried his nose in her hair, bringing her chills of desire and soothing comfort at the same time. She felt herself relax in his embrace and soon his breathing was steady and deep with sleep. Her body melted against his as she followed him into the night.

# Chapter 27

Alexander scowled at Catherina in a veritable standoff in the living room. They glared at one another.

"Are you going to inform me of your plans?" He finally demanded of Catherina, who had ignored his entrance into the room for as long as he would allow.

"My *plans*?" She asked, in her clear, acrid voice; the voice that sounded too much like theirs. She didn't look at him, but chose to watch the wind blow through the trees out the window.

"Yes. Your plans," he replied, reigning in his impatience which was threatening to grow into fury. He pronounced his words slowly, articulating his frustration. "I am attempting to prepare for our engagement with them. I cannot properly do so without understanding what *exactly* it is you intend to do when you confront Jacques."

She looked away from the window and leveled her cold eyes at him. "I intend to kill him," she icily replied.

"And how do you propose that we do such a thing?" he asked.

"I have my own plans," she answered, before turning back to the window.

*That is what I was afraid of,* he thought, but of course she did not respond.

He had blocked Catherina from his thoughts long ago. He understood that she did not like it, but he couldn't bring himself to care. She had taken to staring at him that made him believe she was under the impression that if she concentrated hard enough, some little thought of his might slip through. She had been sorely disappointed time and again.

*I know you're going to say no,* thought Sophie preemptively as she came down the stairs towards him. "But I have to do this."

She stopped and stood beside him, her hands defiantly on her hips, watching him carefully.

Catherina's head shot up when she heard Sophie speak. Laney came peeking around the corner. Dante suddenly appeared in the living room, standing like a sentinel over Catherina, all of them sensing the change of emotion in the room.

"You *do* know what it means?" Alexander asked.

Sophie had been having dreams again; the same type of dreams which had brought her looking for her new family several weeks ago. Alexander knew this of course, but was still not prepared for her sudden decision to pursue them.

"Of course," she replied.

"What is going on?" asked Dante.

Sophie sighed. "I have to go find my mother," she explained.

Catherina looked at her with one raised eyebrow, and Dante became instantly concerned.

"Sophie, it is extremely dangerous," he warned.

Alexander shook his head. He knew better than any of them that any attempt to convince Sophie away from her goal was useless, no matter how much they wanted to—or how hard they tried.

Jim lumbered down the stairs and leaned against the banister next to her. "We'll go with you," he volunteered with a nod.

"Thanks, Jim," she replied, "but I have to do this by myself."

"Not the best idea, kiddo," Jim warned.

"I'll be fine," she insisted and looked to Laney. "What do you think?"

Laney shrugged her shoulders. "I don't think anything will happen, but Sophie, you know as well as I do that I'm not even close to being accurate. I thought we were going to meet with one person and then Celia *and* Chaz and Masumi showed up. Plus, you're ten times better at seeing the future than I am. Please don't ask me. I don't know what'll happen if you try to find your mother. Why do you want to find her so badly, anyway?"

Sophie shook her head and glanced at Alexander before answering her sister. "I can't explain it, but it's the same feeling I had before I came into the family. There's this sort of draw to her. I know it doesn't make any sense, but nothing about *any* of this seems logical."

"I know, Sophie, but it's just scary," whined Laney.

"Fine," replied Sophie, holding her hands out to the younger girl, "come here. Let's see what we can see."

Laney shrugged and reluctantly walked over to her sister, taking her hands. Catherina looked up quickly and stood to join them.

"Allow me," began Catherina with a fair amount of self-confidence.

"No, we've got it," Sophie replied briskly, refusing her help.

Catherina stopped in her tracks and acted like she didn't know what to do. She looked at the remainder of her family sheepishly, and hesitatingly retook her seat.

Sophie turned her back on Catherina and closed her eyes. The images came to Alexander as Sophie received them, but the swirl meant little to him.

The images came at him in confusing flashes through Sophie's mind, but it was not up to him to decipher what they meant; that was not his gift, but theirs. Yet suddenly, just as they had begun to increase in certainty, the images went black.

Sophie's eyes flashed open. "They know." Her voice was grim. She stared straight ahead at Laney without seeing her.

"What do you mean, 'they know'?" Alexander asked.

"They know everything," said Laney just as gravely, returning Sophie's stare.

The two women, still linked, stood perfectly and eerily still.

"Who?" Jim demanded.

Zoey slinked into the room and watched Sophie warily.

Laney and Sophie continued to look at each other and dropped their hands, their eyes still locked on each other as a sense of dread overcame the room.

"I won't be going to find her," said Sophie softly. Laney shook her head.

"What is going on?" Alexander demanded louder.

"Her mother is part of Jacques's coven," explained Laney.

Sophie continued, "They know who each of us are, where to find us, what our weaknesses and strengths are. They know everything: down to the cars we drive and our favorite colors."

"Okay, so your mom's here and that's a surprise, but we knew everything else. What's the big deal?" asked Jim.

Sophie slowly turned to face Jim, blinking as her eyes left Laney's.

"They're coming after us," she replied in a flat voice. "I think they want to take some prisoners."

"When?" Alexander demanded.

"Soon. Today…tomorrow…I don't know," answered Sophie, shaking her head.

"Damn," Alexander whispered to himself.

*I know,* she thought, nodding her head and shooting him a meaningful look. *What do we do now?*

*My thoughts exactly,* Jim thought.

*We can't wait around here for them to come get us,* thought Laney.

*No, indeed, we cannot,* Alexander agreed, pursing his lips and looking to the others as he plotted.

"Since I cannot hear what half of you are thinking," Catherina suddenly interrupted bitterly, "would you *mind* speaking aloud?" She glared accusatorily at Sophie.

"We've gotta go find them," Jim replied.

"The best defense *is* an offense," added Alexander.

"I've heard that before," Zoey murmured.

Sophie sunk down and sat on the bottom stair with a thud. She looked down at her hands, slowly rubbing them together deep in thought. The thoughts flew through her head faster than even Alexander could keep up with. Jim watched him as he heard what Sophie was thinking. He studied Alexander's face and tried to figure out whose thoughts were whose: Sophie's or Alexander's.

"What's up, sis?" Jim asked, looking down at her, frustrated by his own confusion.

"Oh…" began Sophie with a sigh, knowing she could not, and would not, keep the information from him.

"What was it?" he asked, moving to stand protectively over her without thinking.

"She wants to kill me…like actually come after *me* specifically. She either wants me dead or to be one of them," answered Sophie flatly and shook her head back and forth slowly. "I don't know what I ever did to her, other than being born. She asked Jacques if she could have a crack at me." *They also think Laney would be useful for a trade—Catherina for Laney. They've got her in their sights,* she thought only to Alexander.

Catherina mumbled something to herself. The tension was building in the room; it electrified the air around them. Everyone fell silent for several minutes; some of them wondered the same thing about their own biological parents, others decided how best to proceed.

Sophie glanced up at her sister and tried to smile. "Yeah, I'm okay, Laney. Thanks."

"What do you think, Alexander?" Jim asked.

Alexander looked into Sophie's eyes. She let out a shaky breath. He glanced at Jim and Zoey, then at Laney, Catherina, and Dante. His eyes settled on Sophie's again, and he sighed.

"We go after them."

# Chapter 28

Sophie and Alexander exchanged a meaningful look.

"Laney, why don't you help Catherina to bed?" she suggested.

Laney nodded. She and Catherina disappeared around the corner. Alexander looked at Sophie, telling her something that the other three couldn't hear. She suddenly disappeared, just to reappear out of nowhere a second later, with one of the family's various laptops under her arm.

She quickly typed a few things into the computer. Setting it down on the table, she spun it to face the others. It was a map of New Orleans, zoomed in, to show the area where she and Alexander predicted the coven was hiding out.

*When the hell did they do this?* Jim thought

"It's just something we've been working on based on the flashes I've been getting. Turns out I was right," she said matter-of-factly, without a hint of arrogance behind the statement.

"We think they'll be here," Alexander began, pointing to a street on the map as he spoke. He nodded to Sophie, who scooted to the edge of her chair before she began speaking.

"They're planning to make another kidnapping attempt on Laney tomorrow," she explained in a hurried, but hushed and trembling voice. "They're hoping that we'll come after them to get Laney back, and we'll either leave Catherina here alone so they can get to her without dealing with the rest of us or that we'll be willing to trade one for the other."

*They* have *been studying us,* Zoey thought.

"Wait a minute," Jim said, holding his hand up. "What do you mean 'another kidnapping attempt'?"

"That's what they were trying to do the other night when they cornered us," Sophie replied. "Since my flash earlier, I've tried to concentrate and hone in on what they're planning. Ideally they want to change Laney so they can exploit her talents, but they figure she's valuable even dead."

A rush of expletives poured from Jim's lips in an angry whisper. Zoey sighed uneasily.

"We have to take the offensive. We must approach them tomorrow before they have the chance come here," Alexander immediately added, ignoring Jim's reaction. "We must strike before they have the opportunity to do so themselves; it's our best chance for survival."

Sophie exhaled heavily at the word "survival," and Dante's brows furrowed in concern.

Jim could feel his heart pounding and the anger coming up from somewhere deep in his gut. They were coming after his sister, to lure his family away, to kill his…mother, lacking a better term.

"There's about fifteen or so," Sophie said.

"I guess it could be worse," Jim grumbled to himself.

She shrugged; she wasn't scared for herself at all. She worried about keeping Laney safe from them, knowing instinctively that the rest of them—those of the family that she really cared about at least—could take care of themselves.

"So? What's the plan?" Jim asked Alexander.

"First, we keep Laney and Catherina with us at all times," Alexander began. "You are correct about there being five for each of us. I am afraid that it will just be the four of us on the offensive," he said, looking to Dante. "You will need to be with Catherina to keep her safe."

"Catherina will manage," Dante said in an even tone that pulled Sophie's eyes to his, but his thoughts were as silent to her as ever.

Alexander looked at Sophie, "Keep Laney close to you. She will be able to help a bit, but remember that her power is defensive. She will be able to block certain things, but she will not be much use in an attack, unfortunately."

Sophie nodded. She preferred to keep her little sister close by anyway, especially since she now knew how ineffective the younger girl was in the reality of a fight.

"So, what?" Jim asked, looking at Alexander. "We just drive down the alleyway there and call 'em out?"

"Precisely," was his determined answer.

"It's too far to jump back and forth?" Sophie asked him.

"Yes," he replied.

"I'll need to take a lot of wooden stakes and weapons," Zoey said. "There won't be many natural items laying about the warehouse district, I'm sure."

"We'll need your cars," Jim said, looking at Sophie and Alexander.

Sophie looked up abruptly at Alexander as if he said something to her. Her eyes met his as they communicated back and forth, each shaking their head a bit, and their expressions changing along a wide spectrum of emotions in split seconds: frustration, determination, hesitation, and worry, all in a matter of seconds. Jim had a feeling he knew who would win.

"I'll take Laney in my car and we'll follow everyone else, who will be in Alex's" she said swiftly to Jim and Dante, "I'll be fine," she assured Alexander with a penetrating look. "Besides, you'll be in the car right in front of me. Nothing's going to happen. We'll be able to outrun them if we need to. Catherina's their ultimate target, not Laney. They'll hit you before they try to mess with me. You need Jim with you, and Dante won't leave her side."

"I'll follow Sophie's car," Zoey volunteered. "It can't hurt to have one more vehicle there."

Dante nodded in agreement, but didn't say anything.

Alexander sighed deliberately and shook his head, not wanting to accept the decision Sophie had made for them, though he knew he had no choice. Her logic was watertight; he couldn't deny that. They'd need to protect Catherina more than Laney, and Catherina would be safer with all of the men than with Sophie alone and there wasn't any point for the coven to kidnap Laney if Catherina was coming to them herself.

"We'll leave at dusk tomorrow. The area does not seem to be heavily populated, so hopefully collateral damage will be kept to a minimum. I suggest we rest tonight as much as possible, but we must keep watch over Catherina and Laney in case they decide to attack."

Sophie sighed thoughtfully. "We can watch in shifts," she suggested.

"Probably a good idea, sis," Jim said.

Alexander nodded in agreement. It was already after ten o'clock and the night had finally started to settle in around them.

"I'll take the first watch," she volunteered.

"I shall stay with you," Alexander stated, of course he would.

Dante, Zoey, and Jim looked at each other.

"Why not use my room tonight, Dante?" Alexander suggested, since Laney and Catherina were already settled in their shared room.

He nodded and with Jim, began to climb the stairs; planning to trade places at three. They said goodnight to Alexander and Sophie as they went to start their watch and Jim and Dante went to try and get some rest.

"I'll bed down on the couch so I'm nearby," Zoey said. "Don't have too much fun, you two."

Sophie grasped Alexander's hand. "I'm going to make sure Laney's good for the night."

"I'll come with you."

# Chapter 29

"Laney," Sophie called just above a whisper.

Laney opened the door to Catherina and Dante's room softly and closed it just as softly behind her, looking to them both. "Yeah?" she asked, a foreign weight in her eyes, destroying the jovial innocence that had seemed to be ever-present there until recently.

"We need to tell you something," Alexander said.

She looked worriedly from Sophie's face to his.

"What is it?" she asked bravely, blinking back tears of anxiety. She was nearly to her wits' end.

"We think Jacques is coming after you, either to get to Catherina or for other reasons," Sophie began, seeing no reason to beat around the bush. "They're planning to try again tomorrow, but we're going to beat them to it and meet them at their hideout instead of waiting for them to come here."

Sophie could feel the fear raise in her little sister and hated it. She pulled her into her arms and held her as tears of fear welled up in her eyes. Laney leaned her head on Sophie's chest, beneath her chin—she was just that much shorter than Sophie—and grasped onto her.

"We're not going to let anything happen to you," Sophie assured her, smoothing her hair as her eyes met Alexander's and Sophie saw her own emotions mirrored in his pained expression.

"I know," Laney sniffed. "I just want it all to end."

Sophie nodded in agreement. "I know," she whispered and rocked her back and forth a little. "Me too."

"We are running guard shifts tonight just as a precaution," Alexander explained. "I know it will be difficult, but you must try to get some rest."

She shook her head against Sophie's shoulder and opened her mouth to argue.

"Laney, you know your power isn't as strong when you're tired. You're going to stay with me all day tomorrow, but I'll need your help," Sophie persuaded, looking warily to Alexander. He nodded in approval. "I need you to get some rest. We worked well together the other day; you did a great job keeping those vamps off of me. We're going to need you tomorrow."

Laney sniffed, looking years younger than she was, and sighed. "Okay," she gave up with a nod.

"We'll be here until three. Jim and Dante will take over after that. Zoey's over on the couch in the next room. Try to rest and don't worry," Sophie told her. "We're going to handle this and then it'll be over tomorrow night." *One way or another.*

She smiled weakly at them both and Sophie's heart ached for her. Laney turned to the door and silently reentered the still room, shutting the door softly behind her and leaving the other two in the hall. Sophie listened to her for what may have been mere seconds, or several minutes, and was surprised that Laney actually did fall asleep after a while. And with Laney's eventual slumber, Sophie finally felt herself relax, though her instincts remained on edge.

In the meantime, her mind had wandered. There was something deep in her soul, something dark that told her Catherina was—if not inherently evil—then definitely well beyond selfish. Catherina wouldn't hesitate to sacrifice Laney, or the rest of them for that matter, to save her own skin. If it came down to it, Catherina would trade any of their lives for hers or Dante's; she'd told Sophie that much herself once.

Sophie had finally admitted to herself that she didn't trust Catherina as far as she could throw her...in the metaphorical sense, of course. Catherina meant little to her, but somehow, Catherina had become the glue that held the family together, bound as it was. Sophie knew Laney would be in danger, whether from kidnapping or from the conflict itself and she vowed to protect Laney at all costs while helping Alexander fight their enemies tomorrow night. She still couldn't shake the image from her dream of the vampire Catherina hurting Laney. She didn't stop to wonder about her sense of responsibility for Laney, why she was so protective of her.

Perhaps it was because she had been young and vulnerable once…and there'd been no one to protect her.

She finally turned her back to the door, startled to see Alexander standing like a preternatural statue behind her, watching her with unblinking eyes. It was times like this that she remembered where they came from, who their parents were— when one of them acted a little too un-human.

"She *will* be safe," he said in a firm whisper.

She walked over to him and wrapped her arms around his firm waist. He held her against his chest and said nothing, running his fingers lightly atop her hair. Sophie closed her eyes and just let him hold her.

"Come on," he whispered. "Let's go sit outside."

He took her hand and led her out onto the porch that lined the entire front first story of the house. It was a peaceful night and they were afforded a good view of the street from their perch. He stood at one end, she at the other, both of them silently surveying the night, looking for any sign of unnatural movement. Their ears were finely attuned to the sounds around them, their attention pulled to the smallest rustle of a bush, the steps of a neighbor coming home from an overtime shift.

Life was carrying on as usual for those around them. A baby cried out, wanting a late-night feeding; a dog barked at a passing cat. Their own world could be coming to an end tomorrow for all they knew, and the clueless humans around them wouldn't know the difference. They would continue on with their simple lives, the largest challenge coming to most of them was figuring out how to pay some bill or another.

Sophie's condescending thoughts surprised her, though she really couldn't help but think that way, with what they'd already seen, and what they'd face tomorrow, and the blatant oblivion the people around her operated in.

And so they watched; they simply waited for hours, listening. They didn't speak and their thoughts, though open to one another, were void of real conversation for a long time, until a question happened to occur to Sophie well after midnight.

*Why did you hate me so much when I first came here—into the family?*

He sighed inwardly. *I have* never *hated you, Sophie.*

*Why did you act like you did?*

He became still and his thoughts were silent for a few minutes. She waited without looking at him.

*I was angry with myself,* he finally admitted reluctantly.

*Angry with yourself? For what?*

*For being weak.*

*Weak?*

"Yes, I thought I was weak," he answered aloud, but only in a whisper. "I knew the moment I saw you that, for the first time in centuries, I had something great to fear," he paused before quietly adding, "The knowledge was nearly unbearable for me."

"What do you mean?" She whispered back. "I don't understand."

He laughed disdainfully at himself and shook his head, running his hand through his hair. He looked down at his feet in thought before meeting her eyes.

"It's a long story," he answered, avoiding the question. "Why did *you* dread *my* presence?" he asked quietly, trying to divert the conversation which was unlike him. "Remember: I could hear your thoughts, though you could not hear mine."

"I think we have plenty of time for your story," she answered, looking at the night which surrounded them.

"That is true," he replied, waiting for her to answer his question first.

She sighed. *Fine, I'll play along. I'll answer your question if you answer mine.*

"I believe I can handle that," he said, quietly.

She folded her arms and looked up at the dark sky, trying to find the words. "How do I say this?" She asked herself.

"Just say it."

"Well…" she began, turning quickly to look at him, "I've been alone my entire life. I've…I…I don't…" She sighed. "I've never needed *anything* and then…" She shook her head slowly, trying to find the words. "I mean, it's not like I've had good experiences with guys before…and I could at least hear *their* thoughts. And then there was the thing with Danny when I was a kid…" She trailed off.

His eyes clouded in fury.

"...And then I met you," she whispered, feeling like a deflated balloon somehow. "I saw you *everywhere*, even in my dreams. It's like you wouldn't leave me alone. And then...and then the day I came into the family, I realized the strange draw I felt to wherever you were..." She broke off, shaking her head. "All the strange companion stuff...I guess I was frustrated with myself for falling for you so quickly; it defied reason. You know," I shrugged, "kinda like everything else. Nothing makes sense anymore." She laughed under her breath. "And then I realized that I couldn't stop it."

He was nodding his head, with a thoughtful look on his face as he stared across the street at the other house standing there. "It appears we were both too weak to refuse such a force."

"Seems inevitable."

She look at him. It was his turn and he knew it. The silence that fell between them seemed infinite.

*It is difficult to think about. Forgive me,* he finally thought half an hour or so later.

She waited, trying to understand his pain; the pain that began to transfer to her. She began to feel what he felt; the crushing weight of his emotions as he remembered something that he wasn't ready to share, something he would *never* be ready to share.

They all had their own version of tragedy and she waited to learn his, knowing it had to be more significant than hers. After all, what did she have to complain about? So she'd had a few bad breaks and been raised in foster homes all her life. It happened to humans all the time and they survived, and maybe time made her dismissive of most of it. It had all just made her independent, and probably a little more than bull-headed. But Alexander's pain went deeper than just the hassles of being born into this life, deeper than momentary abuse. The utter knowledge of that fact washed over her, and she began to regret asking.

*Please do not regret asking me. This is something you must know. You are correct,* he confirmed her inner thoughts. *You see, my mother bore two children, rather than one when she was transformed. My sister Abigail was born with me. She was the smaller of the two of us and by all accounts should not have survived. Of course, we later understood that her survival was due to our mother's transformation, and the heartiness we inherit at birth.*

*I loved my sister dearly, and kept her with me always. I protected her from harm and kept her to myself, until one day she felt the strange force which we all experience eventually, and began seeing her future companion in her mind's eye. She left to find him one day and I followed after her, unwilling to let her go out into the world alone. She was much like Laney: naïve, young, happy, in need of protection. In those days, there were as many vampires, if not a heavier ratio of vampires in comparison to the human population, as today. It was very dangerous for our kind.*

*Disregarding all dangers, she met Stephen in Philadelphia and there they began a new life together. I settled there as well, to remain close to her and to protect her, when I could.*

*Stephen was a good man and loved her above all else in the world, but did not protect her as he should. He was a foolhardy man, and lived his life in the clouds, much as she did. He did not protect her, did not keep her from venturing out in the dusk, and did not shield her from the potential harm that could come to her...that did come...*

He hesitated; his breath quickened and she was surprised to see him struggle to blink back tears.

"Alex...what *happened*?" She breathed in shock. She'd never seen him like this. He was trembling.

He shook his head slightly.

"She was attacked," he answered in a whisper, his eyes centuries away. "In the hour before the sun retreats for the night, something struck from the shadows. She never saw it coming."

He stopped telling her then, instead showing her what he had seen through his sister's eyes as the images flashed through his mind. He had been keeping tabs on her, but Sophie suspected it was all in vain. He sighed in answer.

She saw Abigail, clothed in colonial dress, walking with a basket over her arm back to her home with Stephen. She thought of the kitten at home who was surely ready for his milk through the innocent negligence of her companion, her new husband.

She was beautiful, and looked so much like Alexander. Her hair was gold and it curled like his, but unlike his eyes, hers were the clearest blue. She walked along, not paying much attention to her surroundings, having been shielded her entire life by her brother, when something moved in the shadows.

The memory of the vampire's smell caused Sophie's stomach to lurch and the memory of the predator's eyes told her what Abigail had not known. Suddenly, Abigail's memory— Alexander's memory—became Sophie's own.

He came at her so swiftly that Abigail couldn't see. His hands were like steel claws on her arms, crushing them. Sophie could feel her bones shatter under his grasp.

Sophie gasped and clutched the railing in pain as Alexander melted to the ground beside her. She knew he was there at her feet, but she didn't see him. All she saw was Abigail's terror; Abigail utterly alone there in that alleyway.

*The smell again. Oh, it's overwhelming. It's so sweet and smells like decay.* Sophie broke into a sweat under its oppression. *He leers at her, savoring the moment and smiling when she cries out in pain; licking at the air around her, thrilled with her horror.*

*She's terrified. She wants to scream for Alex, that's what she calls him, but Abigail can't make her voice work right. She can't open her mouth to scream for him, for anyone. Her arms and legs are painfully weak and cold from the adrenaline and she pushes against his chest, but her arms are too wasted from the terror. She's fighting a losing battle, but she can't give up. She has to live for Stephen, for Alex.*

*Alex!*

*Alex...*

And then it was black.

Then, there was nothing.

*The vampire broke her neck carelessly in his lustful efforts to drain her blood; her bones were crushed painfully under his hands.* Sophie was suddenly aware that her perspective in the memory had changed to how Alexander had witnessed it.

He had seen it all, coming upon the scene too late to save her, but not too late to see the horror.

Sophie trembled and her arms shook as she gripped the railing for balance. She started to cry, feeling all of the emotion and the terror and the rage that he'd felt then—and now, as he remembered it all over again. She clutched the railing for support and felt the horror tear through her body, the tears streamed down her face as she felt the memory that had been Abigail's last, and Alexander's very worst.

"Oh, Alex," Sophie said, grasping his hand as the vision continued. He buried his face in his other arm where it lay on his knee, still remembering.

In a fury of rage, he tore the vampire from his beloved sister, threw him through the brick wall behind him and turned to try to save the lump of flesh which had been Abigail. Too late.

*Too late. Too late to save my angel.*

*'Alex,' she whispered. She smiled at me. She was peaceful, but I was too late to save her, and she was gone.*

*I tore the vampire to shreds; I enjoyed every horrid second of it and then I ran to Stephen,* he began narrating again, but stopped, just letting Sophie see what he remembered. He ran into the house with murder on his mind.

A strangled gasp tore at Sophie's throat. "You didn't!" She exclaimed in a whisper.

He nodded slowly, keeping his eyes trained on the ground. She didn't need to listen to the story any more to know that Stephen had met the same fate as the vampire; an innocent life ended at Alexander's hands.

"Why?" She whispered.

"At the time, in the *moment*, it seemed that he deserved it. He had killed my sister as surely as the vampire had, in my estimation. I could not tolerate his life to continue when…when *hers* was lost forever."

"But, *Alex!*"

"His death haunts me nearly every day of my existence, but not as Abigail's death does," he said, shaking his head in grief. "I was too late to save her."

He grew quiet then and the emotions which flowed so freely between them began to gradually subside. Sophie began to calm down, though she'd been rendered weak from the emotions.

She had no doubt that his actions on that day remained with him. It was clear that the pain and guilt of what he'd done hadn't diminished over the centuries. It was a blessing and a curse to remember everything so vividly…that a memory could never be erased from their consciousness.

*She was the only person that I ever truly loved,* he finally continued, *until...*

*...Until I showed up,* she finished his thought.

He nodded. *And it was so different with you of course, because you meant so much more to me from the start. It infuriated me to care about you so. It was a weakness that I had escaped for centuries and then, there you were, in that miniscule college town, vulnerable to everything, just as she had been. But ultimately I was wrong. You were not like her. You were so powerful, yet so unaware of your potential. It sickened me to know that I could lose you just as I lost Abigail, so I resisted for a time, but I knew I would not be able to avoid you for long. I continually reminded myself that though I'd survived her death...if anything were to happen...to you...*

He didn't continue.

She nodded. Everything from those first few weeks made so much more sense to her now. One minute, he'd looked like he hated her, and the next minute, there was a subtle, seemingly foreign kindness in his green eyes. Everything that made absolutely no sense at the time was perfectly explainable today. He rose to stand by her side.

She looked at him wisely. *So it has nothing to do with boredom then, does it?*

*What do you mean?* He asked with a shake of his head, his emotions keeping him from following her train of thought.

*Hunting vampires,* she clarified.

*No...,* he thought, *but I do think it is something more than vengeance. There seems to be a deeply rooted instinct in us all to rid the world of them—clearly you have felt that as surely as I. For me, it is the innocent human lives I save with the death of each one of the devils that keeps me pressing onward. It is atonement in a way, for my sins of killing Abigail and Stephen.*

*Alex, you didn't kill your sister,* she thought sternly.

He sighed resolutely. *My logical mind tells me so, but I can't help but blame myself for her tragedy.* He squeezed her hand. *I simply cannot let the same thing happen to you.*

"You won't," she vowed. "You've prepared me as well as possible. Jim has trained me in the best way he knows. I've got just as much chance against them as you do. We'll fight tomorrow and we'll live or we'll die, but we'll do it together. You're willing to kill and be killed for me, and I'm more than willing to do the same for you. For the first time in my life, I have something to kill and *be* killed for."

"Please do not think that way," he begged in a fierce whisper, shaking his head.

"I can't help it, Alex. It's just how it is," she replied matter-of-factly. "But we'll survive tomorrow. I *know* it. I promise. I won't disappear on you. For the first time in my life, I have someone to live for."

She looked earnestly into his eyes before bringing her lips to his and gently kissing him.

"I love you more than anything," she whispered before laying her head on his shoulder in an attempt at comforting him. "And it's going to work out."

His memories were now hers. She knew after his rampage at Stephen and Abigail's house, he'd returned to the site of her murder and gathered her body up in his arms.

He buried her himself, clawing up the dirt with his own two hands before tenderly laying her there. He deliberately covered her precious body with the dirt. The pain coursed through his veins as surely as his blood, and he laid on the mound and wept until his tears ran dry.

At dawn, he pulled himself from her grave and turned, never looking back over his shoulder, left Philadelphia, and traveled to Europe. He vowed to never return to the city.

She felt him stiffen suddenly despite the calm that had settled around them, and she looked up quickly. Something had broken the silence, but they both immediately realized that the sound they'd heard was simply Jim and Dante coming to relieve them.

*Is it really three already?* She wondered.

"Three-fifteen, actually," Jim whispered, his face solemn as he studied Sophie's expression. "Everything okay?"

She nodded and swiped the last errant tear from her cheek, forcing a smile.

*I told her about Abigail,* Alexander thought to Jim.

Dante rested a hand on his shoulder and whispered only, "Brother." He knew.

Without a word, Alexander led her back inside. She locked the memories that were now hers deep inside her heart, and would hold them sacred forever. He gently pulled her upstairs and had every intension of leaving her at her bedroom door until she turned in the doorway and looked into his eyes.

"Don't go," she commanded in a whisper, gently pulling him by the hand to follow her inside. He followed without hesitation.

Closing the door behind her, she leaned against it and pulled him towards her. She found his lips in the dark hours of early morning. There was that new, deep desire in her soul that threatened to boil over again; the need to never let him go. She knew that this could be the last night of their lives, despite what she'd said earlier. They'd face the unknown tomorrow and the anxiety in the air was tangible. He felt it too.

He kissed her jaw, her neck and whispered his devotion in her ear, pulling her fiercely against his own body.

"I love you," he said, the desperation catching in his voice.

She simply had to listen to what he said to himself only, what his emotions expressed privately, to know how he felt. It was overwhelming. He kissed her more, his lips pressing against her neck and collarbone, lingering on her lips.

He added, "I do not want to lose you," and his voice caught again when he said it, sharing her thoughts and doubts about the coming fight.

She kissed him again, the passion and fear burning all at once.

"You won't," she tried to reassure him between kisses, though she was unsure of it herself, terrified of losing him too. "Don't think about it."

His hands slipped to her waist and then under the hem of her sweater. His hands were suddenly on her bare back. Without saying a word, he picked her up in one fluid movement and carried her to the bed. She was on her back in a second as he held her in his arms, kissing her fiercely on the mouth. His free hand trailed down her side, lingering at her hip and then caressing down to her thigh. Her breathing accelerated and she felt dizzy. Each touch, each caress, sent a current through her body as if electrically charged, as she clung to him in near desperation.

# Chapter 30

The light from the sunrise was bright on Alexander's eyelids. He blinked against its shine and looked down to see Sophie curled against him, breathing steadily in her sleep. He drew her closer to himself, her body fitting perfectly within his embrace. She sighed lightly in her sleep, a response to the movement.

He laid his head back on the pillow and began to listen for the others in the house. It was still too early for Laney and Catherina to have stirred. He was relieved to know that they were both still asleep; Laney would need her rest to get through what they were planning for the night. Dante and Jim sat outside on the porch, drinking coffee. Dante perused the morning paper, the danger of the night gone with the arrival of the predawn dew.

Alexander closed his eyes, still holding Sophie close. He absentmindedly traced the contours of her back with his fingers, savoring the moment.

"Mmm," she softly moaned after a few moments, causing him to open his eyes.

She smiled at him and stretched forward to kiss his lips.

"Good morning," he said quietly, kissing her soft, naturally pink lips.

"Good morning," she replied, her voice husky from sleep.

She looked at him dreamily and in that instant captivated him with her eyes as she so often unconsciously did. She blinked twice and her expression changed. Suddenly recalling all that had occurred yesterday, she sat swiftly up in bed and looked frantically around the room.

"What is wrong?" He asked, watching her, suddenly concerned. He'd learned quickly to trust her instincts without question. He was on his feet in an instant.

"Oh...," she replied with a sigh, holding her forehead with one of her hands. "I just forgot about yesterday for a minute there." She looked up to smile at him. "You're a good distraction," she said, before gliding over to him and planting another kiss on his lips.

He could feel the desire build in them both, but he pushed her gently away.

"As much as I would love to...," he began.

"I know. You're right," she replied, cutting him off with a grave look in her eyes. "Trust me. I know."

She reached up to kiss him once more and then was gone. He heard the shower running in the attached bathroom and he took his leave.

*

By the time Alexander descended from the second floor, the house was teeming with intensity. It seethed with nervous energy, but it lacked the usual, joyful feel of morning that he had grown accustomed to.

Laney was curled up in one of the living room chairs, her chin resting on her knees. The smile that usually adorned her face was gone. She was lost in thought, vainly attempting to foresee the actions of tonight.

He turned away from her and went to investigate the banging pots and pans in the kitchen. Passing a pacing Jim in the dining room without a word, Alexander walked into the kitchen to find Sophie making a huge breakfast, as if her life depended upon the completion of the menial task. She wasn't thinking about the meal, but about him. She glanced up at him from under her eyelashes and he caught a glimpse of a faint blush, mid-thought, as it spread across her cheeks when she smiled at him.

"May I help?" he asked quietly.

She smiled an affirmative answer. He worked around her in a natural ease.

*Where is Dante?* He asked in a thought as she swiftly chopped onions for omelets, the knife blade a literal blur.

*Telling Catherina everything.*

*How long has Laney been awake?*

*I'm not sure...* She pointed to a skillet on the stove. *Will you stir that one please?*

*Of course...Have you spoken with her?*

*Not yet. Here,* she directed, handing him a spatula.

*I did not know you could cook.*

*Oh, I'm full of surprises,* she thought with a smile, before turning back to her chore. *I was extremely self-reliant at one time, you know.*

*You still are.*

*...I guess so.*

*Is it not better to allow others to shoulder part of the burden?*

*Better? Yes, probably—will you hand me the bowl of veggies there?—But, it's still not easy for me.*

*I know.*

Her thoughts were silent for a moment as they went about their tasks, before his turned suddenly to the previous night and a passionate thought sprinted through his mind before he could stop it. Her cheeks reddened as she heard it, and as her mind jumped to a scenario along similar lines.

He smiled. *I would never have thought you were the blushing type.*

*Well, apparently, I am...especially since I'm waiting for Jim to walk in and somehow hear what you're thinking.*

He laughed silently. She did have a point.

*I'm surprised is all,* she thought.

*You do realize that there is nothing to be embarrassed about?*

She looked at him, amused, took his hand and placed it over her heart, which raced. *I'm not embarrassed, trust me...just surprised. I didn't expect to hear thoughts like those from you. You're usually so in control.* She smiled conspiratorially at him.

He walked up to stand behind her and placed his hands on her hips, nuzzling her neck. *I am not without an imagination.*

She leaned against him and shuddered with a sigh.

*Or desire, apparently,* she thought and he laughed against the hyper-sensitive skin of her neck.

"Stir that, please, or it'll burn," she said barely above a whisper before turning away from him just as Jim walked into the room. She looked at her brother before saying, "Please go tell Laney and the others that breakfast is ready."

She tried to sound positive, but her words came out formally and forced. She knew that it may very well be the last day together as a family. No amount of distractions from Alexander, and no amount of menial busy work could draw her mind from it for long. There was no way of knowing if they would all come back tonight, no matter how hopeful she might be. He smiled sadly at her.

As she and Alexander placed large platters of omelets, bacon, and pancakes on the table, the other members of their family gathered around, taking their seats.

No one spoke as they ate.

The tension in the air was nearly palatable, making it difficult for all to bear. Sophie silently reached for Laney's hand where it rested on the table to her left. She grasped it and gave her a steady smile.

Zoey laid her fork down on the plate, her food largely untouched. She sat back in her chair and absentmindedly twirled her ring around her finger. Catherina kept her head bowed through the whole meal, although Sophie occasionally looked in her direction, and surely Catherina must have felt the younger woman's eyes on her.

Jim stood up abruptly, making the chair scrape the floor tiles with a squeal. "I'm gonna go make sure everything's good to go." He stomped out of the kitchen.

The rest of the family fell apart. Laney silently rose and walked into the other room. She sat at the piano; her fingers lightly brushed the keys, the melody was melancholy.

Dante and Catherina drifted off next to find distraction elsewhere. Zoey suddenly disappeared.

Sophie looked down and studied her hands, sure and still on the tabletop in spite of her uneasy thoughts. She narrowed her eyes and then with a little gasp, she looked up at Alexander, holding his eyes in her gaze.

She suddenly looked away and over her shoulder. "Jim's gone for a drive," she said softly.

She rested her chin on her hand and gazed out the window. Alexander reached for her other hand, absentmindedly stroking it with one finger, just to touch her. Her eyes closed slowly as she listened to the others' thoughts, but she couldn't sit still for long.

"Come on," she said suddenly, her eyes popping open.

She rose so quickly that she nearly knocked the chair over in the process. She caught it without looking and strode in the direction of the basement, where they kept their weapons. He followed her silently.

Typing the code in with lightening fast speed, the door was suddenly unlocked and they entered together. She went to the shelves where their weapons were lined up, waiting for the battle that would come that night. She tried to distract herself with checking magazines, examining the sharp ends of the wooden and silver stakes, all to no avail. She turned on a heel to face Alexander from across the room, frantic fear in her eyes. She couldn't hide her fear any longer. It knocked the breath out of him. He leaned against one of the steel tables for support.

"Sophie," he breathed.

"Alex, what…what if we don't…," she would not allow herself to finish and turned from him.

He rushed to her in three quick strides and placed his hands on her shoulders. "We *will* make it home tonight."

She turned around. "But, what about everyone else?" She asked; her face inches from his, her eyes probing his in uncertainty.

"With you protecting Laney, she has nothing to fear. Jim and Zoey are strong and will prevail."

She nodded. "What about Dante?"

He sighed. "Dante is the master of his own fate. He will survive if he wishes to."

"I think this'll be the longest day of my life."

"I know."

\*

The sun filtered into the windows at a steep angle, and the light had that golden, late afternoon quality to it as dust motes danced and whirled with every subtle breeze that swept their way. It was as if all was well in the world. The house was inhabited, but deathly calm.

Alexander sat across from Dante; the others had decided to rest in preparation for what awaited them. There was nothing—and everything—to say as he sat with his brother.

"Dante," Alexander said, "please tell me what Catherina expects to do tonight."

Dante simply looked at him, regret in his eyes. He had made his decision already, chosen his alliance long ago. He would not tell Alexander what he knew or the choices he had made.

"Brother," said Dante, "it has been a very long time."

"Centuries," Alexander said under his breath, waiting for the blow to be delivered.

"I thank you for what you have chosen to do for me. I do not pretend that it is motivated by any personal affection for Catherina," said Dante. "I have long known your sentiments toward one another."

Alexander thought to interrupt him, but it would have been useless; he couldn't deny that Dante was right.

"You have stood by me through many challenges, and over the years have proven yourself a brother to me. For that, I shall be eternally grateful," continued Dante. "I apologize for anything that may happen tonight."

"What exactly do you mean by that?" Alexander asked, straightening in his seat.

Dante had never spoken this way before. He shook his head. "I shan't say, but know brother, that I am indebted to you in ways that I cannot accurately express."

"Dante, is something going to happen tonight that I should be aware of?"

He would not look Alexander in the eye.

"What's going to happen?"

Dante stood and placed his hand on Alexander's shoulder, looking down on him with a regretful expression.

"My brother," he simply said once more before looking up quickly.

"What is *this*?" the sharp voice of Catherina interrupted. "Saying your goodbyes already?" The tension rolled off of her.

Alexander strangled a growl in his throat. She glared at him with fire in her eyes. Before she could say anything else, Sophie had suddenly appeared beside Alexander, who rose to his feet.

Sophie tensed beside him and met Catherina's glare. A low growl vibrated in her chest before she could stop herself.

"A moment between brothers only," replied Alexander in a guarded voice, stepping between the two women. He met Catherina's accusatory glare with one of his own and stood his ground as Sophie's eyes bore into her over his shoulder.

"What's going on?" Zoey asked, suddenly appearing.

"Nothing," growled Sophie, holding Catherina's glare.

Dante sighed and looked toward the grandfather clock. "It is time," he quietly said.

He reached for Catherina. Grasping her hand, the two of them jumped to the basement get ready to leave, not bothering to wait for the remainder of the family.

Sophie huffed in frustration.

"Everything okay?" Jim asked warily, looking around the room.

"Yes," Alexander replied quietly. "Thank you."

Sophie looked at them all. "Let's go."

# Chapter 31

Dusk had come on quicker than they'd expected as they gathered together in the basement. They checked firearms, counted stakes and throwing stars, and shoved daggers into their boots or waistbands.

Sophie checked to make sure she had her cell phone with her and they all walked out of the basement towards the garage. Most of them were armed to the teeth with whatever they could get their hands on. And despite everything, everyone seemed eerily calm.

That crazy calmness reminded Laney of a movie she'd once seen, with a queen who climbed to the chopping block and her death. The queen had been peaceful beyond reason. Both scenes had an inevitable, resigned feeling to them. She shuddered at the similarity and rubbed her neck.

Without saying a word, Sophie tossed her bag into the backseat of her Mercedes and left the top down. Laney silently slid into the passenger seat and watched her with wary eyes.

Sophie looked at Alexander, but they didn't say anything to each other. He squeezed her hand and kissed her on the forehead in parting. She turned away from him abruptly, hiding a tear, and got into the car. She didn't see the desperation marking his face. It was too much for Laney to watch; she looked away to avoid Alexander's anguished eyes.

He slid into his car where Jim, Dante, and Catherina were already waiting. Zoey pulled her helmet on and straddled the Ducati. She nodded to the other drivers. Sophie looked at Alexander once more, and waited for his move. He smiled at her and pulled out of the garage first. Sophie turned the key in the ignition, and with a resigned but hopeful sigh, Laney felt her sister's mood instantly change.

A small smile crept across Sophie's face and her spirits were suddenly lighter. Her infectious optimism immediately gave Laney some hope. It was like Sophie had suddenly had a revelation, but Laney couldn't tell what caused the change. Whatever it was, Laney was grateful for it—she began to hope.

"Here we go," Sophie said to no one, slid her sunglasses on, and cranked the music up.

Zoey revved the engine on her bike and was inches off the back bumper of Sophie's car as they pulled out of the garage. Laney felt safer knowing she was there.

They sped through the streets, racing the setting sun. Laney looked around and tried to keep her mind open for anything that could help them.

Sophie sighed and patted Laney's hand where it lay on the armrest between them.

Laney tried to visualize the coven's hideout and what they would probably find there, but none of the pictures made any sense whatsoever. She couldn't put the flashing images together into anything that she could easily comprehend. It *seemed* like there were going to be a lot more vampires than they were anticipating. But she was nervous, so instead of thinking about it, she sang a nonsense song in her head to try and distract their thoughts. She tried not to think about what they were doing. She didn't have any faith in it actually working.

It ultimately didn't matter, though, because they made it to the warehouse district literally before Laney realized where they were. Sophie parallel-parked the car behind Alexander's and leapt from the seat over her closed door. Her long leather coat floated back down to her sides as she grasped the bag of weapons that had hovered near her hand at some silent mental command. Alexander looked at her, his head tilted to the side and there was a strange, amused smile on his face, finding a change there that he hadn't expected.

She smiled back at him, and Laney realized immediately what a difference the drive had made. Sophie was ready for this, even if Laney wasn't so sure about it herself.

They came together as a group before falling naturally into a casually arranged formation. Alexander stood at the point of their small triangle and was flanked by Sophie on his left, and Jim on his right. Laney stood behind Sophie, next to Zoey, and Dante stood behind Jim's right. Catherina was guarded in the center, behind Alexander and within arms' reach of both Sophie and Jim. Alexander didn't give the fact that Catherina had placed him between herself and the enemy a second thought; he practically expected it.

Jim cocked his handgun and touched the shoulder strap on his crossbow in anticipation as his lips slowly turned into a grin, feeling a change in the air. He glanced over at Sophie and winked. He was ready too, and probably just as crazy as Sophie...or maybe on further examination, it wasn't insanity at all.

*Maybe they're fighting for the only thing worth fighting for: family,* thought Laney.

Like the other two, Alexander rested a hand on the grip of his revolver and almost arrogantly twirled a stake in the fingers of the other. Laney watched them uncertainly. The confidence of those three was astounding for her. But maybe unbridled confidence and a touch of arrogance was what was needed in that kind of situation.

She glanced over at Dante. He prepared for what was coming with a stake in each hand. He kept glancing sidewise at Catherina, who didn't hold anything. As always, Zoey looked eerily Zen about what was going on.

Laney was caught up in her own thoughts and worries as something from the shadows started to move. She jumped at the movement and slid to stand just a step closer to Sophie. But just as quickly, she was stepping back from her sister.

Sophie opened the bag she'd thrown across her chest. Six throwing stars began floating out of the bag and slowly began to orbit around her, gaining speed as they continued on their invisible paths. Laney took another step back at the sight of her sister. Sophie pulled her gun from the holster, pulled the slide back and cocked it, ready to go. She wasn't even paying attention to the weapons that spun around her. She looked over to Catherina and then to Alexander. He nodded to Catherina.

"JACQUES!" she called.

Laney jumped again; she wasn't expecting her to call him out like that. A door suddenly burst open and several dark figures began slinking out of the building, a hushed hissing coming from the group. It gave Laney cold chills as she fought to focus on the scene playing out in front of her. She seemed to be the only scared one of the group and she struggled to remain calm.

*You're okay,* Sophie thought.

The vampires organized themselves in a tight line with the one who must have been Jacques at the head. Sophie, Alexander, Jim, and Zoey began trading thoughts back and forth in such a swirl that Laney couldn't keep up. She could almost feel their thoughts in the air around her body.

*There's my mother,* Sophie told them. Their eyes locked and the vampire grinned.

"This is *indeed* interesting," Jacques said in a cold, ancient, French-accented voice, and laughed. "We did not expect to see you here."

He was either laughing at the family or his good luck, or both. His physical appearance added to the horror of the evening; he looked like a stereotypical Hollywood vampire, with a widow's peak and jet black hair, paper-thin skin, black, hollow eyes, and shining white teeth.

The wind changed direction and Laney finally caught the vampires' scent; she'd been waiting for it, but was still swept by a wave of nausea. It was the worst smell imaginable: something close to blood, but sweeter somehow, with the tinge of decomposing rot. At her side, Sophie shuddered, but the stars that spun steadily around her maintained their course and pattern.

Alexander watched the eyes of the vampires, unflinching. The clouds above thundered ominously over the assembly, lightning lit up the sky on the horizon.

Both sides froze, keeping absolutely still. They knew why they were there; there was no need for taunting, posturing, or greetings that night.

Laney began to shake with nervous tension at Sophie's side.

*Stay beside me, no matter what happens,* Sophie instructed without looking in her direction.

*Okay,* was all Laney could think in response; she was virtually incapacitated by her fear.

The tension electrified the air around them. Thunder crashed again and in that moment, like a bad dream, it happened.

When the vampires charged the family, their neat formation broke apart to take the vampires on. Sophie sent the throwing stars into the group. Her energy swirled around her in the form of the sharp metallic objects, and she was utterly terrifying. Even the vampires, usually so sure of themselves, slowed their attack on her. Some even stopped squarely in their tracks at the sight of such a foe.

Catherina ran to Dante's side, which placed him between her and the vampires, but removed Alexander from a direct line of attack. Alexander for his part took one side step toward Sophie and sunk down in a feral crouch, ready to spring on the charging vampires.

Laney watched in mute horror as Jim charged full force at a set of two vampires. They hissed and kept low to the ground, waiting to pounce on him when he got closer, probably hoping to take his massive frame down at the knees.

Zoey was fast on his heels, taking down two at once. She pulled a large bottle of water out of her bag. With one hand, she tossed the bottle so the water shot into the air. She swept her other hand in an arc and doused a handful of vampires with it. They fell to the ground with a sizzle and screams, writhing with the slow pain only holy water could bring.

Sophie forced a handful of her stars into the crowd of vampires closest to herself, but only one reached its target, and not in the way she'd hoped. The one that made contact severed the arm of a female vampire and her glass-shattering scream sent chills up Laney's spine. She watched two others turn on her sister.

She swiftly tore her eyes from Sophie as three vampires charged Alexander. He spun the stake in his palm and shoved it through the chest of one while he grasped the vampire's head, twisting and tearing it viciously from the body. He tossed the head to the ground and then leveled his revolver at the chest of another. He fired two rounds through her chest, and the vampire screamed a blood-curdling scream.

He pulled the stake from the other's heart and plunged it into hers so hard that the force of his strike broke the surrounding ribs and the stake within her body. His knife slashed through her neck. Blood gushed from her body; she was finished.

Another charged the blood-stained Alexander. Taking his opportunity in the blink of an eye, Alexander lunged for him, their bodies colliding in a loud crash. The vampire gnashed at his neck. He grabbed the vampire's jaw and tore it from its face. He ripped a stake from his belt and sank it deep into the chest and ripped the head from the vampire's body with his bare hands in a graceful and horrifying movement.

Laney looked around her, wide-eyed and terrified, unsure of which family member was the most frightening, and found that Jim had torn four of the vampires to pieces in the few minutes that she'd been watching Alexander. Jim and Alexander turned at the same instant to look at Sophie where she still fought in front of Laney, and the latter followed the line of their shocked expressions.

Sophie had pushed Laney against the wall while the younger girl watched the fight. Fear had paralyzed her from doing anything other than just watching her family fight. She hadn't even realized she'd been pushed out of the way. She had just enough time to raise her hands quickly to stop a running vampire from charging her sister, as Sophie drove a stake into the chest of another one. Two more came from the right and Sophie unloaded three bullets into each of them. Laney tried to keep two more off of them. Her arms shook under the strain, and her head felt like it might explode.

"I need a clip," Sophie growled desperately to herself. One was suddenly in her hand and she was firing again in a split second.

Sophie finally grabbed one of the vampires by the head. Laney stopped trying to keep that one off of Sophie, and she felt weightless for an instant. She focused on the others who were charging them.

Sophie spun around him, throwing her body in a spin, and twisted the head free from his shoulders, landing on her feet behind him, the adrenaline giving her the extra strength needed to accomplish such a feat. She tossed the head at the wall where it crashed to the ground. Without pausing, she ran up the back of another vampire and plunged the stake into his heart from behind. As he stumbled, she pulled her knife out of her pocket, the blade was instantly exposed, and the head was gone in a bloody mess.

It was all done in less than two minutes. The alleyway was quiet.

Jacques, who had stood by and let the slaughter happen, began clapping his hands slowly and laughing. Sophie slowly turned around, leveling her eyes at him.

"Bravo!" he yelled in a thunderous voice.

Sophie exchanged a look with Alexander and shook her head grimly.

Jacques whistled quickly and the rest of his coven poured out of two doorways into the alley.

Jim groaned under his breath as he counted twenty more.

*It figures,* Jim thought. *We're not that lucky.*

# Chapter 32

Sophie turned on a heel, placing herself securely between Laney and the encroaching enemy. The blood of the vampires she'd killed dripped from her hands as she sunk into a crouch in front of her sister. Zoey mirrored her movements. Her red hair was plastered to her shoulders from the rain that had begun to come down. Black blood ran in rivers down the legs of her pants.

Jim whipped his crossbow around to bring it in front of his chest. Sophie holstered her Glock; she'd need both hands for what was coming. Catherina still stood behind Dante, but Sophie saw a steadiness in Catherina's eyes which—more than anything else in that alleyway—made her nervous.

Sophie looked at Leslie, picking her out of the crowd. Her mother snarled at her, with an evil look in her eyes. Leslie was clearly almost beyond self-control, and Sophie waited for her to charge.

"Time to get serious," Sophie muttered to herself, watching her mother crouch forward, ready to spring.

"Go for the women first," Jacques commanded in a hiss, "but Catherina is *mine*."

Instincts taking over, Sophie felt herself become something completely foreign. She crouched beside Alexander, just like a vampire. She turned herself over to the monstrous part of her nature, the part that continually tried to break free, boiling just under the surface of her self-control. She could feel the eyes of her slightly more composed family watching her, but Sophie's eyes were locked on Jacques's. A low laughter came from deep in his chest as he met her gaze and sunk down into a mirroring crouch; a direct challenge.

Sophie's chest rumbled. It wasn't the human part of her that made the guttural sound. She had her father—her eyes flashed quickly from Leslie back to Jacques—to thank for that. She surrendered fully to that black part of herself; she felt the fury course through her veins.

Beside her Alexander leaned forward, ready to charge or catch, the enemy. He'd follow her into battle, even if it meant death.

Leslie suddenly tore out from the group like a feral animal, her gangly arms unruly in her movements, and charged directly towards Sophie like the deranged creature she was.

Sophie's hands, gripping two stakes each, jerked up. She threw the stakes at her mother, and they twirled through the air, shooting through Leslie's heart, and even through the chest of another vampire who stood behind her, like bullets from a gun. The stakes shot through both bodies and lodged in the mortar of the wall behind the coven.

Blinded by anger, Sophie felt the energy of her rage collect around her as she spun Leslie's head from her body, tossing it viciously to Jacques's feet in a challenge. His beef with Catherina might be centuries old, but Sophie's was personal too. Sophie nodded her head in a challenge to him. His jaw dropped and his lips curled into a deadly snarl.

The other injured vampire lay twisting on the ground, clawing at the stake wound in his own chest. Black blood poured from his lips, further staining the air with the smell of death and decay. Sophie let him suffer there. She stood between the groups, exposed, but unwilling to advance too far away from her family.

Jacques was no longer looking at her though, but was staring at Catherina. His goal was singular. He raised his hand and snapped his fingers. The rest of his vampires charged the hybrid family. Alexander and Jim rushed to Sophie's side. Laney struggled to hold a large group back from them despite her fear.

Suddenly the activity was interrupted by a horrible screeching scream.

Catherina grabbed the female and sank her teeth into the soft tissue of a vampire's neck. The vampire's scream was ear-piercing. Dante stood over her, protecting Catherina from the horde.

Everything stopped. The vampires stopped mid-stride; the family stopped in mid-strike.

*NO!!!* Sophie's thoughts screamed in absolute horror.

An immediate change began to take shape in Catherina. The black blood dripped gluttonously down her chin. Everyone was perfectly frozen in the alleyway, except for the vampire in Catherina's jaws, who clawed vainly against her attacker.

Catherina looked at Jacques as she sucked at the vampire's neck. Her eyes meet his as they changed from their natural green to the deepest, darkest black. Sophie's heart stopped. She looked at Alexander.

His horror mirrored hers. *This is what Dante meant when he said Catherina would be fine.*

*This is what she's been hiding from us all along.*

*This is what he wouldn't tell me.*

This was the choice she'd made weeks ago.

Catherina dropped the drained body of the vampire and straightened herself into a standing position. She was taller than Sophie had ever seen her before; stronger than she'd ever seen her; her eyes never left Jacques's.

"This ends now," Catherina said in a clear, strong voice. It was their voice, like glass shattering and bells clanging; fingernails on a chalkboard. She stood taller than ever and was teeming with strength.

She charged Jacques and the two tumbled into combat like tigers attacking each other. Seeing their leader in distress, Jacques' coven sprang into motion.

The enemy began flying at them, but Laney blocked each individually in mid-flight, finding new strength and determination from somewhere in her soul. They had a chance, albeit a slim one, and Laney chose to fight rather than give up.

Sophie and Zoey threw stakes into the hearts of the vampires as Jim and Alexander ripped, tore and sliced heads from the bodies. It seemed like an eternity, but they fought them off in a matter of seconds, not taking time to think or direct the others, simply working together as a unit, striking them down one by one as they attacked like lemmings.

The last head rolled to a stop at their feet and they looked collectively to Catherina. Dante stood in the shadow watching her, as paralyzed as any of them would be at the sight of their companion submitting completely to evil. Catherina held Jacques like a rag doll in her mouth, her anger and the learned hunger that had been suppressed for so long, visibly raging in her.

"Her thoughts are confused," Sophie shouted Jim and Alexander as they inched towards her. "Watch out."

Sophie could suddenly hear Catherina's thoughts through all the barriers she'd previously put up against her. The transformation was complete.

"She thinks we're here to attack her too," Sophie said quickly. "She's completely identifying with them. She's *one* of them."

Jim looked from Sophie to Alexander. "What do we do?" he asked, panic in his voice.

Zoey pulled another bottle of holy water out of her bag. Alexander held his hand up to her and Jim. He glared at Catherina, refusing to pull his eyes from her, waiting for the moment she would decide to spring. Instead, Catherina froze and looked back in their direction.

Laney stared at her adopted mother in horror. Catherina turned her eyes to the young girl and cocking her head to the side, stared at her with a terrifyingly expectant smile. Laney stepped forward in a trance to stand between the members of her family, reaching almost blindly out to Catherina.

Catherina leered at Laney as if she were something to eat. Sophie's eyes bore into Catherina, but her focus was not on Sophie. Catherina's concentration rested on the weakest target of the group as Laney innocently approached her in shocked, mute terror. She was within reaching distance of Dante, but he stood helplessly by, watching his wife embrace her evil instincts; he did nothing to stop the young girl.

*No one* was stopping Laney. Sophie stood behind them all, furthest from the group, but could see Catherina the best of all. She saw the split-second change the rest of them missed in her countenance. Catherina wanted human blood, and Laney's was close enough.

"*NO!!!!*" Sophie suddenly yelled, pushing past Alexander and Zoey, nearly knocking them down, jumping to traverse the space, and she tackled Catherina before she could charge the family.

Catherina's body was catapulted through the opposite wall seconds before she sprang to attack Laney. Sophie forced Catherina to the ground, but she knew she couldn't hold her for long. Now that she'd changed, she was stronger than Sophie was. Catherina had one goal in mind, and it involved Laney's death. Sophie hurled her keys at Jim without looking, not daring to pull her eyes from Catherina's face.

"I'll kill her," Catherina growled at Sophie. "You can't stop me."

*"Get her the hell out of here!"* Sophie ordered him as Catherina struggled to be free.

Jim grabbed Laney, jumped to the cars, and tossed her into the front seat of Sophie's Mercedes before screeching the tires in a spin and speeding out of the alleyway, getting Laney out of danger as quickly as possible. Catherina glared hatefully at Sophie with her black eyes; the hunger had taken over. She looked from Sophie to Alexander, then to Zoey, to Dante and then back at Sophie from where she held her down on the ground.

"Get a hold of yourself, damn it!" Sophie demanded roughly, slapping Catherina fiercely across the face.

The new vampire snarled and gnashed at Sophie in response. She fought like an animal and was quickly able to struggle free from her grip. Catherina backed away from them slowly, stepping over vampire bodies as she went. The black of her eyes was obvious even in the dark night and her body was deathly pale when the lightning flashed above them. She didn't know any of her former family from strangers. The clouds above opened up and a heavier rain started to pour down, running down their soaking clothes as they stood silently watching Catherina.

Alexander and Sophie waited, ready to spring, while Dante watched helplessly, as if he knew what would happen. He didn't move to stop it. Zoey watched him through suspicious eyes.

Catherina continued to back away from them slowly, crouching low to the ground like a vampire. Her eyes shifted from Sophie to Alexander. She had no idea who they were, anymore than she knew who she was herself. She suddenly froze in place, a fearsome statue before them, standing too still for reality. Sophie didn't move as she watched Catherina's face.

And then, rocking back on a heel, Catherina suddenly charged Alexander and was on him in a moment. All the hatred and violence in Catherina hit Sophie like a tidal wave. She roared in response. Alexander brought his arms up to fend off the attack, but not before one of his stakes flew through the air and tore through her heart. Catherina squealed in pain and fell backward, clawing at the stake like the terrified monster she had become. Alexander stood above the vampire, looking down at her in disgust. She had become one of them completely.

She clawed at the stake, but stared viciously into his face, desperately wanting to attack him again. But the stake prevented her from moving, as if it weighed a thousand pounds. She tried to hiss something out at them, but it came out garbled and like the rants of a demon.

Sophie ran to Alexander's frozen side as Catherina lay there twitching. She bent and gripped the sides of Catherina's head with her hands and looked into her face as Alexander stood frozen above her. There was only anger and madness in the black depths of those eyes.

"I'm sorry, Catherina," Sophie whispered before she brought her knife down on Catherina's neck and twisted her head off.

The body convulsed at the loss of its head, the mouth still moved in an effort to say or bite something, until finally, it was still.

The night was suddenly quiet around them, save for the soft rumbling of thunder overhead and the sounds of traffic and laughter from adjacent streets. The rain had slowed to a drizzle almost as quickly as it had come on. For the first time that night, Sophie's hands shook as she exhaled some of the stress from her body.

Alexander sprang to action, quickly piling the other bodies together and set them on fire as Sophie remained over Catherina's body, a foreign heaviness in her heart, as her hair hung wet down her back and into her face. Zoey stepped towards Sophie and stood at her side.

Sophie looked over her shoulder at Dante, who wept silent tears. He slowly walked over to the body at her feet, and scooping it up gently in his arms. He carried it over to the bonfire in the narrow alleyway.

Alexander appeared at Sophie's side and wrapped his arm around her waist as they silently watched Dante toss his wife's body and head into the fire. He turned slowly to look at the three of them. Sophie's breath froze for his reaction; Zoey held her hand.

Dante sighed, thought about something and then nodded his head. "I think I shall take my leave of you now," he said quietly, almost to himself.

"Dante, I'm…," Sophie started to say, but really had no words. She tried to reach out to him.

His face was gentle and serene as he looked at her. "She would have done the same thing if your roles were reversed. You have saved *many* lives tonight." He looked from Sophie to Alexander and back to Sophie once more. "Regret *nothing* of this night. It is done."

And with that, he was gone leaving the three of them in the street, dripping with rain and dead blood.

"Come with me," Alexander said, pulling her hand in the direction of his car, but not turning his back on Dante who continued to walk slowly away. Zoey backed away from Dante towards her motorcycle.

The fight had taken all of five minutes, yet so much had changed.

He opened the passenger door for her and she slid in, dazed. He slid into his seat. Gunning the engine, they sped for home. Zoey had ridden off in the opposite direction. The Audi was soon passed by two police cars, lights flashing and sirens blaring in the direction from which they'd come, but they knew the cops wouldn't find anything but a few broken bricks and a dumpster set ablaze.

Alexander looked over at Sophie as he drove, but she didn't meet his gaze. Her clothes clung wetly to her skin as she stared out the window into the waning rain.

"Did I scare you out there?" she muttered self-consciously.

He shook his head. "You could never scare me. Besides, you saved my life," he responded equally as quiet, staring at the road in front of him.

"Not then. I meant when…I…," she couldn't say it out loud, but the vision of herself flashed through her mind: violently crouched low to the ground, snarling like one of them, the rage had no doubt been visible in every inch of her body.

She'd seen herself in Laney's eyes, and it was terrifying.

He was quiet for a minute, staring at the road before them.

"Your mind was very open to us all. You may have been behaving like a vampire, but I assure you, you are not anything like one of them," he said, carefully pronouncing every word. "Laney's perspective was a bit skewed by her emotions."

"If you say so," she replied doubtfully, though she did smile a little.

"Trust me; it is not the first time for one of us to act like that. We *are* all part vampire, no matter how much we hate to admit it. Their behaviors are sometimes unsettlingly natural for us."

"I know." She nodded and was quiet, lost in her thoughts which suddenly turned to Catherina.

*Dante saw it coming,* he thought as the car came to a stop.

They were already in the garage back at the house. She looked over to see her car already waiting there and sighed with relief. Zoey had already made it back too. He turned in the seat and took both of her hands in his.

"I do not know how to make you understand this, but you must know that I am not surprised or upset in *any* way. Laney and Jim will have a difficult time with this, but they will always love you for who you are and what you have done for them, regardless of who Catherina was. They will soon recover from this.

"You saved Laney's life for certain, and probably Jim's as well. You and I both know that you saw it would be her life or ours tonight. And Zoey would have chosen you over Catherina any day," he reached up to push a wayward lock of hair from her face and looked deeply into her eyes before repeating Dante's words: "Regret nothing."

She nodded as he dropped her hands and slid out of the car. He walked around, opened the door for her, and held out a hand for her to take. They walked slowly out of the garage and towards the house as she contemplated what to say to the others.

*Don't worry. They love you.*

"Sophie!" Laney exclaimed the moment they walked inside. She ran into her arms, regardless of how filthy Sophie was, and nearly knocked her over.

Sophie looked over Laney's shoulder to see Jim and Zoey standing behind her, watching them expectantly.

Jim smiled. "I'm just glad we're all okay."

Laney was clinging to Sophie as if her life depended on it. She pulled away quickly and looked into her eyes, trying to read her thoughts, and Sophie simply let her hear everything as the memories ran through her head. She watched as Laney's eyes filled with tears. For a few moments, her eyes locked on Sophie's as she heard the story. Then Laney resolutely wiped the stray tears from off of her cheeks and a small, grateful smile spread across her lips.

"Thank you, Sophie," she whispered.

"You're not mad at me?" Sophie asked seriously.

She shook her head quickly, like a little child. "She was going to kill me. That's something *I'll* have to make peace with. And you saved me. I love you, Sophie. I'm so glad you're my sister," she replied before turning from the room.

*I love you too,* Sophie thought as she watched her walk away.

Jim gave Sophie a small, sad smile and turned to follow Laney out. Zoey nodded her head in a bow and disappeared, but not without a reassuring smile for Sophie. Sophie slowly turned to Alexander and let him wrap his arms around her and simply hold her for a while.

It was hauntingly quiet, and the melancholy atmosphere that fell on the house that night would not let up for several weeks.

# Epilogue

SOPHIE PAGE

The weather was changing, spring was coming on. Sitting on the front porch, perusing the morning paper, the sun felt warm on my skin. The house was quiet behind me. Alex was on an interview at Tulane for a professorship there because, well, what else was he going to do during the day? He loved to teach and I'd encouraged the interview.

Laney had enrolled in high school in January and was thriving as a somewhat normal seventeen-year-old. Her idiosyncrasies were either ignored or perceived as charming by her classmates. With a bit of adjustment, she'd really enjoyed the past three months.

Zoey was usually off doing her own thing. I could never really keep up with her. She was taking a yoga class, a dance class, and a pottery class. I think she may have even taken up Buddhism, but I wasn't sure.

Jim kept in touch. He began having dreams of an attractive young girl—I'd seen her in his thoughts—and did what comes naturally to us all and left to seek her out. He hadn't found her yet, but was enjoying the travel in the meantime. He'd left just the four of us: me, Alex, Zoey, and Laney, the only members of our family left in New Orleans, to find the companion of his destiny.

The last time he called, he had been somewhere in the northeast, taking in museums and historical sites. It all made me think of Catherina's story about finding Dante and though I hadn't known them long, it still made me a little sad.

After what had happened, we had simply shut the door downstairs and no one had dared enter the room Catherina had shared with Dante. Subtle changes occurred gradually around the house though—books that they had read, pieces of furniture that the rest of us thought were superfluous, certain ingredients in the pantry—all began to slowly disappear. It was as if while we were healing, the house was healing itself; purging itself of Catherina's and Dante's memory.

I couldn't put my remorse behind me though, no matter how many times my family had either thanked me for what I did or encouraged me not to hold myself responsible. The fact of the matter was that I'd taken their mother away from them, or at least from Jim and Laney. I'd reacted instinctually; maybe that was the most frightening part of it all. I'd embraced my most animalistic and potentially evil nature, the dead part of my heart, and struck down one of our own.

"*C'est la guerre,*" Josephine had said when she'd learned the news: *That's war.*

Most days, I was able to push the guilt back to the furthest reaches of my subconscious; other days it wasn't quite so easy.

Thankfully, today it was.

I lounged on my patio, waiting for Alex to return home. I listened to the sounds of the city and smelled the stale smell emanating from my neighbor's kitchen, leftover from the previous night's gumbo. My patio; my neighbor; my home. It had become largely that. We made the home ours, rearranging furniture, and Laney helped pick out new art for the walls. Catherina would never return and it was hard for my sister to grasp that reality, but freshening things up had breathed fresh life into the home and had given us all hope.

"'Mornin'," the postman greeted in his deep Cajun accent, walking up the sidewalk.

"Hi, George!" I responded to the cute little old man. He'd probably been doing this for the past sixty years.

I swung my feet down from the porch railing and walked down the path that led to the street, meeting him at the gate.

"Here y'are, ma'am," he said, as he always did.

I accepted the stack of mail from him with a smile.

"Thank you," I replied.

He smiled with a nod and continued to the next house. "You have a good day now," he said over his shoulder.

I waved back to George and strolled slowly back up to the porch to reclaim my seat, flipping through the mail. There was a postcard from Jim with a picture of the White House on the front. I flipped it over:

*Miss you guys! D.C. is great. Keep out of trouble, Jim,* was all he'd scrawled out in his large script. I smiled to myself. "Keep out of trouble," yeah, because he'd be angry he were to miss any of it.

There was the typical junk mail, offers for credit cards with no limit, coupons…and then there was a small, unassuming envelope at the bottom of the pile. It was a pretty cream color, but had no return address. On the front, my name and our address were finely written in old-fashioned calligraphy.

I flipped it over and broke the seal. There was a thin piece of paper inside that I carefully unfolded.

"Hello, my love," Alex called cheerfully, coming up the walk, but stopped suddenly. The sound of his steps vanished quickly when he saw my face as I read the paper in my trembling hand.

"What is it?" he demanded fiercely, but I couldn't answer. He dropped his briefcase and ran over to me, gripping me by the arms, giving me a gentle shake. But I still couldn't answer.

I simply stared at nothing as the letter floated softly, lazily to the ground. I tried to remember how to breathe and realized what a complete fool I was to have thought that the actions of last December would go unnoticed:

# *We know.*

# Acknowledgements

There are a few people that every author is indebted to. Writing is a process, but it's not a journey embarked on alone.

Many thanks to Lisa, who read this story in just about every stage of its life…even when it was an ugly little baby manuscript that only I really loved. Thank you for being one of my biggest fans.

Thanks to all the friends—those I know only through social media and those I've known for years—for all the cheerleading, all the support.

Thank you Mike for always encouraging me and reminding me I can fly.

# About the Author

Megan Winkler is a communications coach, author, military historian, musician, and coffee junkie. She lives in the artistic environs of North Texas, draws inspiration from people watching, and regularly test runs characters in RPGs. She writes all the time-- probably more than she should.

Megan is also the author of *Transmissions from Dating Land: The Revised & Expanded Edition* and *Revolution 2*.

www.ingramcontent.com/pod-product-compliance
Lightning Source LLC
Chambersburg PA
CBHW070811180626
46818CB00001B/206